GUT FEELING

VICTORIA BROWNE

Gut Feeling

Who do you trust, if you can't trust yourself

Neville House Publishing

Published by Neville House Publishing

First published by
Neville House Publishing in 2012.

Reprinted 2014, 2017

A CIP Catalogue of this book is available
from the British Library

Paperback: 978-0-9928083-0-3
EBook ISBN: 978-0-9928083-1-0

Printed and distributed by
Createspace

WHY I WROTE GUT FEELING

DYSLEXIA FOR A CREATIVE writer is a cruel disability. I carried a vocabulary in my head that did not match my spelling ability. I would find myself substituting words on paper in order to make my writing legible, unaware that this only detracted from my writing and the impact it had on the reader.

At the age of twenty, I was writing erotica poetry and also some general philosophy. Looking back, I can see the natural creative path I was taking myself on. Just like an artist, I was trying different genres and writing styles. At twenty-four, I sought help, determined to learn to spell. I found out that I also had a weak short-term memory. In short, it went in one ear and out the other! I worked on developing my memory with a therapist, which helped me go back to the basics and teach myself to spell. Toward the end of my program, my therapist asked me to write a diary to help develop my reading and writing skills. I explained that I did not like writing diaries but had written some romantic scenes. My therapist suggested building a beginning and an end to one of the scenes I had written. This was the birth of my first book, *Gut Feeling*.

Being a dyslexic in the world of creative writing will always leave you vulnerable to harsh criticism. My advice to dyslexic writers is this: never be embarrassed of your abilities, only proud of them. And never give up. You are amazing.

Victoria_Browne@yahoo.co.uk

CHAPTER

1

ASHLEIGH PAID AND THEN took a sip from her last glass of Sauvignon Blanc at the hotel bar. The annual conference dinner had finished over an hour ago, but the thought of going home compelled her to have yet another glass. She wondered if anyone she knew was still in the hotel—perhaps outside smoking. She engaged her alcohol-intoxicated legs and wandered out onto the terrace.

Through glazed eyes, she could make out a small gaggle of smokers by the fountain.

"Ashleigh—over here." A girl in the middle of the group waved in the dark.

Ashleigh stumbled toward them. She recognized two faces, but the others didn't belong to anyone she knew. One of the unfamiliar men offered her a cigarette and held his hand out to light the white stick. She took a long, slow drag, blowing the smoke out hard. They chatted for a while, but what about, she couldn't tell. The alcohol had well and truly saturated her blood. Not that she cared, because it numbed the pain.

"Text me when you're home," shouted Samantha, a co-worker, as Ashleigh stepped onto the number 52 bus outside of the hotel.

"Sure," Ashleigh said, swiping her travel pass without looking back.

The doors closed, and Ashleigh fell into the first seat she passed. She watched Samantha laughing animatedly with one of the unfamiliar men as the bus pulled away. She wished she could be more like Samantha, but then she shuddered at the thought. Samantha was cold and callous to everyone, but she did know how to have fun with men—something Ashleigh had forgotten. She closed her eyes as the bus chugged along the route home.

The bus jerked as it pulled away from a stop, knocking Ashleigh's sleeping head off the window where it had been resting.

"Shit. Shit." She startled as the bus rolled past her stop. "Wait—please, stop. Stop the bus. That's my stop. Wait—go back."

"Sorry, miss," the driver said. "I can't go back."

"Then stop. Please—please. I beg you. It's late—I'm on my own—*pleeease*."

The driver checked his rearview mirror and then pulled over sharply. "You're lucky this bus is empty, young lady."

"Thank you!" Ashleigh ran—or fell—out of the open doors.

"Be careful," she heard the driver shout after her, and then she heard the hydraulics of the closing doors.

"Bollocks," Ashleigh muttered repeatedly under her breath as she stumbled back along Knightsbridge High Street toward home. Why had she gotten so drunk again?

A passing car playing loud music tooted its horn at her, and she heard yells and whistles from the open windows. Ashleigh picked up the pace, ignoring her burning feet, and pulled her fur coat tight around her waist.

It was past two a.m. by the time she fell through her front door, then onto her bed, fully dressed.

"Where is it?" Ashleigh fumbled around in her bag for her phone. She poked her finger at the screen and waited for an answer.

After a few rings, the phone went to voicemail. "Hello, you have reached Kelly Lands. Please leave a message, and I'll call you back as soon as I can. Have a nice day."

Ashleigh did the math; it was nine p.m. in New York. "Where are you?" she asked the recording. "Answer your phone, girl. I—I—never mind. I'll call you tomorrow. 'Have a nice day.' " She mocked her sister's farewell and hung up, instantly regretting calling her.

Was every choice she made the wrong one? Why did she feel

the need to call her sister for support yet again? Had it not been long enough? She should be over it by now—she should be over *him* by now.

★ ★ ★

Sunshine filled the room through the open blinds. A piercing pain bolted across Ashleigh's forehead. Reaching for a glass of water that must have been at least two days old, she caught a glimpse of herself in the dresser mirror.

"Oh fuck."

Draining the glass of its stale water, she sat staring at herself. Makeup was smudged down her face, her navy cocktail dress twisted from her sleep, and she was still wearing her unbuckled Valentino stilettos.

"Jesus, what's wrong with me?"

Water ran over her face as she stood in the shower, wondering why she always woke up so early after a night of drinking. Surely her body needed more sleep. She looked at her shaking hands.

"Yep. Definitely need more sleep."

What was she thinking, staying out so late after agreeing to open the office for a workman on her day off? All she wanted to do was wallow in self-pity while lying in bed for the whole day—and possibly even Sunday, too. The last thing she needed was to babysit her boss's antique paintings while some overweight workman fit a window. Had people really not figured out that reliable, sweet Ashleigh was no longer available for service?

Now, on all accounts, she loved her job as a dental assistant in one of the most respectable dental offices in London—just not so much the owner of the practice. He was an arrogant dental professor who terrified Ashleigh at the best of times, so saying "no" didn't feel like an option. However, being positive about the situation was a far jump for her right now. Her life had actually hit rock bottom.

Well, the only way is up. She smiled, but it hurt her head.

She allowed herself to think back to before her family had left, before Lee had left, before happiness had left. She had truly had it all: family, love, and a career that she had chosen—not one that her dad had expected, but at least it was one she wanted. If he'd had his way, she'd be working for his boring oil company over in New York. She had been the envy of all her friends, the one who was so strong and together.

Now what? Now all she had was designer shoes that Daddy sent over from America. The irony, however, was that she was still the envy of all her friends. Somehow, they still thought she was strong and together, that all her drunken nights out were just being young and sticking it to her no-good, cheating ex—living up her early twenties. She didn't know how she had convinced her friends that she was doing fine, but she did know it was definitely easier than dealing with their pity faces.

She patted herself dry, and dressed. She didn't need to be at work until mid-day.

Her phone vibrated. "Oh God," she said, remembering that she had drunk-called her big sister the night before. She picked it up.

"Kelly, hey," she said, trying to sound bright.

"Drunk again?"

"Is that judgment I hear in your question, Kelly?"

"No—concern. What's happening? You're turning into me. I'm the family drunk; you can't have that."

"Why not? You have everything else." Ashleigh instantly regretted her comment.

"And what's that supposed to mean?" Kelly asked. "Ashleigh Lands, what's up with you?"

"Oh God, Kelly, ignore me. I'm hungover and have to go into work. I'm sorry; I didn't mean it." And she didn't.

"Seriously, Ash, what's up? Have you bumped into Lee or something?"

"No—God, no. I've not seen him in four months now. No, I just miss you, that's all."

"Funny way of showing it."

"Sorry."

"You know you can move out anytime," Kelly pressed.

Ashleigh didn't answer.

"Ash?"

"Yeah, I know. I'm good, just had a moment of weakness, you know?"

"You're having lots of those lately. Look, I'm here if you want to talk. It's OK to still be upset. It's totally—"

"I'm good, Kelly. I've got this."

She heard her sister sigh. "I know you do, Ashleigh—you're a Lands. Anyway, you know where I am."

Ashleigh hung up the phone, regretting the night before. It wasn't so much the drinking; that bit was relatively fun. No, it was more reaching out to her sister again. All her life, she had relied on her big sister, but since choosing to stay in England with Lee, she had vowed to do it all on her own. Granted, she hadn't banked on doing it *literally* on her own without Lee as well, but she was still determined to make her own way in life. Her plan was falling apart, but it was time to get it back together.

★   ★   ★

By eleven a.m., she was rolling along a busy Oxford street on the top deck of a bus, wondering again why it was always her who got asked to go in on her day off. "A people pleaser," her mum used to call her, and she was right.

Excited shoppers scurried off the bus at each stop. She remembered that she was supposed to text Samantha once she got home the night before, so she pulled out her phone. She put it away again. She knew Samantha well enough to know that she didn't really mean it. Even if she did, she would not remember saying it the next day. Ashley should have known better than to agree to get a bus home from a night out with Samantha. Samantha always ended up going home with a man, leaving Ashleigh to fend for herself. She also should have known better than to have gotten the night bus on her own, even if it *was* only up the road. Why had she not called an Uber? Her thoughts were interrupted as she reached her stop and rose from her seat, feeling a fresh wave of nausea.

After purchasing a popular brand of hangover remedy from the local Boots pharmacy, she slowly and carefully walked the length of

Harley Street to work. Why did she always have to be the reliable one? Where had it actually gotten her in life? She allowed herself to imagine a life like Samantha's, or maybe her best friend Rachel's. Neither had a boyfriend, but both were happy. No one worried when they got drunk; no one asked them if they needed to "talk" because they made drunken late-night calls and acted irresponsibly. But then, they were never responsible in the first place, and neither had a sister, either. Ashleigh wondered if she was over-exaggerating the situation.

A small ping from her phone distracted her from her self-pity. It was her sister.

Ash—I'm worried about you. [Concerned face emoji]

You're not acting like yourself.

Don't let Lee ruin your life! [Angry face emoji]

"Seriously!" she shouted, and a man walking his dog edged toward the curb as he passed her.

Why are you so concerned about me? She made a mental note: *Stop drunk-calling Kelly.*

And she meant it this time. She was going to stop running to her big sister whenever things got tough. It was time to stand on her own—for real this time. It was also time to stop saying yes to the practice owner's overtime demands. He could open his own office the next time.

Opening the dental office main door, she felt empowered, feeling a hint of nausea but ready for her new stand in life. She had this.

CHAPTER
2

HEAVING HIS BAG OF tools onto his shoulder for support, Dave stood on the pavement. Squinting in the brilliant sunlight, he looked at the oversized front door and stepped up to the intercom. A gold plaque caught his eye.

The Harley Street Dental Practice
Oral & Maxillofacial Specialist Surgery
Prof. Dr. W. J. Matson
Dr. E. A. McDonald

He reached out, pressed the button, and waited.

"Hello, Harley Street Dental," said a small female voice.

Dave could barely hear her over the noise of London traffic. "I'm here to replace your window," he shouted.

There was a click and a buzz, and he pushed the door open.

The light dimmed in a huge entrance hall as the door closed behind him. A deep emerald green carpet engulfed the floor where he stood, and the distinct smell of dental tools hit his nose, dragging him briefly back to his childhood. His eyes wandered around, looking for the owner of the intercom voice. As he stood waiting, he admired paintings of fox hunts and expensive-looking chandeliers dangling from the high ceiling.

A pretty girl stepped into view. "Good morning," she said politely.

"Dave Croft," he said, holding his hand out. He was pleasantly surprised to be greeted by someone who looked to be around his own age, not a housewife with 2.1 children who thought flirting with a man half her age was somehow sexy. "Where's this window then?"

"Hi, I'm Ashleigh." She shook his hand. "This way. Tea? Coffee?"

"Coffee, please—black, no sugar." He followed, admiring her from behind.

She led him to a large, elegant room at the back of the practice where there were more pompous paintings of men on horses playing polo. In one corner was a dental chair, and in the other, a grand Victorian, walnut desk, behind which a large window overlooked a courtyard.

The girl seemed to be the only one in the building, and Dave assumed the practice was closed, as it was a Saturday. She returned five minutes later with a cup of black coffee. Smiling, she placed it on the desk and then left—much to Dave's disappointment.

As he set about removing the glass, he noticed that she seemed to be wandering around the practice aimlessly, so he tried to strike up a conversation. He didn't want her to feel uncomfortable being there alone with him, and he certainly didn't mind pretty girls watching him work.

The sun poured in through the window frame. Sweat beaded on Dave's forehead as he balanced himself precariously on the window ledge. Ashleigh poured a glass of water from the water fountain, offering it to him with a quick smile. She had an odd way about her—sweet, but tainted. Something in her eyes told him she wanted something from life but hadn't found it yet. Or was he just reading into things again like he always did—looking for meaning where there was none, or answers to questions that hadn't been asked.

He took off his T-shirt and sat down in the dental chair for a rest.

"How about you lay me back and give me a check-over?" he said, shooting her an inquisitive wink. He knew how cheesy he sounded and cringed inside. Lines like that only worked on lonely women, not girls as attractive as this one.

"I think you mean a check-up." She turned her head to take a sip of water. "I'm not the dentist—I'm only the dental assistant, but I could book you an appointment for that check-up."

He smiled politely and drank the water in one swift action. He tried to flirt a little more, but wondered if she wanted to bring the atmosphere back to a professional one as she politely explained her role at the practice. She was cute, a little more sophisticated than the girls he was used to, though she seemed to enjoy talking to him. She had a strange, nervous vulnerability as she spoke—he liked that. She was different; there was something about the tone of her voice that piqued his curiosity and made him want to know more about her. He responded by explaining his line of work, aiming to keep the conversation going in the direction she had led them, but out of habit, he was soon digressing into stories of his embarrassing experiences with lonely housewives and of the lavish places he had worked.

He continued chatting in the hope that she was interested, and was also keen to impress her, which was a nice change. He hadn't wanted to impress many girls since losing Caroline, his first love. Women rarely matched up to her. However, not wanting to present himself as a womanizer who had women throwing themselves at him—which they did more often than not—he decided to tell Ashleigh a different story. This girl was not like the others, he thought—or at least he hoped.

"I've got a story I think you'll like," he said. "I once turned up to a job in a barn."

"A barn? I didn't think barns had windows."

"Well, this one definitely did not." He watched her smile. *She is beautiful.*

"Another lonely housewife?"

"Ha, no—a little old lady living in her own world. It took me a few minutes to figure it out, but then I realized she was a sandwich short of a picnic—and in her world, she lived in palace."

"A palace? What did you do?" Ashleigh asked.

"I let her take me on a tour of the most beautiful palace I had ever been inside."

"What?" She smiled that beautiful smile again.

"Yep. It was amazing. You may laugh, but this little crazy lady used to be a famous writer—and no, I will not disclose who." He winked. "She described every room to me in such detail, it was like I had stepped into another world. No joke. I was there an hour."

"An hour?" Ashleigh echoed.

"Sure. It was a big palace, remember."

"Stop—you're kidding me."

"No, God's honest truth—her son gave me a copy of the book she wrote. Said she was trapped in the story in her mind. The palace in the book was the same place she showed me around. He tried to pay me for my time, but the tour of that palace was priceless."

"Oh, that's so sad. And so kind of you."

Dave racked his brain for more stories Ashleigh would like, desperate to keep this girl amused. He loved that she was smiling and laughing at his jokes—the jokes that his brother always told him were not funny. He watched as she threw her head back, laughing; she was honestly the most beautiful girl he had ever met. How was she finding him so funny? His brother always told him he was grumpy and boring.

She left the room to fetch a new water bottle for the water fountain. *Is she just being polite?* She seemed genuinely amused, but then she *did* just leave the room fairly quickly, and she looked a bit pale. *Damn.* Had he just messed it up?

Ashleigh found a fresh water bottle in the store room, desperate to rehydrate her body. She was enjoying talking to Dave. He was funny and very handsome, not the overweight workman she had expected. She was curious to know more about him—about what was beneath his surface-level, brash persona. That last story told her this guy wasn't interested in telling lonely housewives' stories; those tales must be just boy talk. He was deep, and she wanted to know more about him. But first, she needed water—this hangover was not shifting. She wanted to ask more questions but felt sick when she talked. She hoped he hadn't noticed.

Ashleigh heaved the water bottle back into the surgery and let Dave help her fix it in place. She poured herself a cup and drank it quickly before refilling.

"Thirsty?" Dave asked.

"Bit hungover, to be honest," she said sheepishly.

He smiled and sat back down again, and Ashleigh's eyes moved down to his bare chest.

My God, I could kiss him. She struggled with her imagination for a while. *I could just stand up and walk over, and then straddle him and see what his reaction is.* She giggled in her head. *Is that what Samantha would do? Who cares what she would do—she's no role model for my new empowered self.* She had noticed that he hadn't mentioned a girlfriend or wife.

The more he talked, the more she watched his body language; and each tiny gesture made her desire him more. She had not felt this way about a man since Lee. She had been on numerous dates and had lots of fun, but she never felt the same lust she had with Lee. This guy was different, though. He wasn't a bad boy; he was a real-life, modern-day gentleman. She watched Dave's mouth as he talked, imagining the warmth of his tongue sliding around in her mouth, her hands gripping his broad shoulders as he ravished her right there on the dental chair.

"So would you?" he asked awkwardly.

Bugger. She cursed inwardly as she was torn back to reality. "Um . . . yeah," she said warily, unsure what to say as she had not heard his question.

"You would?" He sounded surprised.

"No, yes, sometimes." *Oh shit.* Her heart was racing, and she was increasingly aware of how stupid she was sounding. Why had she not just said pardon?

He smiled. "What about me?"

"What about you?" she replied. *This should throw some light on his question.*

He looked confused. "Would I go out for dinner with a guy like me?" He hesitated, thought about his own question, and then said, "Yes—if I was me, I definitely would go out for dinner with me. And I think you should too."

She smiled in relief. "I'd love to," she said, feeling the excitement spread across her face.

★   ★   ★

As Ashleigh walked home through Hyde Park toward her flat in Knightsbridge, she giggled to herself as she thought of Dave, her prince from an imaginary palace. She actually felt happy—her cheeks were filled with color, and she had to refrain from a sudden urge to skip. She knew that if she *did* skip, she would more than likely throw up. Reaching for her phone, she stopped.

No—you don't need to tell Kelly about this; it will keep. Remember your new, empowered self.

The July heat and the fumes from the city fused together so that distant buildings shimmered like a film of gas. Hyde Park was full of children and rollerbladers whizzing up and down. The sound of people enjoying the summer made her smile as she strolled along the path. She stopped and sat down on the grass, watching the rollerbladers showing off to each other. One blader tried to catch her eye by jumping onto a stone ledge and doing some fancy footwork. She smiled to herself, lying back on the grass and thinking again of the window glazer man and what she should wear on their date next week.

Dave, that's a nice name—sounds solid and trustworthy. Unlike her previous boyfriend. Gently, she drifted off to sleep in the sun, listening to the sounds of skaters.

When she woke, both the bladers and the sound of children playing had vanished.

She got up and glanced at her watch, which read 5:28 p.m. She strolled through the park, jumped on a bus, and got off just past Harrod's, feeling energized after her nap in the park.

As she walked into her mews just off Knightsbridge, she stopped. All the happiness and excitement instantly drained from her entire body. Standing by the steps to her flat was Lee Preston, her ex, whom she had dumped five months ago.

What the hell?

Lee Preston was a good-looking, confident, twenty-nine-year-old lawyer whose confidence overreached his knowledge. Even so, coupled with his father's name, he was doing very well for himself, and he knew it. But what was he doing here? Ashleigh had known this day would come. She had known he would find out where she'd moved, and she also knew the one thing he hated most was being told no.

Lee had had a privileged life but had been raised by a father with imbalanced morals—like father, like son. She knew this, but she had always thought she could be the one to change him. How wrong she had been.

Ashleigh walked forward with hesitation in each step. Looking at him, she could feel knots in her stomach as she remembered the bad times he had put her through, and she didn't know if she could go back there again.

No, don't get carried away. You don't know why he is here—just smile and say hi. The ball is in your court, Miss Empowerment.

"Lee. Hi."

"Hello, Ashleigh," he replied, flashing his perfect white teeth. He still looked drop-dead gorgeous as he stood there wearing the same cocky smile.

"How did you know where to find me this time?"

"Nice place." He gestured up toward her front door. "I bumped into Samantha—she told me."

"Did she now?" Ashleigh asked, not too happily. "And what do you want, Lee?" She urged herself to be strong this time.

"To see how you are."

"Fine, I'm fine, can't you tell?" She also gestured up toward her front door.

"Yeah, looks like you are—a little mews tucked back from the main road. Nice." He looked past her at the cobbled stone driveway. "Still got your Classic MG?" He nodded at the garage door beneath the stone steps that led up to her front door.

"Yes, thanks."

They stood on the cobbles, Ashleigh not wanting to invite him up but curious nonetheless.

Lee looked hard at her. "Ashleigh, I've been a fool."

And here it comes—the "I've fucked up" speech. Do not fall for it.

"I can't live without you." He moved closer to touch her face, taking off his shades to reveal his sharp blue eyes that still paralyzed her with lust. "I still want you." He moved her hair behind her ear.

"Lee, don't." She tried to step to the side, but he wouldn't let her. *I can't let him seduce his way back into my life like this. Not again.* She let him stand close for a moment before pushing away.

"I can't," she said quietly.

"Can't what?"

She knew he could feel her self-doubt and was ready for her to run back into his bed like she always did.

Not this time.

"I can't be with you again—too much has happened. I'm happy with my life now," she lied.

He looked into her eyes, demanding her full attention as if she were one of his clients who didn't understand what was at stake.

"Do you think about us making love like we used to?" he asked, stepping closer again. "Ashleigh, I can't get you out of my head at night—your smell, the way your body moved underneath mine, the noises you made when we were making love."

"Stop! Lee, just stop it."

But he had moved her against the garage door, bending to kiss her, pushing his body hard against hers. In the heat of the moment, she kissed him back for a split second, but then she broke away.

"Go," she said.

"Ashleigh, it's still there—can't you feel it? Our life together—we can still get it back," he pleaded, just like he always did.

"Yeah, Lee—until something else takes your fancy," she shouted, running up the step to her front door. "Now, just go—and leave me alone."

"I'll prove it to you, Ashleigh Lands. Just give us some thought."

"No. I've met someone else." The words fell from her mouth without her thinking. She slammed the door behind her and, through the door's spy hole, watched him stare up at the door. Finally, he rolled his eyes and turned to walk away.

Ashleigh stood with her back against the door, her heart pounding, her head in a spin. She put her keys on the table in the hall and picked up the phone to call Rachel, her closest confidant, but decided against it, placing the phone down again. She couldn't call and offload her problems about Lee again. She thought about calling her sister—no. She needed to move on from him and stop leaning on Rachel and her sister for support.

Be strong. She hoped Lee would stay away, but who was she kidding? He would be back. She walked over to her couch and slumped down. She couldn't let Lee do it again. He was bad for her—she knew this. Did she deep down like or even invite the excitement and power he had over her?

Ashleigh stood up. *Snap yourself out of it. You're in control of your own feelings.* But this was no good; she wasn't strong—no, she was weak and easily led. She always had been; even as a child, she had clung to her big sister and friend Rachel at every given opportunity, copying everything they did and said. She sighed. Everyone had figured out their lives, but Ashleigh felt as if she had never gotten it quite right.

A loving family, who had all moved to America without her—even if that was her choice, maybe she had made the wrong choice to stay in England like she had made the wrong choice with Lee. Then there was her average job as a dental assistant. Ashleigh didn't think it was average, but she knew her parents did. A dental assistantship was not a worthy job for the private school education they had spent thousands on. But somehow, she managed to make people believe she had it all together. All she wanted was a faithful man to love her and have babies with .

"Is that really too much to ask?" she said out loud. *A family of my own.*

CHAPTER

3

"OUCH!" DAVE GRITTED HIS teeth in pain.

"What'd you do?" shouted Peter from his room up the hall.

"Stubbed toe," was all Dave could say through the pain as he clutched his foot.

Dave had been living with his twin brother Peter ever since their parents had split up three months after their eighteenth birthday. By the time they were twenty, they had gone into business together as window glaziers. From a young age, it had always been clear that Dave had the brains, and Peter, the gift of gab. Now, the boys were happily living south of the river in Wandsworth in a top-floor, Victorian, converted house overlooking the Common, even if the mortgage *was* proving to be a strain.

A week had passed, and Dave's date with Ashleigh was finally here. Dave was nervous about taking out such a beautiful, well-mannered girl.

"I've got someone coming to look at the room," Peter shouted.

Dave ignored him, gripping his toe as it throbbed. Peter had put forward the idea of a female roomie on the condition that she could cook, drank beer, and liked football; also, she would have to be reasonably hot. Obviously, both brothers were in favor of the idea—Peter more so than Dave, who suspected that women like that did not actually exist.

However, this had all been before Dave had started speaking to Ashleigh every day on the phone since they had met. It was as if he couldn't get enough of her; their conversations lasted for hours. He didn't like to compare, but he hadn't felt this easy with someone since his first love. He enjoyed the way he could talk to Ashleigh about total nonsense, and she laughed at all his dry jokes. Dave found her a breath of fresh air—she didn't play games, and there was no worrying about calling her too much or coming across too keen. If he sent her a text, she would reply straight back with none of that twenty-minute rule some people did just so the other person might think they were busy or not being overly keen. Not Ashleigh. She was different.

Peter came down the hall to help his brother get to his feet since Dave was still holding his toe in pain, rocking like a mental patient.

"So where are you taking her?" Peter heaved Dave to his feet, and Dave hobbled into the lounge and dropped onto the sofa. "And don't be too loud later; I've got Sasha over tonight, and she's a bit prudish."

"Sasha, hey? Things must be bad on the lady front." Dave laughed.

"She ain't that bad. Anyway, a shag's a shag. So where are you going?"

Dave shrugged. "I've got a few ideas." He sat back, thinking some more about where to take Ashleigh. He liked this girl. She was sexy, elegant, and kind, and she made him laugh—which, in fairness, was not the easiest thing to do. Dave was the first to admit that he could be quite serious at times. Since they had met, he had lain in bed most nights thinking of her—what she would be like to kiss, and whether she would be wild in bed or, at worst, frigid. This behavior on Dave's part was quite out of character. After all, she was just a girl he had met for a few hours on a job—and not the first, either. Why was he so bothered this time?

He remembered the last time he had been in love. It had been with Caroline Fletcher, the stable girl from his home-town in Cornwall. He wondered what she would have been doing now. He often wondered this. Peter got angry when he talked about her, telling him to move on, to stop living in the past. He knew his brother meant well, and he also knew he too struggled with the loss of Caroline as a friend. However, this brotherly love only closed Dave off from his emotions. He had to keep them locked inside with no one to talk to, along with a past that he found so hard to let go of. It was a happy past, but one that had died when Caroline Fletcher had fallen to her death when they were just seventeen.

Since then, Dave had found opening up to people so hard. He didn't really understand why—it wasn't as if he had been through bad relationships. But something inside him had died that dreadful day when Caroline died. No one had ever matched up to her since—no one until now, anyway.

So, what was it about Ashleigh? All he knew was that Ashleigh Lands was on his mind every day, so this first date had to impress.

★　　★　　★

Ashleigh was dressed with just her hair left to do. She sat in front of her dresser, pinning bits of her long, dark hair into an elegant style that would show off her pale, slender neck.

There was a knock at the door. Hoping Dave was not this early, she rushed to answer it. Standing there was Mr. Schnitzer, one of her neighbors. He held a box out in front of him. He was a nice man in his late fifties who had a thick German accent and kept to himself. They rarely crossed paths, and when they did, there was just a quick exchange of pleasantries, then on with their separate lives. Mr. Schnitzer didn't seem to have many visitors—just a young man whom Ashleigh assumed to be his son. He also didn't go out much, so she assumed that he either worked from home or didn't work at all. No lady friends ever visited—just the young man who looked like a younger Mr. Schnitzer. Ashleigh always felt sad that he didn't have love in his life; he seemed like such a nice man.

"Hello, Mr. Schnitzer," she said, looking at the box.

"Evening, Ashleigh. Zis came for you today ven you vere out." He handed her the box.

"Thank you."

"You're velcome. Have a lovely evening." Mr. Schnitzer's mouth curled into a stiff smile as he looked at her standing there, and then he retreated down the steps.

Ashleigh turned and closed the door behind her, placing the box on the hallway table. Stepping back, she stared at it with folded arms. Lee used to send her gifts in the post throughout their relationship. She pondered for a moment and decided to open the parcel. She quickly tore back the brown paper to reveal a cream box with black writing on it.

"Links of London," she read out loud.

Opening the box, she peered in and saw a black velvet dust bag. Reaching inside, she slid out a beautiful silver picture frame. It held a black and white photo of Ashleigh with her arm around Lee's dog, Max, in the park. Ashleigh smiled. She loved that picture—she had always wanted to have it blown up and framed. She missed Max, a friendly, bouncy, yellow Labrador that wouldn't leave her side and cried each time she left the house.

Poor thing. How he must miss me. She went into the living room and placed the picture on top of the fireplace, stepping back to reminisce about that summer's day in the park, which had only been last year.

What was Lee playing at, sending her this? He knew it would pull at her heart. He was not leaving without a fight, and she now knew that for sure. To him, she was a case to be won.

Well, not this time, Lee Preston. She addressed the framed photo and sighed. She was annoyed by the gift's attached intention but still missed him. All the heartache and betrayal he had put her through, all the lavish gifts in the post trying to win her back time and time again, and she still missed him. Why? How was she meant to move on if she still missed him?

"Enough," she told herself.

Lee was not going to spoil her night with Dave. She owed herself that, at least. She needed to give this guy a chance. All week, she hadn't thought of Lee, but she had spoken and laughed with Dave every day—and it felt natural, not forced or awkward. She had even decided not to confront Samantha about giving Lee her address—she just wanted to move on. An argument was the last thing she needed, and her week had been good—better than the previous weeks, at any rate. She had even turned down a night out drinking to spend it as she had in the past, on the sofa watching

Netflix. Dave was a breath of fresh air. She just hoped this date ended the way all her fantasies of him did: with a kiss that would melt her soul. She giggled.

Stepping up to the picture of her and Max, she traced the dog's coat with her finger. She missed her life with Lee. Who was she kidding to say otherwise? But it was done—time to move on, to find someone who would treat her right. However, she left the picture on the fireplace.

Just for a few days. Then, she jumped at the sound of the doorbell.

By the time she got to the door, she had composed herself—Max and Lee would have to wait. Dave was speechless for the first few seconds when she opened the door. She had been told that she had such beauty, and there were times like this when she felt it, too. She hoped he was admiring her long, slender, bare legs as she rushed back to pick up her handbag from the living room.

She locked the front door, and Dave gestured for her to walk down the steps before him. The air was heavy and close with no breeze to cool their clammy skin. Dave opened the cab door for her to slide in. She looked up at him, and he looked back at her for a moment with a stare that made her nervous. Smiling, he shut the door.

On the way to the restaurant, Dave sat close to her and held her hand on his lap. She could feel his body warmth on the back of her hand through his smooth trousers. Thoughts scattered around her mind, making no sense. She wondered if a glass of wine would refocus them.

Oh God, am I alcohol-dependent these days or something? She shook the thought away fast. Alcoholism was definitely not part of her empowerment plan—not even a failed empowerment plan.

"Do you like French food?" Dave asked.

"Yes," she replied. *I also love the sound of your deep voice. How does he do that? He's like a catalyst to something deep inside me.*

They drove through London to Richmond, where the cab dropped them off at a French restaurant opposite the river. Dave escorted her by the hand in a true gentleman's fashion. All thoughts of Lee had been pushed far away, and she intended for them to stay there.

The evening was turning out to be just perfect. They had so much in common; even before the wine, they were flirting.

Ashleigh couldn't take her eyes off him and felt quick quivers every time he touched her. Even small gestures like putting his hands on her waist to guide her to the table made her feel powerless with desire.

Ashleigh had frogs' legs on Dave's recommendation, as the whole menu was written in French. To her surprise, Dave could read everything in what seemed a perfect accent. The waiter left them, and Dave explained that he had learned French at school and was not fluent, just well-practiced at reading the menu he held as he and his brother enjoyed the food and dined at the restaurant regularly.

"So you're a fraud, then. And I thought I may have found a nice Frenchman," she joked.

"*Oui, oui, mademoiselle.*"

The waiter returned with a bottle of champagne and silently popped the cork into a towel. Dave asked Ashleigh about her job and sat listening intently as she explained that she had studied for two years while working for a small practice in a town called Downton near Salisbury, Wiltshire, where she had grown up with her parents and sister Kelly.

Dave took a sip of champagne. "So, what brought you to London?" he asked, placing his glass back on the table.

"I took a job in London to be close to my friend Rachel, who followed her career to the big city. She's a buyer for Hopscotch, the children's clothing company—do you know it? She's done so well for herself."

Dave smiled and nodded.

"So enough about me, Dave—what brought you to London, then?"

Dave didn't divulge a huge amount about his younger years, but from the fragments he let slip, he seemed to be well-loved even though his parents were divorced. She learned a lot about his childhood and laughed at his boyish tails of adventures over the Downs with his brother. But he seemed more interested in her, asking question after question. She liked that—Lee would spend a whole dinner talking about himself. Sometimes, she had wondered if Lee would even notice if she got up to leave. What had she actually seen in Lee in the first place, she thought.

Damn it—forget Lee, will you? She pulled herself back to the present.

"Do you miss your family?" Dave asked her.

"Oh, no. Well, I do, but not enough to leave—England's my home, you know," she added hastily. "My dad helps me out with money a lot even though I tell him not to. I'm more than capable of supporting myself, but you don't know my dad. If he wants to help me, no one can tell him not to."

Dave nodded. Ashleigh thought he would ask why she hadn't gone to America with her family, but he didn't, and she was glad. Their conversation was interrupted by the arrival of the waiter, who placed a plate of what looked like tiny chicken wings down in front of her. She wondered if the frogs' legs had been such a good choice after all.

After dinner, they took a walk along the river, intoxicated with passion that had been accelerated by copious glasses of champagne, and they stood looking out at the water, holding hands for a while. Was this happiness, or was she just drunk again? Whatever it was, Ashleigh liked it. She liked *him*. Dave was strong and romantic. Maybe a little too nice at times, but as a whole, he was as good as any prince she had ever met. Was Dave the one to get her over Lee? Or was Dave the one?

Slow down, slow down. She silenced herself.

"I think you're amazing." Dave looked her up and down in a way that made her feel vulnerable.

He moved in front of her and touched her face with the tips of his fingers. She smiled, putting her hands around his waist.

Sod slowing down. Just kiss me already. He bent slightly and then moved in closer so that her breasts were pressed against his chest. She was lost in his kiss, shivering at the way his hand felt against her face. His tongue slipped around inside her mouth. Time slowed, and the sound of her heart vibrated throughout her body. This kiss was everything she had hoped it would be. If Dave's only down point was being too nice, she was sure she could get over that. Nice boys did not kiss the way he was kissing her. This man had depths she wanted to explore.

★   ★   ★

They arrived back at Ashleigh's flat just after one a.m. Dave walked her up to her front door.

"I had a lovely night—thank you," she said, putting her arms around his body again.

"So did I. I hope you will let me take you out again."

"Of course." She leaned up to kiss him, trying to suppress an excited smile. She chose not to offer him a nightcap—not this time, anyway. And she was pleased that he didn't ask to come in.

A true gent, and a shockingly sexy one at that. She shut the front door.

As she lay in bed that night, her head was full of conflicting emotions: excitement, worry, desire, fear, and happiness all churning her up inside. She wriggled around beneath the sheets and then kicked them off, laying exposed, staring at the glow of the city emanating through the thin blinds. She struggled with her misplaced feelings for Lee, and anxiety pinched as she thought of the picture and frame he had sent. Surely he would now pay her another visit.

She pulled her thoughts back to the evening she had just had with Dave, her very own real-life prince. Was life actually starting to go her way? Was she really going to let Lee spoil that?

CHAPTER

4

A SHLEIGH AWOKE THE NEXT morning on top of the world. Pulling up the blinds in the living room, she sat down to drink her tea just as the phone rang. It was Rachel.

"Is he still there?"

"No, I didn't offer, and he didn't ask."

"Argh . . . is that a good sign?" Rachel said inquisitively.

Ashleigh laughed. "I hope so."

"Let's meet up—Jules is back in town, and you can then tell all."

"OK, lunch at the Harp. One p.m.? You ring the others."

Ashleigh hung up and sat back down in front of the TV. She hadn't seen Rachel in over a week, which was a lifetime in their relationship. She didn't like distancing herself from her friends, but she did need this small amount of time to regroup her life. They had texted, and she was sure Rachel hadn't noticed a difference, which was good. Miss Empowerment transformation was underway—and without detection. She had this.

She was excited to tell everyone about her date with Dave, but first she needed to tell Jules about her and Lee. Ashleigh now regretted keeping it from her. She thought she was doing the right thing—the last thing Jules needed was Ashleigh offloading on her about Lee while she was working away. It wasn't their first breakup, and it felt wrong to concern her. She hoped Jules would understand.

Pulling out her phone, she dropped her sister a quick text letting her know about her first date with Prince Dave, his new secret nickname between Ashleigh and Kelly.

OMG date was sooo good. No—awesome.
Prince Dave is too good to be true.
Text me later.
x Ash x

A few moments later, there came a knock at the door. Still in her nightie, she answered it. To her horror, Lee was standing there in the brilliant sunshine, holding a dozen red roses in one hand and one single white rose in his other hand. He extended the single white rose toward her and tilted his head the way a confused Labrador would.

"Lee, what are you doing? This is exactly why I didn't want you to know where I lived." Unwanted butterflies awoke in her stomach. She pulled her bathrobe tight.

What was Samantha thinking when she told him where I lived? What is she playing at? Ashleigh had known Samantha was a troublemaker from the first day Ashleigh started work at the dental practice nearly two years ago. Not to put too fine a point on it, Samantha was a bitch at times and had always fancied Lee—so why she had told him where Ashleigh had moved to baffled her somewhat.

"Can we talk?" Lee asked, still holding out the single white rose.

Ashleigh stepped aside, and with a roll of her eyes, she accepted the rose. Lee walked into her hallway and looked around, waiting to be shown the way.

"You can wait in the living room while I get dressed," she said, leading the way. Without a thank you, she took the other roses as he held them out to her.

"I can put them in water for you," he offered.

"Thank you, I'll do it. Just wait here."

Her reply was polite but blunt. This was her home, not his. She made him a coffee and then left him to get herself dressed.

She watched him through the crack of her door as he wandered around the room. He reached up, touching the framed picture of her and Max on the mantel, and then picked up a business card next to it. Dave's business card. He discarded it with a flick of his fingers down into the open fire below. *How dare he?* She closed the door.

Old desires pinched at her emotions. *Oh God.* He was in her home, her new home. *Be strong. Do not take him back.*

Ashleigh pulled out the first pair of jeans she saw and pulled on a T-shirt laying on the floor. She needed him out of her flat, and fast.

Walking back into the living room, she watched Lee stand up. She continued quickly to the kitchen to fetch a vase, buying herself more time before facing him. She put the roses in a vase and carried them to the windowsill, separating them slightly after placing the vase. Lee picked up the single white rose and walked over, pushing it into the middle of the bunch. Just the sense of him being close to her weakened her slightly.

"Can't leave that one out, can we?" He gave her a sideways glance.

"Shall we take a seat?" she replied hastily, disregarding his comment.

She sat on the sofa, and Lee followed suit, taking a seat next to her. She didn't say anything; she just sat there cross-legged with both hands on her lap, straight-backed, feeling awkward in her own home.

Lee sighed. "We were good together, Ashleigh." He tried to take her hands, but she slowly moved them to her knee.

"I think you'll find that *I* was good, Lee, and you were not."

"I messed up big time, I know. I don't know what to say to take it away." Ashleigh carried on looking straight ahead without replying, and Lee continued. "I tried to find you, but you'd changed your number."

She still had nothing to say. What did he expect from her?

"I love you, Ashleigh," Lee insisted. "Please talk to me. We can work through this."

Ashleigh turned to look at him. She normally had so much to say for herself, but now she just sat there, lifeless, eyes fixed on his face. She didn't know what to say or what to feel this time. She was still attracted to him, but did she *want* to go back? They had broken up plenty of times in the past, but never for this long. Had it been too long for her to want to try again? She thought of her date the night before and how Dave made her feel important, and then about her life with Lee. She saw it now: how he controlled her, how he put her down with smug comments until her self-esteem was so low the only person who could make her feel better was him, the victor. So why was she still letting him affect her emotions? Why not just tell him to leave?

Eventually, looking directly into his eyes with cool, calm composure, she said, "Lee. Nearly two years ago, my whole family emigrated to America, including my only sister, whom I miss every day. But you know that—you could see how dependent I was on her, and you exploited that. I can see that now." He tried to speak, but she held up her hand. "Let me finish. I had a new life set out for me—a job and a home. But I stayed for you, decided it was time to stop clinging to my big sister, to do what I want, make my own decisions and my own mistakes—you being one of those mistakes."

Her eyes started to well up, but she blinked back the tears and continued. "You became mean and vindictive. All the client functions you took me to started to become nerve-racking because you noticeably flirted with most of the female guests. Not to mention your unhealthy relationship with *that*." She pointed at his phone. "You stopped taking calls in front of me, claiming them to be 'just some client, honey.'"

Lee shook his head. "I don't know what to say." He tried to convey regret. "You just have to ignore these silly thoughts you have. It's you I love." The words flowed like polluted water from his mouth.

Fighting the new desire to scream at him, Ashleigh took a deep breath. "I don't regret staying in London. I loved you, still do in a small way, but I trusted you. You broke that trust in so many ways."

He fidgeted slightly, but she knew his arrogant personality believed that she would not find a more eligible bachelor than himself.

Lee straightened. "It was the biggest mistake of my life losing you—one silly, silly mistake." He looked at the floor.

"One mistake it certainly wasn't, Lee—more like the one I found out about." Her earlier emotions of lust were subsiding into hate.

"Ashleigh, you know that's not true."

"Do I? At most parties you took me to, I always had a funny feeling that your ex-girlfriends might not have been so ex."

"People like me; it's not my fault. I have to mingle, and you just got jealous. It's business, honey." He took a sip of coffee, sitting back in the sofa.

"Oh my God. Lee, you're so self-sure." She laughed. "You mean like your client's twenty-two-year-old, Swedish niece was just business?"

Ashleigh had just about had enough, so she stood up and walked over to the balcony door. He followed behind, stepping out and standing close as she stared out over the chimneypots of London. She had loved him. God knows how or why, but she had, and hard. In the beginning, he made her feel like a prized possession. But she didn't want to be his possession any more. She didn't want to be mad at him; she didn't want to be *anything* with him. But she was. She was balancing precariously on that fine line between love and hate, and she was sure he knew it.

"I'm so, so sorry," he whispered. She didn't move. He stood close, placing his hands on her shoulders. "Ashleigh, I wish I could go back and change the past."

His touch was familiar, and she let him gently touch the back of her neck as he bent to smell her perfume. She urged herself to stay strong, to move away, but she couldn't.

"She meant nothing." His lips were close to her skin.

His warm breath brushed against her neck. The words rang through her head like an air-raid siren during a blackout, people running for shelter from the bombs about to drop, to destroy life as they had known it—only she had nowhere to run. He was in her house, and she couldn't run away from him, his words, or her unwanted feelings for him. How dare he seduce his way back into her life only to drag up painful memories of his infidelity?

"Get out!" she snapped, turning to face him. "Just get the hell out, Lee. And never come back. We're over. *Over.*"

He stared at her and then slowly walked away without a word, not even a single glance back. He slammed the front door. She fought back tears, pushing away the pain, the unwanted desire she felt, and all the memories. Who did he think he was, showing up in her life and expecting her to just take him back? Not this time, not again.

Never again. She hoped she could stay true to her own decision.

The sound of her house phone brought her back to reality. She let it ring for a while and then hurried to answer before they rung off. It was Dave. A feeling of guilt flooded her as she stood listening to his deep voice, as he told her of his trouble-free day without a care in the world. She didn't disclose her encounter with Lee to him as this time, things were going to be different. She wasn't going back. Things had changed—she had managed without Lee in her life; she had moved on, met someone else; life was fresh. And more to the point, Dave had just called the day after their first date; surely this was a good sign. Her new, empowered self took over—Lee could well and truly go to hell.

★　　★　　★

It was nearly one o'clock when she finished talking to Dave, realizing she had to meet the others. She hurried around the flat, getting ready and grabbing her things before rushing off to the Harp, a pub opposite Victoria Station. Surprisingly, she arrived at the pub with a good five minutes to spare. She found a table and sat drinking a glass of Sauvignon Blanc. The door to the pub opened, and she heard Rachel's loud voice followed closely by Jules and Leon.

"Ashleigh, darling, hello." Rachel's voice filled the pub as she bent down to kiss the air on either side of Ashleigh's face.

"Hey, Rachel; hi, Leon . . . Jules. How are you? It's been too long." Ashleigh gestured for Jules to sit down next to her while Leon rushed to the bar, leaving them to ponder over the lunch menu. Jules looked a million dollars, as usual, dressed in the latest fashion, her long, thick blonde hair pushed back by Gucci sunglasses.

"So," Ashleigh said as Jules sat down next to her, "how was it living in Milan for the last twelve months? Do tell all."

"Fun, but glad to be home, if I'm honest." Ashleigh thought she caught a hint of relief in Jules' voice. "Anyway, less of my boring work life. Just another day in the life of a magazine editor's assistant. So—how's things with Lee?" Jules asked, unaware of past events.

Ashleigh didn't know what to say and looked around the table at the straight faces. Rachel quickly jumped in, explaining the whole story while Ashleigh sat back and listened. Jules looked back and forth from Rachel to Ashleigh, visibly shocked that no one had told her before.

"Why didn't you say something?" Jules asked the whole group. "It's not like we haven't spoken."

"Sorry, it's my fault," said Ashleigh. "I didn't want to bore you with my problems. You sounded so busy whenever we spoke, and if I'm honest, it was nice to talk about something else. I should have told you sooner."

"You should have, yes. All of you should have." Jules gave an icy stare. "I'm your friend, no matter where I am in the world. I'm friends with *all* of you, so don't you ever do this again."

"Cheers, Ash. I told you." Leon flicked his wrist.

"It was me," Ashleigh said again. "Don't blame them, Jules. I asked them not to."

"Well, that was wrong of you, Ashleigh. I'm your friend, and I want to be there for you."

"I know, I know." Ashleigh felt terrible.

A waitress appeared beside their table, notepad in hand. One by one, they gave their orders.

"It's been five months since I left him," Ashleigh said, moving her drink out of the way so the waitress could lay their cutlery down.

"She's met a new man, though, haven't you, Ash?" Leon announced. "She's been texting me every day with updates. He sounds dreamy."

"Yeah, he's lovely." Ashleigh smiled, glad that the conversation was lighting up. "He's tall, dark, and handsome." She took a sip of her wine, still smiling. "He took me for dinner last night to a French place on the riverfront in Richmond. It was the most perfect, romantic first date *ever*, and everything was the way it should have been."

"I'm happy for you, honey." Jules softened. "You deserve better than Lee."

"Lee wants me back," Ashleigh said quickly.

"What?" Rachel's shocked voice bellowed.

Three faces stared at her from around the table.

"He said Samantha gave him my new address and he turned up at my door last week."

"And you're only telling us now?" Rachel questioned.

Jules laughed. "Now you know how I feel."

"If you go back to him, you're a fool, and you know it," Leon said, looking away sharply.

"He came over with flowers today and wanted to talk," Ashleigh told them. "I get so weak around him; it's so frustrating—but this time, as I listened, I got mad at him. I screamed at him and told him to get out. And he did. He just left."

"He left without a fight?" Rachel looked confused. "He's up to something, Ash."

"Yeah, I know." Ashleigh sighed.

"You still love him, don't you?" Jules said plainly.

Ashleigh shrugged. "No . . . no. Oh, I don't know."

"That man is up to something—trust me, I know," Leon said. "And you, girl, need to wake the hell up and move on." He shook his head and clicked his fingers at the waitress. "Mark my words, girlfriend, if you go back, he will shatter your heart just like all the other times."

Jules slapped Leon's arm, reprimanding him for clicking at the waitress. "At least you have two men who want you," she said, breaking the tension.

Leon chuckled. "Yeah, look at poor Rachel. It's been so long she probably has cobwebs down there."

"Bitch, *please*," Rachel said. "That's by choice. I'm far too busy for a man."

"It's ironic," Leon said. "You work for a children's clothing company, but you're the least maternal woman I know."

"I'm twenty-six; there's plenty of time for all that," Rachel retorted. "However, you're thirty this year, Leon—where's *your* Mrs. Right? You can't rattle around all on your own in your posh riverside apartment paid for by Daddy forever."

"In African culture, we like to sow our wild seeds." Leon grinned sarcastically.

"African culture, don't talk crap." Ashleigh laughed. "Your dad loves your mum."

"Maybe I don't take after my dad. Maybe I want to sow my wild seeds for eternity."

Ashleigh threw her head back, laughing. "Stop—let's change the subject from Leon's seeds."

Leon smirked and raised his hand toward the waitress, who had ignored his previous finger snaps. "The service in here is shocking, don't you think?"

Jules shook her head in disbelief.

"You know what we all need?" Rachel said. "A holiday."

Silence fell around the table. "Oh, come on, guys! It would be fun."

Jules caught the waitress's eye and politely waved her over. "Can we possibly get another bottle of wine please?" She turned back to the table, giving Leon a sideways glance. "If I'm honest, a holiday is the last thing I need after spending a year in Spain. I just want to get back into my life in London, but I promise to think it over, honey."

"We understand," Rachel said. "I could do with a getaway, though." She smiled at Ashleigh. "Let me do some research on destinations. What do you say, Ash?"

"Maybe. I've never been on a holiday without Lee." Ashleigh thought about it for a moment. "Maybe I should."

"Yesss!" Rachel clapped. "See ya, Lee."

"So what are you going to do, Ashleigh?" Jules asked. "Will you give Lee another chance? Maybe a holiday is just what you need."

"I am not getting back with Lee," Ashleigh told her. "Not this time."

"You sure about that, girlfriend?" Leon asked. "You've said that before."

"This chick isn't having none of it this time." Ashleigh snapped her fingers, knowing full well her friends could see though her charade. Would things really be different this time?

CHAPTER

5

THE NEXT MORNING, ASHLEIGH woke late. She made a mad dash to get to work on time, jumping on the bus at Knightsbridge instead of walking through Hyde Park. She got off at Oxford Street and then ran through Cavendish Square and down the whole length of Harley Street.

"Excuse me." The quiet voice of an elderly, well-dressed lady stopped Ashleigh as she opened the door. Ashleigh swung round.

"Is this the dental practice?" the lady asked.

"Yes, please come in."

Ashleigh put her key in the door, still panting under her breath from her dash.

Thank God I made it. She showed the lady to the waiting room and then rushed off to set up for the day, nearly knocking over the receptionist coming down the hallway as she went.

The dentist Ashleigh worked with was Eliza McDonald, one of the best maxillofacial surgeons in England. Like Ashleigh, Eliza was a brunette, but she was slightly curvier and in her early forties, though her pale skin made her look a lot younger. The two had worked with each other for over four years and had become more than just work colleagues. Before Ashleigh took the job two years ago, she had worked alongside Eliza at the Eastman Dental Hospital in King's Cross. Over time, they had formed a friendship, making work even more enjoyable despite the principal of the practice, Prof.

Matson, being an arrogant jerk at times. She loved her job, and while she was regretful that she hadn't achieved more from her schooling, she was grateful that she had picked a career that she excelled in.

By lunchtime, there was a thick heat haze across London—a lethal combination of hot sun and car fumes. Ashleigh and Eliza strolled along the pavement toward the high street. Ashleigh adored Marylebone High Street. It still had a small-town feel to it—the only place in London that could sometimes make her forget she was in the middle of a big city. They stopped at some of the small boutiques dotted along the road to the lunch café. The only thing to remind her that this was the capital was the traffic and countless people, not to mention the celebrities going about their business.

Ashleigh barely ever recognized famous people—she was usually too lost in her own thoughts to notice—but the other nurses would come back from lunch telling everyone whom they had seen: Liam Gallagher at the cashpoint, or the Beckhams leaving a Harley Street building.

Ashleigh wasn't really interested in stardom. She had grown up around more money than she ever really needed. When she was a child, her mum and dad would throw extravagant parties, inviting important men from the oil business world, some low-profile celebrities or their relatives, but mainly suits and politicians. Ashleigh was never interested in these parties like her sister Kelly was. Ashleigh would whine at the announcement of the next party and refuse to help her mother and sister prepare the invitations or entertainment.

"Why do I have to help? I'm just a child," she would say.

"It will teach you how to be a good host when you're an adult. Now go and help your sister design the invites," her mother would insist.

Ashleigh had never wanted for anything, and she still had the financial support of her father. When she called America after her breakup with Lee, her father had demanded that she come and live with them.

"Ashleigh, I admire you for staying in England and fighting for something you believe in," he said, "but it's over now. There is no need to be apart from your family anymore, is there? I have a position here in the business for you."

After Ashleigh explained her reasons for still wanting to stay and not wanting to leave her friends and her life in London, her father reluctantly accepted her decision to stay. However, he insisted on paying for her to break her rental agreement, and then he paid for her new flat in Knightsbridge; all so she could get away from Lee and make a fresh start. This was another reason why getting back with Lee was a bad idea. Her father was a kind man, but he would not take kindly to Ashleigh taking Lee back this time.

"Enough is enough, Ashleigh. Drop this deadbeat for good," he had said. "You do what you need to do in England, darling. Your mother and I will always be here if you need us. You know that, don't you?"

Ashleigh loved her family and missed her big sister dearly, but she wanted nothing more than to stand on her own two feet and find a loving man to have a family of her own with. She knew deep down this man would not be Lee, and she couldn't bear to think what his parenting skills would be like. But Prince Dave—now *this* guy was ticking all the boxes.

★ ★ ★

Ashleigh and Eliza sat outside a small sandwich shop enjoying the lunchtime break, waiting for their food to arrive. It was a humid afternoon. The air was heavy, and there was little breeze in London. After a few moments, the coffees arrived on the table. Facing the passersby, they drank their drinks and relaxed. Cars drove along the high street, and the smell of their coffees wafted into the paths of pedestrians, occasionally making them glance at Ashleigh and Eliza as they hurried past.

"My friend suggested a holiday," Ashleigh said, looking across at Eliza.

"Sounds nice."

"It does," Ashleigh agreed. "Somewhere hot, maybe."

"Like where?"

Ashleigh thought for a bit. The waitress brought out their baguettes, placing them down on the table.

"Thank you," Ashleigh said to the waitress. She turned back to Eliza. "Ibiza."

"Ibiza?" Eliza echoed.

"Yeah. I've been thinking, and you're only young once. You know what they say—live your life to the full, and Ibiza is the place to be at my age."

"You're not wrong there," Eliza said. "You go for it, and live it for me, too. Two kids kind of puts a stop to holidays in Ibiza," she added with a laugh. "So, have you spoken to Samantha about why she gave Lee your new address?"

Ashleigh sighed heavily. "No, I don't see the point—I mean, if I really want him out my life, why create an issue? However, something does feel off about it all. Why would she want him to find me? I mean, it's no secret that she fancies him, so why tell him where to find me?"

Eliza nodded. "I agree, but you should say something to her. I understand that you want a clean break from him, but you should tell her not to disclose personal information. What if he was a violent man and you wanted to escape him?"

"He's not." She wondered why she was defending him. Violent or not, he was no god.

"I know, but what if he was? I'm just saying she needs to know not to get involved in your private life. So what are you going to do?"

"I have no idea—running away to Ibiza is my best plan at the moment." Ashleigh tried a small laugh. "I hate confrontation, and Samantha is the last person I want to pick a fight with. My plan had been to just ignore it. We have been getting on so well these last few months."

Eliza grimaced. "Only because you have started going out drinking with her after work. Be careful, Ashleigh. You're a nice girl—don't let people use you."

★   ★   ★

That evening after work, she went straight home to call everyone. Eliza was right—Samantha wasn't a real friend. Her real friends were the ones she should be having fun with. She also didn't want to go out drinking after work all the time anymore; that was not helping anyone. This holiday would represent her new beginning.

First, she rang Rachel, who thought Ibiza was a fantastic idea and was already on the internet checking for cheap, last-minute deals. Ashleigh was excited. Her excitement faded as Rachel explained that she had called Jules, spending the best part of an hour trying to convince her to join them, but Jules was not having any of it. Ashleigh rang Leon, and much to her disappointment, he was less than enthusiastic about the whole thing. As she listened to the excuses coming from the receiver, Ashleigh said nothing. She just twirled the phone cord around her fingers, making the right grunts, "mms," and "ahs," pretending to understand when really, she couldn't understand why anyone would rather not go away to a hot island in the sun to eat, drink, and dance.

Hanging up the call with Leon, she said out loud to herself, "Just me and Rachel, then."

She could still have her new-life holiday celebration with just Rachel. She smiled. Just the two of them, like old times. As she turned to walk into the living room, the phone rang; and like a gunshot in the distance, it triggered a thought—Dave. She had just met a drop-dead gorgeous man and now was planning a girls' holiday to Ibiza.

Oh God, what if that's him calling?

The phone kept ringing.

What do I say?

She couldn't invite him if it was just her and Rachel. Anyway, she hadn't known him long enough for a holiday with him. The phone rang on, and she knew if she didn't pick it up soon, whoever it was would give up. Snatching the receiver, Ashleigh placed it to her ear warily.

"Hello?" Her heart was beating.

"Hello." Sure enough, it was Dave.

"Dave, hi, what a . . . nice surprise." Her heart was beating hard against her chest.

Don't say anything yet. Nothing is set in stone; it's only an idea. Just be normal.

"How's your day been?" he asked.

"Normal . . . you know, just normal."

"Just normal—hey, sounds good."

There was an awkward silence for a while. Ashleigh tried to act as normal as possible, but it was making her sound abnormal. She took a slow breath in, composed herself, and started again.

"It was good. I had my normal lunch with Eliza." *God, no, did I just say normal again?* "So what did you do today?"

She relaxed after listening to Dave for a few minutes, completely forgetting any hot holiday thoughts. Once again, she found herself drawn into his world, and it was a feeling she was starting to really enjoy.

CHAPTER

6

A WEEK WENT PAST. LEE had not tried to contact Ashleigh, which she was grateful for, and she was enjoying talking to her sister about Prince Dave and not Mr. Nobody—Kelly's nickname for Lee. She was also enjoying not drunk-calling her after a night out with Samantha. It had been three weeks since she first met Dave, and in the last week, she had seen him twice for lunch and once after work for a cinema date. She would see him every day if she could, and she didn't think he would mind, either. Being with him was so easy. He made her feel confident about herself, was always pleased to see her and complimenting her clothes or hair. She was actually starting to move on from Lee this time, and it felt good.

Rachel and Ashleigh had agreed on a holiday destination: San Miguel, a small port on the coast of Ibiza, and they were leaving in three weeks' time. Now she would definitely have to tell Dave, but when? She had put off the idea of telling him every time they had spoken, and that was a lot. He didn't seem the jealous type. On the contrary, he was super laid back. But what if he met someone else while she was away? Ashleigh knew her insecurities were clouding her judgment—she also knew that she ran away from difficult conversations more often than not. She still hadn't confronted Samantha, and now she was putting off telling Dave she was going on holiday.

"Oh my God, Ashleigh, we are so going," Rachel said.

"I know, just me and you, like old times. It's a shame the others won't come."

Rachel walked into Ashleigh's bedroom and pulled out a small floral dress.

"If you take this one, can I wear it?" She held the dress up to herself, looking in the mirror. "I want to look sexy and elegant like you, Ash."

"Only if I can wear your little light blue denim hot pants." Ashleigh patted her own bottom. "I will look hot and sassy like you."

Rachel sat back on the bed and tilted her head in thought. "Well, it looks like we are going back to borrowing each other's clothes again, so . . ." Rachel beamed as she jumped up off the bed with the floral dress in her hand. "I need to raid the rest of your closet," she said with a squeal. "So have you told Dave yet?" She pulled out another dress.

"Er . . ."

"Ashleigh . . ."

"What? Nothing was for certain. I'll have to tell him now that it's booked, though." Ashleigh slumped onto the bed.

"See? Men are too much hassle. But you do need to tell him, honey." Rachel sat down beside her. "What's the big deal?"

"What if . . ." Ashleigh paused. She knew deep down that she wasn't worried about Dave being jealous. It was deeper than that. "Well, what if he, you know . . ."

"Um, actually, no. I don't know. What if he—oh, what if he cheats on you while you're away?"

Ashleigh didn't reply.

"Ash, honey, if he does, then he's a fuck-whit. But you can't put your life on hold for a fuck-whit, can you?" Rachel lifted Ashleigh's chin and smiled at her. "Can you, Ash?"

"No . . ."

"Or worry about it. Dave is not Lee. Trust me—even I can see that. So come on; let's have a look at what you've got in the way of beachwear."

Ashleigh agreed but still dreaded the conversation.

Rachel rummaged through Ashleigh's bikinis, tossing out any old or out-of-fashion garments and then cooing over others. She left Ashleigh's flat late in the evening on top of the world, bouncing down the steps as she left and waving frantically over her shoulder. Ashleigh waved her off and then went inside. She had a date with Dave the following night and would tell him at some point during the date—but at what point was her new issue. Her mind bounced around his possible responses. Would he be hurt that she hadn't told him, or disappointed not to be invited? Would he get bored waiting for her and go off with someone else?

It's only a week.

Trying to sleep that night was impossible; there was so much in her head that she couldn't sleep. She lay awake, turning from one side to another. Bikinis, holiday outfits, how much money she would need, would Dave cheat? She pondered on not telling him tomorrow night and leaving it for the next date instead.

No—just tell him. Stop avoiding the conversation. She tried to banish the thought and started to plan out how many sunbeds she could fit in before leaving.

At least an hour went past, but still she couldn't sleep. She sat up. *Right, Missy. You will sleep.* Lying back down, she tried to clear her mind by concentrating on her breathing, and after some time, she slowly eased into a soft, senseless sleep.

★   ★   ★

The evening air was close, and there was a faint smell of bonfire smoke in the air. Ashleigh sat in front of her mirror, pinning back her long, dark, wavy hair. Every style she tried hadn't worked, so she decided to let it hang loose. She put some hair serum on her fingers, smelling its sweet licorice scent, and then ran her hands through her hair, separating the waves into loose curls. She opened her closet door and pondered which shoes would go with her small black dress. She decided on the new Manolo Blahnik her dad had sent over, and then she was ready to go.

Dave had driven to Ashleigh's and was dead on time. After a brief embrace followed by a kiss, he opened the passenger door for her.

"Not quite a convertible," he joked, holding out a hand to help her inside the small white van.

She smiled. "At least it's clean." Her nerves were mixing with each other—excitement and anxiety, what an odd concoction.

They drove through the West End over Chelsea Bridge into South London, arriving at Dave's flat in Wandsworth at eight o'clock, just as Dave's brother was leaving the flat. Dave ushered Ashleigh along the hallway.

"Pete, mate, you've not left yet?" Dave rolled his eyes and turned to Ashleigh. "Ashleigh, this is my brother Peter. Pete, this is Ashleigh."

"Hello, Ashleigh, it's a pleasure." As Peter greeted her, she realized he looked exactly like his brother.

"Hi," she said with a curious smile.

"Just leaving, bro, have a good one." Peter darted out of the flat, slamming the door as he left.

"You never said your brother was your identical twin!" Ashleigh exclaimed.

"Oh, yeah. Sorry, I know, I never do. We had some fun when we were younger with girls that had no idea. Now I just don't think to point it out—habit. Oh God, that sounds bad. I didn't mean—I'm not like that now. Here, take a seat. I'll fix you a drink."

She laughed nervously. Comments like that were the last thing she needed to hear right now.

Dave left the room to get the drinks, and Ashleigh tried to focus on the latter part of Dave's sentence. She noticed he had already set the table for dinner. Beneath the silverware was a white embroidered tablecloth—a little old-fashioned, but cute. She smiled to herself and bent down to smell the red roses set as the centerpiece.

Dave entered the room with their drinks. "You like it?" He walked over to give her the glass.

"Thank you—yes, it's lovely."

"Only the best for you." He leaned in to kiss her gently on the lips. Where had this man been all her life?

They sat opposite each other with a view of the streets below as the day drew to an end and the twilight set in. She smiled across the table at him. It was refreshing not to be with someone like Lee, who would have booked a caterer to set the table and cook the food.

He would have droned on about his boarding school in Sweden and how privileged he had been to have had such an upbringing, yadda, yadda, yadda. After that would have come the rugby talk, and finally, his father's brilliant law firm.

In contrast, Dave had obviously planned everything himself, down to the last detail. The food was divine: lots of small Thai dishes that were light and easy to eat, which pleased her, as she couldn't have fit much in while wearing her little black dress.

After dinner, they sat at the table talking and drinking with light, easy conversation. After some time, they went to curl up on the sofa. Ashleigh chatted nervously for a while—she wanted to tell Dave about the holiday but couldn't bring herself to do it. The night was going so well, she couldn't risk ruining it. They were also alone and still had not made love. If she told him now, would that spoil the moment?

She attempted to counsel her tipsy self. *It will keep.*

Finally, they fell into silence. She could feel the tension deepen, and she longed for him to kiss her. He moved closer a few times but never made the move. It was getting late, and she hoped he would kiss her again before his brother came home.

She didn't have to wait long before Dave lifted her chin with his hand. Staring back at him, she felt her heart pound with anticipation. Moving his hand around the side of her face, he pulled her into him, kissing her slightly harder than he had done before and pulling her close. She found herself entwined with his body, and she felt the warm air on her back as he unzipped her dress. His hands moved over her shoulder blades, down to the base of her spine; she arched her back, yearning for him, and then fumbled with his buttons, trying to undo his shirt. Dave slowly eased himself inside her, gently moving in time with her rhythm. They tried to make love for as long as possible, but the excitement was too much. Before they knew it, they were having fast, heated sex, grinding hard against each other until finally, Ashleigh climaxed with a sharp gasp, followed by Dave.

She lay in Dave's arms as he held her close against his naked chest. She wished the night would never end. Her body still trembling, she felt as if she had just gotten off a fairground ride and needed time to regain her emotions. If only she could freeze this moment forever and just remain in his arms. She knew he would let her stay the night if she wanted, but she preferred to wake up in her own bed and was conscious that Peter would be there in the morning, maybe with another girl.

Later that night, Dave called a cab for her. She felt selfish for not telling Dave about the holiday in case it ruined their first time. *This is silly. It's just a holiday.* She still couldn't bring herself to tell him. Selfishly, she didn't want to ruin her perfect night.

Dave told the cab office that he would be taking the cab with the lady and then returning. Ashleigh protested that she would be fine on her own, but he insisted on taking her home. She was blown away. He was going to get in a cab all the way to the other side of the river just to make sure she got home safely. How unbelievably chivalrous.

They drove effortlessly through the late night streets toward the center of London.

"Are you OK?" Dave asked. He was obviously picking up on her guilt.

Just say it, for God's sake.

"I'm fine." She hesitated. "Dave!"

"Ashleigh!" he echoed, mocking her.

She smiled lightly. "I've been wanting to tell you something for a while."

"OK . . ."

"Rachel and I have a girls' holiday booked." She exhaled as if letting out a secret she had been harboring for many years.

Dave shook his head. "I knew that Rachel was bad news." He read her facial expression and immediately laughed. "I'm joking, honey. What's wrong? Ah . . . will you miss me?" He pinched her cheek in jest.

"I wanted to tell you last week but was . . . well . . . well, I'm not sure."

The cab took a sharp bend a bit faster than necessary, sending Ashleigh sliding into Dave.

Dave tapped the driver's shoulder. "Easy, mate." After receiving an apology, he continued. "Ashleigh, you didn't think I would get mad at you, did you?" He looked concerned.

She shrugged, not wanting to tell him that she also thought he would cheat on her. "I'm sorry."

"Why are you sorry?" Placing a hand on her leg, he asked, "Your ex? Did he get angry at you a lot?"

She shrugged. "Not really. But he wouldn't have let me go on holiday without him."

"Let! Oh, he was one of *those* guys, was he? Listen, you do whatever you want. I will *never* tell you what to do—unless it's a foot massage, and then you don't really get a say."

"Eww, Dave. No way."

"What? It's romantic."

Shaking her head, she refused. "You rub *my* feet, then."

"Eww, no way." He laughed and pulled her under his arm.

When they reached home, Ashleigh kissed Dave goodbye and watched as he left in the cab. That had gone better than she had expected. He didn't seem to mind about the holiday at all—was that a good thing or a bad thing, though? She remembered hearing that some people hide their true feelings with humor. She poured a glass of water and kicked off her shoes. She then pulled out her phone to text her sister, but reconsidered. "Drunk again?" she could imagine Kelly saying. And she would be right—Ashleigh *had* drunk more than she had meant.

Note to self: don't turn into an alcoholic before the age of thirty. She giggled but meant it. Since leaving Lee, she had ramped up the drinking, and she needed to watch that. She didn't mind being the family black sheep, but the family alcoholic? No. That wasn't cool.

Ashleigh got into bed, and her thoughts were soon back on Dave. He hadn't even asked her where or when she was going, but then, he did seem genuine. Deciding to sleep on things, she turned off the bedside light, feeling somewhat easier now that she had told him. She would judge the situation when she saw him next—and when she was sober.

CHAPTER

7

DAVE LEFT THE YARD and drove home in the rush hour traffic. Throwing his keys onto the table, he opened a beer and fell onto the sofa. Fleeting thoughts of Ashleigh's holiday had interrupted his concentration that day. The night before, he'd been so focused on making her feel easy and conveying contrast to her ex, he'd not even asked where she was going. He didn't even know when she was leaving.

Picking up the control, he switched the channel to the football game. She had trusted him—opened up to him about her ex—but he still hadn't told her about Caroline. He would tell her the next time he saw her. It was only fair for her to know about his life— where he came from and who he was. Although he didn't think Ashleigh would ever judge, they were still from different classes in life, and this concerned him a little. Was he good enough for her? Was he just a bit of rough while she got over her ex? She had told him that her ex was a top lawyer, and he knew her father owned an oil company. His dad was a painter, and his ex-girlfriend had been a stable girl—not to mention the fact that he hadn't had another girlfriend since.

Girlfriend. He let the status sit for a while. Normally he would be breaking out in hot sweats at the thought. Dave heard the door open, followed by two voices. One was Peter's, the other a female voice. He got up from the sofa to meet them.

"This is the living room," Peter said to the girl. "This is Dave, my brother. Ignore him—he just lives here."

"Hiya," said a smiling girl with long, dark, wavy hair and a beautiful Latino complexion.

"Hi." Dave stood there for a second before it clicked. She was looking at the flat to rent the third room. He smiled awkwardly, offering a hand for her to shake.

Peter continued to show her around the rest of the flat before escorting her out.

"So what do you think?" he asked when he came back in.

"I thought a girl flatmate was a joke, Pete—if I'm honest with you."

"It kinda was, but then she rung up today, so I made an executive decision to let her view the place. Bro, don't be so uptight. She's hot, and get this—she likes football, and she knows how to cook a curry."

Dave shook his head. What would Ashleigh think of a girl flatmate? Dave ran a weary hand through his hair.

"Come on, Dave, she's perfect. She wants the room—"

"You've already said yes, haven't you?" Dave interjected.

"Um, well . . . yeah. But I did say I would clear it with you first."

Dave paced the room. *It might not be such a bad thing. Does it really matter what sex she is?* After all, a flatmate was a flatmate—as long as she paid the rent on time, why should it be a problem? He thought about it for a moment, reflecting on what Ashleigh's take on a female flatmate might be. He continued to pace the room as his brother watched. Ashleigh didn't seem the jealous type—after all, she trusted him enough to go on a girls' holiday. Psycho jealous girls didn't do that. And he trusted her enough about her going on a holiday, so why wouldn't she trust him enough to have a female flatmate? Dave had never had such conflicting thoughts before—not over a woman, anyway. He stopped pacing and turned to Peter.

"Tell her we'll draw up a contract for a three-month trial," he said, walking into the kitchen. He didn't have the energy to fight his brother on this one, not today. Ashleigh was consuming every ounce of him, but he liked it. She was all he wanted to think about.

"OK. I can do that—I'll have a coffee if you're making one. But Dave, you have to admit: she has a nice ass, perfectly formed breasts—" Peter rubbed his groin in jest.

"Nothing on Ashleigh, though." Dave filled the kettle, still irritated that he had not asked Ashleigh when she was going away.

"Yeah, Ashleigh looked quite hot from what I saw. Fancy sharing?"

Dave glared at Peter. "Back off. I really like her. You just stick to your new conquest."

"You like this girl, don't you?" Peter teased.

"Yes, I do," Dave said. In a warning tone, he added, "So don't go messing up for me."

"OK, OK. But seriously, bro, I'm glad. I know it's been tough for you since—" He stopped.

"Caroline. It's OK, Pete. You can say her name. I'm not going to fall apart at the sound of her name."

"I'm just saying I'm glad you've met someone you're into." Peter patted his brother's back awkwardly.

Dave nodded. He appreciated the gesture. "So what's our flatmate's name? Please tell me you know her name."

"What do you take me for?"

"Do you want me to answer that?"

"Nah, no need to answer that one. It's Isabella—she's Spanish. She works in IT. See? Beautiful, smart, and paying our mortgage."

"Just don't screw this one," Dave said. "She's going to be living with us. And dude, don't go offering rooms out to people again before asking me first. This is my home as well—don't take the piss." He stared across the kitchen at his twin, and Peter grinned back like a scolded school boy.

★   ★   ★

Just as Ashleigh sat down at the table to eat dinner, the phone rang. Picking it up, she heard a very upset voice at the other end. It took her a moment to recognize that it was Rachel.

"In your own time," Ashleigh said softly. "Slow down."

Rachel was in floods of tears and spluttered out that her grandmother had died, instantly stunning Ashleigh.

Rachel had lived with her grandparents since the age of six after her mother and father had been killed in a helicopter crash off the coast of Scotland. Her grandmother had been battling against cancer successfully for so long, but everybody had known that it was only a matter of time before the cancer would take a firm hold upon her frail body. It had become increasingly hard for her to fight it.

Rachel sobbed, and Ashleigh's heart ached. Mary was a lovely lady, and Ashleigh had loved her like her own grandparent.

"Rachel, honey, slow down—breathe," Ashleigh urged her.

"Not again—I can't go through it again," Rachel cried out in pain.

Ashleigh thought back to the day when Rachel found out her parents had been killed in a helicopter crash. The weekend they died, Rachel and Ashleigh had both stayed over at Rachel's grandparents' house in the Wiltshire countryside near Salisbury, where Rachel and Ashleigh both lived, while Rachel's mother and father went to visit friends in Scotland.

She vividly remembered that dreadful day. It had been Sunday afternoon when Ashleigh, Rachel, and her grandparents had returned from church. The girls ran laughing into the house, heading upstairs to play with the big, old-fashioned doll's house they adored. Ashleigh remembered hearing the phone ringing downstairs and then what sounded like crying, but being only six and a half, she took little notice, stopping to listen only for a split second. Rachel's grandmother hadn't told them until that evening, presumably after she had composed herself in order to be strong enough for her only grandchild.

As the girls grew up together in the same village, they both developed a great respect for Grandma Mary, as Rachel only knew her really as a mother. She was a strong, dignified woman—a hero to both Rachel and Ashleigh, who would help any soul in need, often putting others' needs before her own. Mary taught the girls so much; she was a young soul trapped in a frail, old body. As a child, Ashleigh loved visiting Rachel's house and helping Mary bake cakes and pick apples from their orchard. She enjoyed trying out new games Mary had created for them to play on the front lawn, and all the bedtime stories she told. Mary was a strong, brave woman.

However, Rachel was clearly not coping with her loss quite as strongly as Mary had coped over the death of her daughter and Rachel's mother all those years before. For Rachel, her pillar of strength had been taken from her, and now she wanted Ashleigh with her for support.

"Rachel, of course I'll be there. D'you need me to drive you?"

"No, thanks." Rachel sniffed. "I'm leaving now."

"Are you sure you should drive?" Ashleigh asked, concerned. "I can come with you. I'll just get my things togeth—"

"No, Ash, really—I want to go on my own. You stay. Come down tomorrow. I'll be fine. Promise."

Ashleigh wasn't convinced but had to respect her decision. "OK, if that's what you want. But if you start to tear up, please pull over."

Rachel agreed and reassured her that she was fine to drive.

"I'm so sorry, Rachel. So, so sorry." Ashleigh hung up the phone before breaking down into sobs on the floor.

★   ★   ★

Waking before her alarm the next morning, she packed some things for the journey. Calling work, Ashleigh explained as best she could before sobbing into the phone. Understandingly, Eliza told her to take time off to be with Rachel and her grandfather, reassuring her that she would manage without her. Late that morning, she set off for the countryside. The journey through London was slow. She drummed her fingers on the steering wheel as she sat sandwiched in between two large trucks. The traffic fumes she was breathing sat heavily around her as she waited in the queue, edging forward bit by bit until she finally reached the on-ramp to the M4 motorway. Putting her foot down, she picked up speed, and before she knew it, the trucks were far behind her as she whizzed down the fast lane. So many thoughts danced around in her head. She switched on the radio to distract herself, but she couldn't drown them out.

Memories of Mary playing with her and Rachel when they were younger made her smile. Thoughts flashed though her mind of riding Tarquini, Rachel's silver horse, and how Mary had taught her to ride bareback. There had been picnics in the fields with her family and Rachel's grandparents, and Robert, Rachel's grandfather, would get all the young kids in the village to come over to play a game of rounders on the front lawn with them. It was such a happy time.

Ashleigh checked her speedometer—ninety mph. Trees and fields flew past her. She had given up trying to listen to the radio and moved into the left-hand lane, slowing the car down to let down her car roof, and then racing back up to sixty, seventy, eighty, and then ninety mph, where she stayed for most of the way.

Thoughts of Dave kept popping into her head; she thought about stopping at the next service station to phone him but carried on, not wanting to waste any time. Hearing her phone ring, she hoped it would be him, but as she glanced over at the name on the screen, she saw "Lee" flashing across her phone.

"Oh, bugger off!" she shouted, letting it ring. *Not now.* Of all the times to start messing with her heart, now was not one of them. Why was she still letting him into her life? He was like a painful hangover.

At least two hours had passed. She found herself stuck behind a tractor on a small, twisty country lane, her head pounding with stress after the motorway drive. She reached inside her bag to find her cigarette case while she sat in another queue of slow-moving traffic. She got close to Downton, the village where she had grown up, and decided to stop in a small pub for a drink and unwind from the journey.

Sitting on the grass in the pub garden with a glass of orange juice, she looked around. There were horses in the adjacent field grazing on the grass. She tried to clear her mind again, taking in a long, deep breath. She wondered what Dave was doing and pulled out her phone. She tried to call, but it went to his voicemail. Deciding not to leave a message, she put her phone away. If she spoke to him in person, she could judge how things were between them—hopefully, this holiday hadn't changed anything.

With a heavy heart, she listened to the birds and sounds of the countryside that she hadn't heard for so long. This part of the world had been a distant memory for long enough. Maybe that was what she liked so much about Dave—he too had grown up in the country. She wondered what his childhood town was like. Then she lay on her back and soaked in her surroundings, grateful to be home even if it was on such a sad occasion.

★   ★   ★

After another short drive, Ashleigh arrived at Rachel's grandparents' house; she took a deep breath as she drove up the long, bendy, shingled driveway. She noticed they still had the wooden swinging chair she had loved as a child situated in the same place, motionless on the front lawn.

After parking, she walked around the outside of the house to the rear. The garden and garden furniture had changed from the last time she had been there; she stood looking over a new patio with sun chairs and a wooden table set. There was a water feature beside her, a fountain trickling into some kind of odd-shaped cylinder and then back out the top, starting the cycle again. She remembered Rachel telling her that Robert and Mary had redecorated the house when the kids in the neighborhood had stopped coming around so much. Ashleigh looked down to the far end of the garden; she could still see the horse stables with Tarquini grazing in his field. Turning, she noticed fresh drinks on the table, so she wandered inside to find everyone.

Stepping into the dining room through the French doors, she looked around at the newly painted walls. Even though it had changed, it still felt like the same old house. There was the same grand piano in the corner, and the armchairs may have been new but were placed in the same positions as the old ones. She saw the same brick fireplace with a new mirror above it, but again, it was in the same place where the old one had hung before.

Hearing a noise, she walked into the hallway. She looked up to see an old collie running toward her.

"Saber . . . hello, boy." She bent down, rubbing her hands all over his coat and burying her face in his fur. "Where are they, boy?"

Standing up, Saber ran off into the front room. Ashleigh followed, but no one was in there. The dog picked up a ball, dropping it at her feet.

"Later, boy, later," she said, looking out of the window to her car. It was then she realized her car was the only car there; they must have gone out somewhere.

Couldn't have gone far. The house is unlocked. She brought her stuff in from the car with Saber at her heel, still like a puppy wanting to play. *He must be nearing the end of his little life too.* She took her things up to Rachel's room, finding the same two single beds on either side of the room. Happy memories of sleepovers flooded back. To her delight, the big old doll's house in the corner was still intact. The room hadn't been touched; it was as if she could still hear the sound of Rachel and herself giggling as children.

From behind her, she could hear Saber's tail banging against the door as he waited with his ball in his mouth, saliva dripping from the corners of his jaws.

"Oh, come on then, boy. Down we go," she said, clapping her hands.

She followed him out to the front lawn, throwing the ball for him as she sat on the swinging chair.

Dogs—they never seem to grow up. Saber was still a young puppy at heart.

"Hello."

A voice from behind her made her jump. Turning, she had to do a double take to be sure. Was that Gemma—Gemma Collins? Gemma was an old friend whom Ashleigh had not seen in over six years. Damn, she looked good now.

"Gemma!" Ashleigh said with a surprised grin, eyeing her with delight. Gemma gave Ashleigh a huge hug. Ashleigh stepped back to look her up and down, taking in the blonde, shoulder-length hair instead of the long brown locks Ashleigh remembered.

"You look great, Ashleigh."

"So do you, Gems. It's so good to see you."

Taking her hand, Ashleigh led her around to sit on the swinging chair. She asked about the village and if she had seen Mary recently.

"I moved back to the village two years ago, after I broke up with Steve. I was going to divorce him." Gemma's smile faded as she looked at the ground. "He cheated on me with a girl from the gym. I tried to stay with him, but it didn't work, so I moved home." She looked at Ashleigh and smiled wryly. "But he begged, and I stupidly went back to him—silly, really, as he cheated on me with her again."

"No!"

"Yep. The divorce came through last week, so I'm a single woman again."

"I'm sorry, Gemma. Same kind of thing happened to me. Men are all pigs. God, I've missed you." Ashleigh smiled.

"I've missed you too." Gemma joined Ashleigh on the swing.

Ashleigh felt selfish. All this time living in London, she hadn't once thought about calling her old friend. She had thought Gemma was happily married, but that wasn't a good enough reason to forget about someone—a friend. It was as if all the memories of good times they shared had been hidden away. There had been school holidays exploring the countryside and vacations on Ashleigh's family yacht with Rachel, Gemma, and Kelly. How had they lost touch so easily?

"Did you see much of Mary before she—" Ashleigh felt a lump in her throat.

"Mary was a real pillar for me when I came home the first time," Gemma said. "I sat with her every evening after work, drinking tea and eating biscuits. I would cry, and she would rub my back and hand me another biscuit."

Ashleigh laughed. "That sounds right—Mary's answer to any problem."

"Mm." Gemma sniffed away her tears at the memory. "Then the second time I came home, she supplied me with the same, but I could tell she was getting weaker. She caught a cold, and—"

"I know."

"My mum and dad moved away last year," Gemma said. "Did you know?"

"No. Where have they gone?"

"Jersey." Gemma rolled her eyes. "They bought a B&B. They want me to help run it with them."

"I take it you don't want to."

"Ash, please. No way—a bed and breakfast hotel at my age?" Gemma laughed and pushed her feet into the ground, making the chair swing. "Mum and Dad are coming over for the funeral."

"Are they? It will be nice to see them again. I just wish it was under different circumstances. So where are you living?"

"Here."

"Here," Ashleigh repeated, "with Robert?"

"Yeah, Mary insisted I stay. I think she wanted to make sure I didn't go back to Steve again—plus Mum and Dad had sold the house and moved, so I kinda didn't have anywhere to go."

"Mary never mentioned it—"

"I know. I told Rachel last night—I asked Mary and Robert not to tell anyone until I was back on my feet. You and Rachel have done so well for yourselves; I just wish I could compete. It was bad enough I chose married life at the age of twenty over moving to London with you two, but to then have it all go wrong . . . I just didn't want you both to think badly of me."

"Oh, don't be daft. God, so much has happened. How did we lose touch?" Ashleigh shuddered with a fresh wave of guilt.

"I know it was my fault," Gemma said. "I never called anyone once the wedding was over. It was like I turned into a fifty-year-old housewife overnight. I was so obsessed with making Steve happy, I forgot to make myself happy."

"Wow, your wedding was the last time I saw you. God, we were all so drunk that night. Did you know Rachel shagged Tom Kimpton in the bushes?"

"No way!"

Ashleigh grinned. "Yep, and after you left for the honeymoon, we sneaked into the hotel pool and went skinny-dipping. Well, Tom and Rachel did. I just dipped—you know me. We got caught."

"No!"

"Rachel and Tom blamed it on me—said I told them it was allowed. My mum made me write a letter of apology."

"Oh. My. Goodness. Why didn't I call you guys!"

Ashleigh laughed. "Don't beat yourself up over it. We should have called you, too."

Gemma's smile faded. "Still hurts like hell when I think about him with her, and I know I shouldn't be selfish, but I wish Mary was here to listen to me moan on about it all."

"That's not selfish, and I'm sure she can still hear you. Anyway, you can moan to me now. We are not losing touch again." Ashleigh hugged her.

CHAPTER

8

"HOW MUCH STUFF DOES she have?"
Dave looked at the boxes of shoes and books, bending to pick up a giant, fluffy pink pen from one of the boxes.

He raised his eyebrows in shock at what he had let himself in for.

"I thought she was into football," he said, looking at Peter and passing him the pen.

"Thank you," Isabella said, taking the pen out of Peter's hand as she walked down the hallway to her new room.

Peter shot Dave an icy look and walked after her. "He's touchy about new people," he said, standing in Isabella's doorway. "Always has been, ever since he was a kid."

"I'll bear that in mind," Dave heard Isabella say sardonically.

Dave sat down in the living room, finishing off his lunch before heading back to work. He still hadn't told Ashleigh about Isabella moving in.

"No time like the present," he said out loud, picking up his phone.

But as he listened, he felt helpless; she talked about Mary so fondly and sounded soft and fragile, trying to put on a strong voice. He hung up the phone still wanting to tell her about Isabella. It wasn't the right time—or was it because other emotions stirred inside him? He found himself scrolling through his Facebook photos until he found his first-ever profile picture. He and Caroline were sitting together on her horse, her hands wrapped around the

59

beast's neck, squeezing it with delight while Dave held her waist precariously. The memory was as alive in his mind as it was the day the photo was taken. She had been more than a girlfriend—she was his best friend, and she was gone. Ashleigh's mourning had pulled out feelings he didn't know how to process.

He stood and walked into the kitchen to fetch a glass of water. When he returned, he saw the photo of Caroline still illuminated on his phone. Familiar feelings arose, but he felt content, not sad. Caroline would have liked Ashleigh—or so he hoped—and he closed the app.

Taking a bite of his sandwich, he decided to open up to Ashleigh before she went away, whenever that was—he needed to find out. He wanted her to know he trusted her and that she could trust him. She had been open to him with her feelings, and it was only right to do the same. Not that he knew how well she would take the news of his dead first love and a new female roommate.

"Who was that?" Peter asked from outside the room.

"Ashleigh—she's gone away for a few days."

Peter emerged from the hallway. "Where's she gone?"

"A funeral." Dave got up, not finishing his sandwich.

"Did you tell her about our new roomie?"

"Not the time, bro. See you later." Dave grabbed his keys and headed out the door.

Telling Ashleigh about Isabella was a concern, but adding Caroline into the mix terrified him. His past experience of girls hearing that his last true love died never ended well—they always thought he was still in love with her. And until now, they were right.

★   ★   ★

That night, Dave, Peter, and Isabella got a takeout with some beers. They all sat around the table, finding out about each other. Isabella was swiftly proving herself to be anything but an angel, and Peter was soaking it all up with glee. However, Dave was the brains of the two brothers and read between the lines. He watched Isabella—her hair flicks, the way she constantly fixed her jewelry and garments, her nervous laugh when Peter asked about her past, the questions she avoided, and conversation decoys she thought she had mastered. He knew the signs. He wondered what she was holding back—a bad relationship, or maybe a loss like his. She wasn't so bad, though. She was easy-going, intelligent, and pretty too, admittedly. She had long, dark, wavy hair with tanned Latino skin, but she didn't have the same elegance as Ashleigh.

Later, they all agreed to go out to a bar and show Isabella the night life—the idea obviously was Peter's, and Dave took it for granted that his twin would be hoping to get to know Isabella with a few drinks in her.

"Just remember she's living with you—there's no 'one knob and gone' in this situation," Dave warned Peter as they stood at the bottom of the stone steps outside the flat, waiting for Isabella.

Moments later, she appeared in the doorway, looking great—long, dark, curly hair falling over her bare shoulders, trying to reach her slim legs. She hurried down the large steps to join the gaping twins, and off they set.

★   ★   ★

Dave placed the drinks down on the table. The bar was all but empty apart from the three of them and the young bargirl dressed in black, who was pouring away unfinished beverages and stacking the glasses into the washer. Dave looked around the over-lit room, feeling a slight breeze from the open door.

"So . . . why Wandsworth, Issi?" Dave asked. "I can call you Issi, right?"

"Yeah I don't mind," Isabella said. "I like the name Issi. I moved to be closer to work, and I fancied meeting a new circle of people." She sipped on her straw and stirred her cocktail, giving a soft smile.

"Any boyfriends?" Dave thought he would ask what Peter definitely wanted to know.

"I had a boyfriend. He turned out to be a bit of a dick, so I thought it would be easier on him if he didn't have to bump into me anymore."

"That's big of you," Peter said. "Come on, there's more to it. What did you do—sleep with his best mate?"

"No . . ."

"His best mate's sister?"

"You wish." She laughed that same nervous laugh.

"What, then?" Peter pushed.

She looked uncomfortable. "OK, I'm just going to tell you. And I hope you don't judge me. My ex is in prison. I don't want him bumping into me when he is out!" Isabella dropped eye contact.

Dave broke the silence. "So in other words, *you* don't want to bump into *him*."

Issi laughed. "I suppose so."

"What's he in for?" Dave continued, wondering if this new flatmate was such a good idea after all.

"Attempted robbery on a charity shop." She shook her head.

"You're joking, right?" Peter asked.

"Nope—the dick. And that is why I figured I needed to move away and find some new friends, ones with some morals."

"Well," Peter said before apparently deciding he didn't have anything more to say.

"Looks like you need a fresh start," Dave suggested.

"Here's to a fresh start." She raised her glass.

Dave touched her glass. She seemed genuine, but robbery? He was glad of the three-month trial agreement.

The three of them moved on down the road to a busier place. Dave noticed how much easier Isabella was now that she had told them about her unsavory ex. She had told her secret—she was trying to make a new life and stop living in her past. He needed to do the same.

Peter went to the bar, returning with three tequilas, lemon, and salt. They sat in a Mexican-themed bar with sombreros on the walls and all the bar staff dressed up and shouting in Spanish.

"Here's to new times." Dave raised his glass and nodded to Isabella.

"New times," she replied.

A while later, Dave excused himself to use the restroom, but instead of returning to the bar, he sneaked out the door toward home.

He knew his brother would figure out where he was because he often sneaked off. It was easier than arguing with his brother about staying out for "just one more, bro." It was late, and Dave wasn't in the mood to be getting wasted midweek.

★ ★ ★

Ashleigh woke up in her old room and looked over to see Rachel still sleeping in the bed next to her. Then she looked at the doll's house, rubbing her eyes and registering her surroundings. Getting up, she put on her robe and wandered downstairs. Fresh, morning air drifted in from the open front door, and she stepped out onto the porch to find Robert sitting on the wooden bench with Saber at his feet. He looked out over the lawn beyond the driveway to the fields through the trees.

"We used to watch you playing races on this drive when you were both little," he said, not looking at her.

"It was just an old mud track then," Ashleigh said, walking over to sit next to him. Saber watched her out of the corner of his eye and gave his tail a wag, but he didn't move from where he lay. They sat in silence in the morning sun. The old grounds had changed so much.

"Years of work that didn't mean a thing to Mary if it wasn't for you kids." He took her hand. "Thank you for coming, pet. Don't be sad. Just remember all the happy times. She would want it like that."

Ashleigh smiled. *Two of a kind. Two of the kindest, strongest people I will ever know.*

Saber sat up suddenly.

"Rachel's awake." Robert looked at the doorway. "I'll go and see to her."

"No," Ashleigh replied, putting her hand on his arm. "You stay here; I'll go. I'll make us all a cup of tea."

Ashleigh met Rachel at the bottom of the stairs. They smiled at each other but didn't speak before Rachel went out to join her grandfather on the porch while Ashleigh made tea.

Over the next few days, not much was said in the house, but it felt comfortable nonetheless. The day of the funeral came and went.

People brought flowers, staying for coffee and paying their respects to Mary, a much-loved member of the community. Ashleigh struggled with her own emotions, missing her own family and wishing she could see her mum whenever she wanted.

★   ★   ★

She thought of Dave and still wondered why he hadn't asked any more questions about her holiday. Was he not interested? Did he not care? Having no other reference other than Lee to value her emotions against, she stewed on the situation. She couldn't confide in Rachel now, and when she spoke to her sister, she was too upset over the loss of Mary. Selfishly, she felt lonely.

★   ★   ★

"How are you today?"

Each day, Dave called to speak to her, and each day, she wished he was there.

"I'm coming home today. Rachel is staying on for a while with Robert," she explained. "I can't take more than a week of work. They've been kind to let me take this as a holiday leave."

The mention of holiday seemed to stifle the conversation for a moment. She wondered if she was overthinking things.

"Would you like me to come over?" he asked. "I could stay with you tonight."

"That would be lovely, thank you."

"No need to thank me; I want to see how you are."

"I'm OK," she said, reassuring him as best as she could.

"I'm sure you are, honey, but everyone needs a cuddle sometimes."

"Yeah, you're not wrong there, but I don't want to grieve anymore. It's over now, and anyway, she would want me to be laughing, not crying."

"Well, laughter you will get, then. Ring me when you're home."

They said goodbye, and Ashleigh gathered her things.

On the long drive home, Ashleigh found it hard to stop her mind from drifting back to Lee and when they were happy. She always knew he was a ladies' man, but she never thought he would hurt her the way he had. It still pained her to think of him, but this time, it felt more like a sad chapter in her life that had closed. Her new life occupied her thoughts, including Dave, the holiday, and even reconnecting with Gemma. She would stay in touch this time, she decided as she drove through the lanes and swiftly onto the motorway.

By early afternoon, she was sitting on her balcony, basking in the sun. Dave wandered through the front door she had left unlocked for him, and she ran to meet him. Laughing, he opened his arms and hugged her tight before kissing her.

This feels right—so right. Maybe she had overthought the whole holiday thing.

Sitting in the sun, she told Dave all about Gemma. She told him old childhood stories and talked more in depth about the funeral. She watched him move uneasily in his chair and wondered what had changed—when they embraced moments earlier, it had felt so right. Maybe this holiday was a bad idea. Maybe it had scared him off—he still hadn't asked when she was leaving.

"Ashleigh?" Dave shifted in his seat.

Oh God. Was this it? Was this the breakup conversation?

"Yes?"

He sighed. "I've not been that open with you."

She nodded slowly. *Oh God—he has a wife.*

He continued, "You've told me so much about yourself, and I've not told you much at all."

"That's OK," she lied. "We've only know each other a month."

He smiled. "No. It's not OK. Listen, I don't want to scare you off by getting too deep too quickly or anything, but . . ." He trailed off.

Deep? What was going on here?

"I'm not really that good at opening up, and when I do, it never ends well."

Oh, great.

"So I'm just going to say it. Lay it all out—I really like you."

Ashleigh blinked. *What the fuck? So not a breakup talk, then.*

Dave's eyes didn't meet hers, and he didn't speak for a moment. She wondered what had happened while she was away. Placing a hand on his knee, she nodded gently, asking him to go on.

A sadness glassed his eyes as he started with juvenile stories of Peter, Dave, and a little girl called Caroline. She was fun to hear about, and Ashleigh liked the sound of her, but something in Dave's words led Ashleigh to think he didn't know this girl anymore. Dave's uneasy manner stopped her from asking any question, so she just let him talk. Dave, Peter, and Caroline had so many adventures—finding stray dogs that actually ended up belonging to a neighboring farm, or making swings that swung out over the river at the bottom of the lane. She enjoyed listening.

He was sixteen in his stories now and had relaxed into their conversation. Ashleigh had asked him about his parents, and they sounded kind. Dave confessed to being embarrassed that his dad was a painter, and she scolded him. Had she given him the impression that she would judge him? She would never judge anyone. She loved the sound of Dave's family. It sounded normal, like the families she had read about in childhood books, like Enid Blyton's *Famous Five* stories, her favorite.

Dave's stories moved back to Caroline and him—Ashleigh now knew this girl had been his first girlfriend. Dave looked uneasy as he started to talk about his seventeenth birthday.

"I didn't want to go," he said. "I hated horse riding, but she wouldn't take no for an answer."

"She doesn't sound like she would have taken no for an answer." Ashleigh laughed.

"She wanted to show me the sunset up on the rocks, so I agreed. It was terrifying." He laughed at himself. "I sat behind her on that horse and gripped her waist like a big baby. The sunset was beautiful, though." He fell silent.

"Dave, are you OK?" Ashleigh sat forward.

"When it was time to leave, I couldn't mount the horse. She jumped off to show me, and the horse startled as she was throwing her leg over. Just took off toward the rocks."

"Oh God, no," Ashleigh couldn't keep from saying out loud.

"The horse stopped before the edge, but Caroline was thrown over."

"Oh, Dave."

He swallowed.

"Enough. Don't—you don't have to say any more, Dave. It's OK."

He looked awkward. "Anyway, I wanted to tell you, and I hope you won't let this change anything or think I'm still in love with her."

"What? No. Why would I think that?"

"Past experiences," he said simply. "And until now, they would have been correct." He leaned in to kiss her.

Until now. She smiled to herself as they kissed a deeper, more intense kiss.

"Well, while I'm confessing," Dave said eventually, "I have something else to tell you." He explained that he thought Peter had been joking when he wanted a female roommate. "It was the first week you and I met. I didn't know where we were going."

"Where are we going?" She smiled.

"I don't know, but I know I want to go with you."

"Oh, Dave, that's so cheesy sweet." She punched his arm playfully.

Her heart had just been broken, and she knew how naïve she could be at times. She wondered what this Issi girl was up to, moving in with two men. Was this girl for real?

"Honestly, I thought Peter was kidding," Dave said. "Then he was showing her around the place." He laughed at the memory.

"Ha—what a joker." She tried to sound genuine.

What a dick. Why was Dave's brother so blasé about it all? *Oh God, I really hope the identical bit is looks only.*

"You'll have to meet her—I think you'll like her. She's had a bad relationship and just wants a new start, you know." He grinned.

Oh, just super. She harbored her mocking thoughts behind a false smile.

Something in his voice sounded excited, like a child who had made a new friend and wanted his best friend to meet them too. Maybe she was being overly sensitive—maybe she should give this Issi girl a chance before casting judgment.

But the first sign of trouble, and I'm out. I'm not competing with any more girls in my relationship.

Relationship. She liked that—she and Dave were in a relationship.

A gentle breeze blew over her pale skin as the sun started to lower. Dave suggested getting some food for dinner and left to find a takeaway. As she waved him off and closed the door, the house phone rang. She picked up the receiver, and her heart jumped as she heard Lee's voice on the other end. She managed to ask him what he wanted and listened to his reply, her heart thumping in her chest the whole time. He gave the same old "I'm sorry" speech, and she told herself to be strong and firm in what was best for her.

Taking a breath, she knew what she had to do and say. "Now listen—what you did was heartbreaking, and I will never be able to forget it, but if it's forgiveness you are after, then forgiveness I'll give you so that you can move on like I have."

She stood holding the receiver, staring at the wall and not wanting to move in case she weakened. Lee talked on about how he could change, how life was lonely without her. He used the same old lines, like how all he wanted was her forgiveness and to feel her body next to his again. But this time, it was different for her.

"Lee, I think you have your wires crossed." She paused, looking into the living room, where she saw the photo of Max. She didn't want him in her life anymore. "I forgive you, but you need to move on like I have, please. I would never take you back. I have to go— please don't call again. It's over for good this time."

She put down the phone and walked over to the photo of herself and Max, looking at it for the last time before she moved it to a safe place at the back of the cupboard. Could she have feelings for two people at the same time? She placed the picture frame under her winter sweaters. Falling out of love with someone was the reverse of falling in love. As her lust for Lee lessened, it increased for Dave, and as she cared more for Dave, she cared less for Lee.

Moments later, Dave returned, blissfully unaware.

"That was quick," she said, slipping her arms around his waist. Then she noticed he wasn't carrying anything.

"I didn't get anything because I am going to take you out to eat instead." He pulled her closer. "You're so special, Ash, and I want to treat you right, so let's go somewhere nice to eat."

She slid her hands up over his shoulders and kissed him. *Lee has nothing on Dave.*

Gently, she unbuttoned his shirt, and in a moment, they were on the floor.

★   ★   ★

That night, she lay in bed next to him, looking up at the ceiling and thinking how lucky she was to have found someone so perfect. Dave had finally asked about her holiday. He had explained that he didn't want to ask too many questions in case she thought he was being like her ex. She felt content. She was apprehensive about this new roommate, but that worry could wait. She curled herself into the nook of his masculine arm, catching a waft of his aftershave as she moved; he pulled her tight, and she smiled to herself. Everything was going her way.

CHAPTER
9

ASHLEIGH FOUND HERSELF RUNNING up Harley Street so as not to be too late for work again. She got to the practice just in time for a morning cup of coffee downstairs in the staffroom and a quick read of the Metro before she rushed up to the surgery to set up for the day. If there was one thing she hated more than being late, it was arriving at work without time for a coffee before the mad rush of the day. As she approached the stairwell, she heard a sound behind her. Turning, she saw Samantha hurry past without greeting her.

That's strange. Samantha must still be avoiding her for telling Lee where she had moved to, and Ashleigh didn't think much else of it. She didn't care. *Let her avoid me.*

Eliza strolled along the corridor. "Morning, Ash."

"Morning. How were things while I was away?"

"Er, OK . . ." Eliza sounded hesitant, quickly asking about the funeral.

As she talked about the funeral and reconnecting with Gemma, Ashleigh couldn't help but notice a vacancy in Eliza. Something was off with her. First Samantha and now Eliza—what had gone on while she was away?

★   ★   ★

Later that morning, Ashleigh stood at the X-ray developer machine, wondering why things seemed a little off-kilter. Samantha continued to avoid her, and Eliza didn't seem her normal self. Maybe they were just busy, or perhaps she had stayed away too long and was out of the loop, sidelined, and out of their little clique. This thought didn't last long, as Ashleigh knew that Eliza would never sideline their friendship, and the only clique Samantha had was her own. No, something odd was up.

She pulled out her phone and selected her sister's number. She quietly explained the odd atmosphere to Kelly in a low voice, aware that anyone could walk past.

"Do you think I'm reading into something that's not there?" Ashleigh whispered.

"No, I don't," Kelly replied. "I always listen to my gut feelings, and they're normally right. Call her out. Ask her straight up what's wrong."

Ashleigh cringed at the thought of a confrontation. "No—oh, no. I don't want to do that. I'll just wait and see—" Ashleigh stopped. "Oh, Kelly."

"What?"

"I just had a thought—what if the practice owner wants to get rid of me?"

"What? Why?"

"He might be upset that I took time off for a non-family bereavement. He is mean and would do that," Ashleigh said, gathering up the films from the machine.

"OK, now you're overthinking things. Just talk to Eliza. Look, Ash, sorry, I've got a meeting and—"

"It's fine; go, you're right. I'll talk to Eliza," Ashleigh lied, and then she hung up. She made her way back to the surgery. Surely Eliza would have explained to the principal how important Mary was to her.

She opened the surgery door and handed Eliza the X-rays. Her stomach dropped when Eliza took the films and addressed her without eye contact again. Something was definitely wrong, and she was going to have to talk to her about it at some point. She was just grateful that they had a full day of patients to give her some more time to think it over, which equated to putting it off some more. So much for her new, empowered self.

★   ★   ★

Later that day, Ashleigh was dressing in the staffroom, getting ready to go home. She had managed to convince herself not to confront Eliza, instead wait it out. Raised voices from upstairs startled her, and she hurried to see what all the commotion was about. By the time she got up there, the only people around were Samantha and Eliza, who were standing in the reception. As she walked past, they both seemed a little tense—awkward, even.

Say something. "See you in the morning," Ashleigh said and kept walking down the entrance hall to leave.

"Bye," shouted Eliza.

Samantha didn't say anything.

"Way to go, Ash," she said under her breath as she stepped onto the street.

What's going on? Have I done something to upset Samantha? She let out a big sigh—she couldn't spend too long mulling it over. She knew how temperamental Samantha could be, and if it was important, she was sure Eliza would talk to her when the time was right. *Maybe Samantha is having life problems, and Eliza is helping her through them.* Feeling deflated, she continued her journey home, annoyed that she hadn't found the courage to talk to Eliza. Eliza was her friend, and she should be able to talk to her about anything.

Taking her normal route through Hyde Park, she stopped to sunbathe for a while on the grass. Thoughts of the weird atmosphere continued to plague her mind; her stomach churned, and she wondered what she had done. She hoped Eliza was not upset with her in any way. Why the raised voices? Why the odd behavior all day? What had gone on while she was away? Could Samantha, the ice queen of all people, really have personal issues that she would confide in Eliza? Ashleigh and Samantha had known each other for a few years as work colleagues and even enjoyed nights out together after work, but they were far from friends, and Eliza and Samantha even less so.

Ashleigh wondered if she was being paranoid. Had Lee gotten under her skin? Was she deflecting her emotions onto other people?

Now I really am *overthinking it. This is ridiculous.*

She took out her phone and selected Eliza's number; it rang for some time before a small voice answered. "Hello?"

"Eliza, it's me—Ashleigh. Are you OK with me?"

Ashleigh's heart sank as Eliza told her that everything was fine—she could tell she was lying. The conversation had the same tense feel that had been present all day. She tried to deepen the conversation, telling her about Lee playing games and how he had called her at home.

"Eliza, I kind of still miss him. But when I'm with Dave, I don't even think of him at all. He sounded so sorry. I don't want him back or anything, it's just—oh, I don't know. It's just strange." She slumped on the grass.

"He's not sorry—he's a pig!" Eliza snapped angrily.

Eliza's reaction took Ashleigh by surprise. She had personally never met Lee and knew of him only through what Ashleigh had told her. Ashleigh was stumped by her reaction. There was clearly something wrong with Eliza, but *what* was the question.

★   ★   ★

Leaving home early the following morning, Ashleigh sat outside a coffee shop on Oxford Street, enjoying a cup of coffee and a copy of the Metro that had been left on the table. While she was engrossed in the article she was reading and unaware of her surroundings, a bus sounded its horn at a car, pulling Ashleigh's attention away from the paper and across the road to the commotion. She watched, amused by the irate drivers screaming at each other through open windows. The bus driver flipped the middle finger at the car driver and drove on, clearing Ashleigh's previously blocked view of the street. It was then that she caught sight of Lee and Samantha standing practically opposite her. Gasping, she quickly stood up, walking as fast as she could down the walkway beside the coffee shop to where she could watch them without being seen.

She felt nervous seeing him, and her heart raced. She tried to guess what they were talking about—had they just bumped into one another, or had they meant to meet? Lee worked in the city but did see clients in the West End at times. Maybe he was coming to see her, and Samantha had found a new form of loyalty and was trying to talk him out of it—perhaps this was a skewed attempt to make up for giving him her address. Ashleigh's stomach gave way to a fresh jolt of nerves. Why did he still have this effect on her? She wanted to run and hide but stayed watching as Lee laughed at something Samantha said and shook his head. Samantha flicked her hair the same way she always did around men. What was going on here?

She was about to turn away when she saw Lee put his hand out and grasp Samantha's buttock as he walked off. Shocked, Ashleigh watched as Samantha laughed and turned back to kiss him. Ashleigh stood numb as she saw them embrace. Her mouth fell open slightly. She couldn't move, and her eyes stayed fixed to the spot where they had just stood. How could he do that to her—with Samantha, of all people? She jolted, realizing Samantha was probably going to be walking through the same walkway to get to work.

Quickly, she ran as fast as she could down the alley. Instead of turning left and going to work, she turned right. Her heart was thumping, and her emotions mixed as she ran past the back of John Lewis and carried on straight into the entrance of Cavendish Square park for refuge. Panting, she sat on a bench to catch her breath. Thoughts scrambled in her head. What was going on? What was he playing at? Ashleigh breathed heavily as she braced herself for more heartache.

Her eyes were watering from running but also from an emotion she couldn't quite identify—love? Betrayal? Why was this upsetting her? Her chest felt tight. Was Lee ever going to get out of her life? Would he ever give up? Breathing heavily, she watched the London workers walking to work across the square like ants, doing the same walk every day. Her pounding heart and anger now rumbled through her body like a train speeding through a tunnel. What were they doing? What was Samantha up to? First she gave him her address, and then they hooked up? The penny suddenly dropped, and Ashleigh pulled out her phone to call Eliza, her heart hitting her chest with dull thuds as she waited for her to answer the phone.

"Hello," Eliza said.

Ashleigh took a deep breath. "Something you want to tell me, Eliza?"

"What do you mean?"

"I saw them."

"Saw who?"

"I saw Lee and Samantha—together, Eliza. You knew, didn't you? Why didn't you tell me?" An irresistible urge to scream into the phone flooded her soul.

"I'm so sorry." Ashleigh heard Eliza close the surgery door. "He came looking for you the other day—said you weren't picking up his calls."

"I was on my way to a bloody funeral, for God's sake!" Her voice raised in fury.

"I know, honey; that's what I told him. I'm sorry." Eliza carried on, "He took Samantha for lunch—I don't know why, but he did. I then saw them after work the next day having a drink in some bar off the high street."

Ashleigh was silent for a moment, and Eliza said nothing. In the background, Ashleigh heard an opening door and a small voice.

"Is that her?" she asked. She listened as Eliza said hello to Samantha.

"Yes, it's her," Eliza whispered.

"Don't say I know."

"I won't. You are coming into work, then?"

"Of course. You need a nurse, and I need a chat with old Sammy girl. Time to stop avoiding her, I think."

"Ash, I did have it out with her. I told her to—"

"Eliza," Ashleigh interrupted, "it's not for you to explain. That's Samantha's job. God, she's such a bitch, and I've been way too nice to her recently, considering what she's done. Where does she get off meddling in my life?"

"Hate to say it, but I told you to have it out with her. She fumbles through life intimidating people, and no one confronts her. Look. There are no patients until ten thirty, so that will give you time to talk to her. Keep cool—don't let her rile you up; she's good at that, and I'll see you when you get here. OK?"

Passersby glanced at Ashleigh as she walked slowly up Harley Street, fresh tears rolling down her cheeks. All her life, she had tried to be a good person—kind, without judgment. Living in her world, that was no easy task. She wasn't like the women in her family. They were strong, driven, without self-doubt. It was always Ashleigh who brought home stray dogs or injured birds. Once, she cried for an hour straight after the vet couldn't save a sick fox she had found. Her mum scolded her for touching the diseased animal, but it was Kelly, her sister, who had talked her tears away. She always knew just what to say. As she walked slowly closer to work, she wondered what Kelly would say now.

Suck it up and give her a piece of your mind. She smiled at the thought. All she wanted to do was move on from Lee, with Dave and without any drama. She stopped as she neared her work, knowing life wasn't always that simple, and avoiding every confrontation she came up against was never going to get her anywhere in life.

She wiped her tears away and walked boldly into the practice, saying hello to everyone as normal before continuing downstairs to the staffroom where she found Samantha changing. Eliza was making coffee. Ashleigh smiled at her as she picked up a freshly made cup and left the room.

Samantha did not turn to look at her, just gave a quick hello while she buttoned up her tunic.

"Morning, Samantha," Ashleigh said, sitting at the large, oval table. "Sit with me for a while, will you? I'm interested to hear about you and my ex."

Samantha swung around. "What?"

"I saw you this morning—kissing! So don't feed me any bullshit. Just tell me the truth, if you can manage that." Ashleigh was shocked at how brash she sounded.

"I'm sorry, Ashleigh. I didn't know how to tell you." Samantha sat down quickly.

Samantha didn't feel bad; Ashleigh knew her well enough to see through her puppy-dog eyes. She stared at her face across the table; adrenaline shook her inside, but she hid it well. She wanted to scream at Samantha, lash out and pull her hair, but she could never do that. Instead, she listened as Samantha tried to explain, and then she realized exactly what Lee was doing. He was reading her like a book—and she was reacting just how he wanted her to. She paused for a moment, composing herself and wondering if she was just talking herself out of another confrontation.

No. Lee was not worth this fight. He wanted her to fight with Samantha over him. *Well, not this time.* But she did need to tell Samantha to stay out her business if she was going to move on. A fresh wave of anxiety hit Ashleigh. Could she do this? Could she stand up to Samantha and tell her to stay out of her life?

"Ashleigh, it just happened, you know? We didn't mean—"

"You know what, Samantha? I was angry. Fuck—really bloody angry. But if you want him that bad, then have him. I've got a new boyfriend, and quite frankly, you are welcome to Lee."

Samantha smiled as if trying not to smirk at Ashleigh, which riled her and gave her the boost she needed to carry on.

"However, there are just a few things I don't understand, Samantha." She leaned toward her. "Why did you tell him where I had moved to, knowing I didn't want him to know?"

Samantha sighed. "I bumped into him—I'd had too much to drink. I don't even remember telling him." She looked away, starting to flick through the pages of the newspaper on the table, irritating Ashleigh further.

God, this girl is such a bitch. "OK. Well, in that case, I suppose you don't remember giving him my new number, either."

"I don't know, Ash." She shrugged.

"Not one of your best moves, hey? The other thing I don't understand . . ." She paused, wondering if she should say the next sentence. Samantha didn't look up from the newspaper. "Why do you want to be with a man that phoned me last night telling me that he wants me back?"

Samantha raised her head. "I know what he's like. I can't change that, but I have feelings for him now."

Ashleigh laughed. Samantha sounded as pathetic as she once had.

"OK, Samantha, whatever. You two are so similar you may even work out."

"What's that supposed to mean?"

Ashleigh stood up to get her uniform out of her locker. "The words 'thoughtless' and 'selfish' come to mind."

Samantha stood up to leave.

This is it. It was time to be very clear and tell Samantha to back off for good.

"Samantha," Ashleigh said, watching Samantha stop. "Stay out of my life from now on—I mean it."

Samantha left the room without a word.

Ashleigh knew Samantha didn't care—the exact opposite, more than likely—which was why she couldn't let herself care either. Ashleigh was just glad she had finally confronted her, whatever the outcome. She had stood up for herself, and it felt good—nerve-racking, but good.

★　★　★

On the bus home, Ashleigh sat opposite two lovers who couldn't keep their hands off each other. She watched with irritation as they whispered into each other's ears. *Oh, great—just what I need.* She averted her eyes. The bus stopped at the end of her road, and she got off.

Once home, she hurried around trying to get herself ready and over to Dave's in good time for a meal with the new flatmate, Isabella. She grabbed her keys and rushed down the stone steps to the garage, stopping as she saw Mr. Schnitzer coming home from work. Mindful of the time, she kept the conversation to small talk and went on her way. It didn't take long to get to Wandsworth, which was not such a blessing on this occasion. Ashleigh could have done with a bit longer to prepare for this meal with Isabella, especially after her day of Lee drama. Dave saw her arrive outside and met her at the top step.

"Hey, how are you?" He bent to kiss her.

"I'm good." She loved the way he was so happy to see her and hoped she didn't look as uptight as she felt.

Ashleigh walked through the door to the communal hallway, guiding herself up the darkened stairway by the handrail. She could smell the light scent of cooking and realized how hungry she was.

"Indian?" she asked as she walked into the flat.

"That's correct," said a voice behind her.

She turned to see Peter, who ushered her into the living room.

"So what dish are we having, then?" Ashleigh inquired politely.

"Tikka masala—Issi has to prove she can cook a curry if she wants to stay. It's in the tenant's contract, you see." Peter smirked.

Ashleigh gave a stiff smile. "Yes, Dave told me."

Oh God, this is going to be an awkward evening.

A few moments later, Dave brought Isabella into the living room. "I thought I would give her five minutes out of the kitchen to meet you." He winked.

Ashleigh tried to relax and think of something nice to say. She couldn't.

"Hi." Isabella smiled nervously.

"Hello, so you're on a cooking break, then?" Ashleigh asked, hoping she didn't sound as dry as she felt about the situation. After all, this poor girl was probably very nice. However, she would be even nicer if she hadn't just moved in with Ashleigh's new boyfriend.

Isabella's smile lightened. "Yes—it's nearly ready." She walked back to the kitchen, returning with four open bottles of beer. "OK, cheers, everyone. Now sit down; it's just about ready."

"See, that's why she got the room," Peter said, looking at Dave. "Wanna hand, Issi?" He followed her out.

Dave watched them walk away and laughed to himself. He turned to look at Ashleigh.

"What's up, honey? Don't you like her?"

"No, no. She's fine. Seems nice," Ashleigh lied. Isabella seemed like a hot girl living with two men she didn't even know.

Dave smiled, stepping toward her. "What, then?"

She lowered her voice, smirking. "She looks a bit, you know, rough."

Dave looked confused. "What?"

Ashleigh was immediately disappointed in herself. She wasn't one of those girls, the ones she hated so much at school for thinking they were better than others just because their families had money. What must Dave think of her now?

"What do you mean by rough?"

"Oh God, Dave, I'm sorry. Forget I said that—I had a bad day; I didn't mean it."

She couldn't read his expression. Was he confused, or did he know that she had just judged Isabella? And this was after Dave had told her he was worried she would judge him like that. What had she done?

"She's had a bit of a rough upbringing, if that's what you mean?"

"Oh, Dave."

"Are you jealous of Isabella?"

Am I? This is not a good look.

"Ashleigh, look—it's not her fault. She just replied to an advert. It's Peter's fault for being Peter." He kissed her forehead. "Come on; let's sit down for dinner. You know, you're kind of cute when you're mad."

Remorse, mixed with shame, cleansed Ashleigh's mind of negative thoughts. She needed to give this girl a chance and quit feeling bitter about Samantha and Lee. What was she thinking, being so mean?

They sat for dinner, and her first impressions of Isabella were just as alarming. Ashleigh could see chemistry between her and Peter; however, Isabella appeared to flirt with both brothers, leaning over the table toward Dave and revealing her full cleavage. Ashleigh watched wide-eyed as Isabella flicked her hair and giggled at Dave's dry jokes.

You're not his type, missy. Ashleigh laughed faintly. Dave didn't seem to be reciprocating Isabella's gestures, which pleased Ashleigh, but she really wasn't warming up to this girl at all. She excused herself and went to the bathroom for some space. As she sat her bare bum down onto the toilet seat, she wondered if she was reading into signs that weren't there. Had seeing Lee and Samantha skewed her judgment, maybe? She washed her hands and took a long look in the mirror.

Give this girl a chance.

After she returned to the table, the conversation eventually delved into their different lives. Isabella no longer flirted with Dave, and from what Ashleigh saw, she seemed genuinely attracted to Peter and his sometimes offensive jokes. Ashleigh felt bad for judging her. Isabella's life had been rough, and Ashleigh's earlier comment was out of order. She just hoped Dave hadn't judged her. She still would keep an eye on this Isabella, but for now, Ashleigh was actually starting to enjoy her company—and Isabella might even teach her something. Isabella didn't give the impression that she "gave any fucks," and that was something Ashleigh needed to start doing. It was time to stop apologizing for herself and start living the life she wanted.

By the end of the night, Ashleigh was sorry to leave. Now convinced Isabella was just misunderstood, she air-kissed everyone goodnight. Isabella was just a confident, pretty girl who needed a few lessons in life about correct etiquette—especially on how to act around other women when you're living with their man.

"Thanks for inviting me over," she said to Dave as they stood in front of her car.

"You looked like you were getting on with Issi by the end of the night."

"Oh, yes—yes. Look, I'm sorry again for what I said."

"It's OK." He touched her face. "What happened at work today?"

Now that was one thing she couldn't tell him. "Oh, nothing. Just my boss."

"Who, Eliza?"

"No—oh goodness, no. The practice owner. I just hate it when he sees patients at our practice, that's all. Most of the time, he's at the hospital teaching."

"Is he that bad?"

She nodded.

"Well, you can always call me. I'll be down in a flash—unless that's a bit rough for you?" He laughed.

Great. He does *think I judged her that way.* "Dave, I'm sorry; I honestly don't—"

"Shh." He placed a finger on her lips. "I was just joking with you."

She kissed him goodbye and watched in her rearview mirror as he waved her off. Suddenly, she felt goose pimples all over.

"Oh, my," she said out loud. "Am I falling in love with this man?"

CHAPTER

10

T HE WEEKEND CAME AROUND quickly. Ashleigh had arranged a night out with Dave, Peter, Isabella, Leon, and Jules, though Rachel was still away. At six forty-five, she stood alone outside a pub in Soho looking for Jules and Leon. She hoped that by the end of the night, with her friends' valued opinions, she could really get to know Isabella.

"Ashleigh," said a voice from amidst one of the swarms of people smoking and drinking outside the pub.

"Jules, Leon, hi." She raised an arm and made her way toward them.

She stepped sideways past a few people into the swarm. A man moved his beer glass out of her way, but another did not, and beer splashed onto her bare leg.

"Ow," she said as the man apologized.

"Guys, hi. Shall we go inside and get a drink?" Jules grinned and then led the way.

They walked up to the bar quite easily, as most people were outside. Ashleigh dried her leg with a napkin.

"So where is he?" Ashleigh looked around. Jules had promised to bring her new man tonight. "I'm dying to meet him. I can't believe you've met someone."

"It's not that difficult to imagine, is it?" Jules laughed. "He won't be long. He's finishing up at work, but we can leave as soon as he gets here." She leaned forward over the bar, waving a twenty pound note.

They took their glasses and found a free table.

"So tell me, what does he do?" Leon asked, picking up his usual beverage of Jack Daniels and Coke.

"IT."

"Oh." Leon sounded surprised. "So not in the fashion industry, then?"

"Thank God he's not!" added Ashleigh.

"And why's that?" Jules straightened.

"Honey, your track record isn't a good one, and they all come from the same industry in one way or another."

"She's right, Jules," said Leon. "Your man taste is shit, honey. What exactly does this new bloke do in IT, then?"

Jules thought for a moment. "Well, I'm not too sure, but he has a boat!"

"A boat?" Ashleigh raised her nose to the ceiling.

"A boat for work, you jokers. He fixes the computer systems on the Thames, but that's kind of the extent of what I know about his job. His business card says Network Operations Manager, if that helps!"

"Oh, right." Leon's face lit up.

"Do you know what that is, then, Leon?" asked Ashleigh.

"Er . . . no. Not really. I was being sarcastic, darling. So anyway"— Leon directed his next question to Ashleigh—"Dave has a female roomie, then? Anything we need to know before we meet her? What's the mission? Sabotage or destroy?"

"No, no, nothing like that. I want you to meet her because you'll like her," Ashleigh lied.

"Well, I'm calling BS," Jules said.

Leon smirked at her with folded arms.

Ashleigh spoke again. "OK, so—"

"Knew it. What do you have on her?" Leon leaned over the table.

"Stop, will you?" Ashleigh said. "I don't have anything on her."

"Let us be the judge of that." Leon elbowed Jules.

"Honestly, guys, it's not that exciting, really. I've met her, and I honestly think she's OK. I just want a second opinion, you know?"

"It's fine," Jules said shaking her head at Leon. "We will watch from afar. Right, Leon?"

"Sure," he agreed. "So all good for me to hit on her, then?"

"Whatever. If you really can't control yourself—and like you would listen to me anyway."

Ashleigh could feel Jules staring at her. "What?"

"I don't know—you tell me, Ashleigh. What's bothering you about this girl?"

"More like what's bothering me about *me*." Ashleigh explained the curry night introduction. "I can't believe I said it."

"I don't get it," Jules said. "You didn't say it to her, and you apologized to Dave, right? What's the big deal? Is Dave upset at you?"

"I don't think so. I just didn't think I had it in me to be that bitchy."

"Oh, honey." Jules flicked her hair. "If you think that's bitchy, try working in the magazine industry. You, my lovely, have a heart of gold and really need to stop giving yourself such a hard time."

"And if Dave looks at me differently now?"

Jules patted her hand in her normal, non-offensive, patronizing way. "Honey, men like it when you show a bit of jealousy. I'm sure he knew you didn't mean it any other way than the bitchy girl code way." She laughed. "You were marking your territory—so what? Trust me, it's fine. I bet he's forgotten all about it by now."

Ashleigh nodded. "Maybe."

A few moments later, a big smile spread rapidly over Jules's face, and she stood up. "Hey," she said.

They turned to look at a guy now standing by their table with strawberry-blond hair and a stark resemblance to Prince Harry.

Oh, so Jules has also met a prince. Ashleigh thought. He was certainly charming. *Dimples, nice.* He smiled at them all.

"Hi," he said, leaning over to kiss Jules. "Hi," he said again, addressing the table.

"Everyone, this is Jon. Jon, this is everyone," Jules said in her normal, nonchalant manner.

"Hi, I'm Ashleigh, and this is Leon."

"Good to meet you all finally. I've heard lots about you—all good, obviously." Jon laughed, showing off his dimples. Ashleigh could see exactly what Jules saw in this guy. "Anyone want a drink?" he offered.

Ashleigh checked her watch; they didn't have time. Jules sent Leon outside with Jon to hail a black cab and followed behind with Ashleigh.

"Oh, Jules, he is dreamy," Ashleigh said as three black cabs drove past, all with passengers on board. "Well done, honey."

"You like?"

"Do I ever." They giggled like school girls.

"Hey." Jon raised his hand at a free cab. He even looked hot hailing a cab.

★   ★   ★

At eight thirty, Ashleigh's phone vibrated in her pocket. She and her friends stood outside the noodle bar on Wigmore Street, waiting for Dave and the others.

"Hey, Dave. Where are you guys?" she asked, looking up and down the busy street.

"Just walking through Cavendish Square. See you in five."

"OK, we'll get a table. Just come in when you're here." She slipped her phone back into her pocket, while letting the others know what he had said. "Let's go in and get a table."

They stood inside the doorway, waiting for a table to become free. Leon and Jon had been in constant conversation ever since they got in the black cab at Dean Street. Jules looked pleased at this, but Ashleigh knew she would be slightly concerned at how well they were getting on. They were all more than aware of Leon's deep interest in women who didn't want commitment—the last thing Jules needed was Leon rubbing off on Jon.

The restaurant was hustling. People were talking over one another, and the sounds of pots and pans hitting the cooker tops blended in with the spitting of the fat from the flames that spread under the large woks as steam and smoke wafted through the air from the open-plan kitchen. Moments later, a waitress came over, leading them to a pine table bench that stretched the whole length of the restaurant. The bench behind them and the bench in front were both completely full. They squeezed in alongside some noisy Chinese tourists.

"I bet the noodle bars aren't like this in China," Ashleigh said to Jules, looking at the tourists.

"No, they're busier—trust me, honey. This is quiet compared to some places I've eaten in over there."

Suddenly, there was some movement along the table. They looked up to see Dave, Isabella, and Peter making their way to a seat. Dave bent to kiss Ashleigh.

"You look beautiful," he said over the noise of the restaurant.

She blushed as she introduced Jules, Leon, and Jon.

"Hi." Dave reached over to shake Leon's hand and then Jon's. "Ladies, you all look lovely tonight. This is my brother Peter and our flatmate, Isabella." He sat down next to Ashleigh.

Ashleigh smiled. Dave was such a gentleman, and she beamed with pride as everyone jostled to sit down. She caught Jules staring at Isabella and tried to catch her eye. *Oh no, she's judging her already. No. Give her a chance.*

The waitress took their orders, distracting Jules, and Ashleigh started to relax. She looked over at Leon, who sat next to Isabella and Peter. She smiled to herself. The poor girl was sitting between two men who shared the same pastime: chasing women. And by the looks of it, they saw each other as healthy competition. She watched as Isabella laughed, turning her head from side to side like a tennis umpire trying to keep up with the witty jokes and innuendo. *Male ego.*

"You OK, honey?"

Ashleigh jumped back to reality, turning to Dave and nodding.

The food came and went. Dave seemed his normal self, and Ashleigh was pleased she hadn't messed things up with him. She still had her prince.

The noise in the restaurant didn't die down. The more people came in, the louder it became. There was now a large line of customers waiting by the door. When they had all finished their meals, Dave asked for the bill, splitting it equally between them all—Ashleigh included, much to his annoyance.

"But I want to get this," he said.

"No, Dave," Ashleigh told him. "I'm paying for you, or I'm paying for myself—you're always picking up the bill for me."

"That's because you're my girlfriend."

"Girlfriend?" The word hung in the air between them.

Dave kissed her. "Is that OK with you?"

Was it, heck! She nodded.

Once they had spilled out onto the street, Ashleigh led them to a bar up the road, trying to contain her excitement. A pretty girl ticked off their names from a list on her clipboard, and another pretty girl walked them into the bar. The lights were low, and behind the bar were more types of spirits and liqueurs than you could imagine, all lined up in front of the long mirror. Walking to the rear of the room where it opened out into a much larger area, they were led to a reserved table.

Ashleigh looked for Jules to tell her about Dave's girlfriend comment. However, Jules and Jon were practically sitting on top of each with interlocked tongues. It was nice to see Jules simply being herself around a man, rather than bragging about how successful she was. Jules glanced up. Curling the corner of her mouth she winked.

"They're getting on well." Dave nodded toward Jules and Jon.

"They are—it's nice. I like him."

"C'mon—I want to dance with my girlfriend." He pulled her to her feet.

After a few more champagne bottles had been turned upside down in the silver buckets, it was clear that Leon's and Peter's persistence toward Isabella was paying off—but not in the way anyone would ever have guessed. Isabella was not swaying toward one or the other. As she had told the girls in the ladies' room, "Why choose? Why not have both?" Ashleigh wondered just how far she would take it. By now, it was getting late, and everyone was about ready to go home—but *whose* home was the question in some cases.

"Wait." Ashleigh stopped Jules as Isabella left the ladies' toilet.

"What's up?"

"Do you like Isabella? She's not that bad is she—a bit crazy, but I like her. Do you?"

"She's all right, I suppose." Jules shrugged. "Why are you smiling at me like that?"

"OK, OK, Dave called me his girlfriend. I've been dying to tell you all night."

"Ashleigh." Jules laughed. "Honey, you sound like you're sixteen."

"Jules, I love you, but stop being a cold bitch and be excited for me. This is good. He obviously likes me, and I didn't fuck it up by saying what I did about Isabella."

Jules glared at Ashleigh.

"You know, when I called her rough."

Jules grimaced.

A familiar voice spoke up from behind her. "You called me rough?"

Ashleigh swung around. "Issi."

"When? Why?" Isabella leaned against the wall, blocking the entrance and not caring that other girls struggled to pass.

"Let's go outside," Ashleigh suggested, trying to buy more time to think.

"Nope. Here is just fine." Isabella didn't move.

Ashleigh felt light-headed. Was there no getting out of this confrontation? "I'm sorry—it was before I had gotten to know you. I had only seen you for like five seconds. I was wrong—so wrong. I was jealous, that's all—I promise I would never judge someone."

Isabella didn't reply. "Oh God, you hate me, don't you?"

"Honey, stop." Isabella threw her arm around Ashleigh's shoulder, smiling back at Jules. "Like you're the first rich bitch to call me rough. It's fine, I get it." Isabella led her back outside, and Jules followed. "It's fine; forget it," she shouted over the music, and then she danced off to find Peter.

Ashleigh pushed Jules back into the ladies' toilet. "Fuck, Jules. Fuck."

"Yep. Not your finest hour. I tried to warn you."

"What? No, you didn't."

"I did! I was widening my eyes at you."

"Jules, your eyes are abnormally large naturally; how would I tell if they got any bigger?"

Jules shrugged.

"Fuck. Do you think she's really OK with me?"

"How would we know? We are just rich bitches," Jules said, reapplying her lip gloss.

"Jules, now is not the time for being like that. She is living with my new boyfriend, and I *need* her to like me."

"Ashleigh, stop that. Dave has known you longer than her, and trust me, you do not need a skank like that liking you."

"Skank? I thought you liked her."

"I did, until she called you a rich bitch all patronizingly." Jules offered her lip gloss to Ashleigh.

"No, thanks. Look, Jules, she is not a skank, and you can be just as patronizing when you're hurt—actually, you can be patronizing pretty much all the time—but anyway . . . I really need you to be supportive right now, OK? What do I do? What if she tells Dave, and he is disappointed in me? I don't want him to think I'm just some 'rich girl.'"

"Bitch—rich bitch," Jules corrected her.

"Jules!"

"Fine, fine. Look. It's done now. She's OK about it. You said sorry. If it makes you feel better, then tell Dave what happened, and then it's all out in the open."

Ashleigh nodded.

"Come on." Jules opened her arms wide. "Bring it in."

★   ★   ★

Outside, they waited for cabs. Isabella appeared friendly toward Ashleigh, and Jules talked to Jon, avoiding Isabella. However, Ashleigh still felt terrible. She noticed that Leon got into the cab with Peter and Isabella.

She turned to Jules. "Unless I'm very much mistaken, as I am really drunk, Leon's flat is not on the way to Wandsworth, is it?"

"No," Dave butted in, "and I'm glad I'm staying at your place tonight."

"So are they?" Ashleigh asked.

"By the looks of it," Jon added.

"Skank," Jules whispered in Ashleigh's ear.

Ashleigh glared at Jules.

"See? Like that." Jules pointed at Ashleigh's widened eyes. "That's what I tried to do to you." Ashleigh shook her head. "OK, I'm sorry." Jules kissed her cheek. "Just joking—I'll stop now."

"Stop with the skank thing," Ashleigh said. "She isn't."

Dave opened the cab door. "Who isn't what?" he asked.

"No one. Don't worry, I'll tell you later."

"Sounds ominous." Dave nodded. "Right, well, we don't live in the same direction—unless you two fancy a foursome at Ashleigh's place, that is."

"As much as I fancy the pants off your girlfriend," Jules replied with a wink, "I think I'll take a raincheck, but thanks for the offer all the same, Dave." She pushed the door closed and waved them off.

★   ★   ★

Dave and Ashleigh woke early the next morning, returning to Dave's flat for his van keys.

"Morning, lads." He walked into the living room with Ashleigh following hesitantly.

"Hey, boys?" There was no reply to this comment. "So I take it everything went well last night, then?"

Leon was sitting on the sofa and grinned. "Hey, Ash."

"Hi, Leon," she replied, looking around the room.

"Well?" said Dave. "If any of you want to come, me, Ashleigh, Jules, and Jon are going to the park. I just came back to get the van keys."

After grabbing the keys, Dave started to head out the door.

"I'll ring you later," Peter called after his brother.

"You do that. See ya, Leon!" Dave shouted back as he opened the front door, laughing to himself.

"Bye, Ashleigh." Isabella appeared in the hallway just as Ashleigh was about to close the door.

"Oh! Hi—bye, Issi. See you later, maybe?"

"Maybe," Isabella said.

"Issi, I'm . . . sor—"

Isabella cut her off. "It's fine. Honestly. You're a nice girl, Ashleigh—don't sweat it. I'm not upset at you."

"OK." Ashleigh believed her.

Isabella turned and disappeared into her room. Ashleigh thought she seemed sad, but she hurried to catch up with Dave.

She was sure Isabella wasn't mad at her, but something was definitely wrong—was she regretting the night before with two men?

Catching up with Dave, Ashleigh felt unsettled. He threw his arm around her shoulder, guiding her toward the van.

"I'm glad I met you."

"Thanks—I'm glad I met you, too." She smiled and hugged him just as Isabella looked out of the bedroom window above them.

Ashleigh waved, but Isabella didn't wave back. Ashleigh watched her as they drove away in the van. Was she imagining, it or was Isabella crying?

"You all right, Ash?" Dave asked.

"Dave?" she ventured.

"Yes?"

"I just saw Isabella looking out the window, and she looked like she was crying."

"Really? Are you sure?"

"No, not really—I couldn't see clearly. But maybe." She wondered if she had imagined it. "You don't think she is regretting last night with Leon and Peter, do you?"

Dave laughed but stopped after he glanced over to see Ashleigh's face.

"Oh, Ashleigh, don't be worried. I live with her, and trust me, Isabella would definitely not be regretting it. I know I was less than keen when she moved in, but she's a super cool flatmate, and I'm sure she is fine about it."

"Well, she didn't wave back at me, and she definitely looked anything but fine."

Dave rested his hand on her knee. "I love that you're so caring. Look, she probably wants what we have, you know?" Ashleigh didn't follow. "I think she wants Peter all to herself, but Peter just isn't a commitment kind of guy." Ashley understood this. "Peter has this way of getting girls to do whatever he wants when really all they want is a boyfriend—and Peter is not a boyfriend type."

"Maybe. It's sad, though."

"Honey, are you OK, really?"

"Sure, I'm fine," she lied. "Well . . ."

Dave stopped at a red light. "What is it?"

"Last night I was telling Jules how bad I felt for calling Issi rough, and she was standing behind me—she heard me." The memory made her cringe.

"Oh." The light changed to green, and he drove on.

"I apologized immediately, and she was fine about it, but I still feel awful . . . Dave, do you think badly of me for saying it?"

"No, of course not. You don't think she is crying over that, do you?"

"No, I don't."

"Look, Isabella is a big girl, and I've seen her when she is out and about. She would get bored if she landed Peter exclusively. They are like two peas in a pod—she loves male attention."

"Does she like *your* attention?"

"Are you jealous?"

"No."

"Are you sure?" Dave smiled.

"Maybe a bit."

"Well, don't be. I'd never do anything—well, nothing that you would find out about, anyway." He winked.

Ashleigh stared at him in disbelief.

"Joke, honey—it's a joke. I'm joking."

If only he knew how many jokes like that Lee used to say. Breathe. He is not Lee—he is Dave. Your new boyfriend, Dave. She smiled.

"I know you are."

CHAPTER
11

ASHLEIGH HURRIED OUT OF the shower to answer her house phone, nearly slipping on the tiled floor in the process.

"Hello?" Out of breath and shivering in the hallway, she stood clutching the phone receiver to her ear.

"You'll never guess what," Rachel said brightly.

"What?" Ashleigh asked as soapy water slid down off her body and onto the floor.

"Guess," Rachel demanded.

"Rachel, honey, I'm dripping wet from the shower; just tell me."

"All right. OK, so Gemma is coming to live with me. Exciting, right?"

"You're kidding! How did that come about?"

"Long story, but the short version is that she needs a fresh start, and I need a flatmate."

"Brilliant." Ashleigh tried to sound interested while looking around. "Hang on sweetie—let me go get a towel quickly." Ashleigh rushed into the bathroom, threw a towel around her shoulders, and hurried back to the hallway phone. "Right, now tell me all. Does she have a job? Can she afford London? You always said you liked living on your own—are you sure about all this? It's all a bit sudden," she said, patting her body dry.

"Chill, it's fine, she's super cool—and I've set her up some interviews already. Anyway, I've got better news. I just got off the phone with Jules and convinced her that she needed a holiday, and Gemma is coming, too."

"Oh, my God, Rach! That is fab—how the hell did you get Jules to change her mind? Wow, so much to take in." She was still processing the Gemma situation.

"Oh, she just needed some time to settle back into things. Maybe my promise of sun, wine, and hot men was too much for her."

"Men?" Ashleigh asked urgently. "But she *has* a man, Jon—did she not tell you? I need to call her."

"Relax, she's still with him." Rachel laughed. "Girlfriend, you definitely need a holiday. Why are you so uptight? Are you and Dave OK?"

"I'm fine," Ashleigh lied. Dave's comment about cheating earlier that week was still playing on her mind, and after being cheated on by Lee, she felt hypersensitive. A part of her wanted to confide in Rachel, but she was desperately trying not to lean on other people— to instead trust her own thoughts. She just didn't know which ones to listen to anymore, and now there was the news of Gemma moving to London and living with her best friend. She needed time to think.

"Did you hear about Issi sleeping with Leon and Dave's brother last week?" Ashleigh continued, hoping she hadn't. She didn't want Rachel disliking Isabella before she had even met her.

"Yes, I heard. So she's like that then, is she?" Rachel sounded disapproving.

"Look, it's her life. As long as she doesn't get Peter and Dave mixed up and sticks to the right brother, she can do whatever she wants, I suppose."

"If you say so."

"What do you mean by that?"

"Nothing . . . look, sometimes you really are too nice. That girl sounds like a skank, but I'm entitled to my own opinion, aren't I?"

Jules. "Jules told you. Well, yes, you are entitled to your opinion, but trust me—you have it wrong this time," Ashleigh said, remembering Isabella's vacant face at the window. "I think she's just trying to fit in but doing it all wrong," she said, disappointed that Jules had pushed her judgments about Isabella onto Rachel. She understood why; she had thought the same, but that was before. And was it so wrong to want her best friend to get along with her new boyfriend's flatmate, if only to make life easier? She just wished she had spoken to Rachel about Isabella before Jules had. However, it looked like that ship had sailed.

"Whatevs," Rachel said. "Anyway, we are all meeting at Leon's flat tomorrow to sort out Ibiza," Rachel said.

"Oh, is Leon coming too?"

"No, he's a stubborn git sometimes—said Ibiza is '*sooo* overrated.'" Rachel giggled. "But he doesn't want to be left out. See you there."

"Yeah, see ya." Ashleigh hung up the phone.

Gemma is moving to London. Well, I didn't see that coming. Is it such a bad thing? Ashleigh thought it over. It would be another girl in their group, and one she had loved so much growing up. She let the idea sit a while—the old trio back together. No, it wasn't a bad thing, it was brilliant, she concluded. Mary would have been so proud that the girls were looking out for each other.

Rest in peace, Grandma Mary. We'll look after her now. And what a better way to introduce Gemma to Jules than a holiday to Ibiza, just the four of them?

★　★　★

Ashleigh had been on a high ever since the holiday meeting at Leon's the night before. Even talking to Samantha at work that day wasn't a problem. Ashleigh had decided that Dave's comment was, as he intended it to be, just a joke. Dave was the perfect boyfriend. He never let her down and always kept his word; he bought her small, romantic tokens and not lavish, expensive, meaningless gifts; and he was an amazing lover. Samantha was welcome to Lee. This holiday was the marker for Ashleigh's new, empowered life.

Ashleigh hopped onto the bus home, which proceeded to chug at a pace slower than a walk toward Marble Arch. Her thoughts were interrupted by a low buzzing in her sweater pocket. It was Eliza.

"Hey, did I forget something?" Ashleigh asked.

"No, you didn't forget anything . . ." Eliza hesitated. "I just thought I should let you know that Samantha has booked a weekend away while you're in Ibiza."

"OK . . ." Ashleigh struggled to see what this had to do with her.

"With Lee."

"Oh."

"I just overheard her talking to someone, and she said Lee was taking her to Switzerland to his villa. Isn't that where he used to take you?"

"He wishes it was his—it's his father's," Ashleigh spat.

Twice a year, Lee would whiz Ashleigh out to Switzerland into the mountains, where they would spend a long weekend. In the beginning, she was amazed by the sincerity of his actions, finding rose petals on the bed and champagne on ice ready for when they arrived, but after a while, she tired of watching Swiss television while Lee took client calls in the office on the top floor all day. She tired of the same TV shows and the pretentious restaurant they had to eat in, just because Lee knew the owners from his childhood. The villa was set high in the grassy mountains overlooking the town below; it even came with its own helipad, as did most of the surrounding residences. The town below was too far to walk, so she felt stuck. After seeing the same views, Ashleigh felt trapped and often bored during the day.

Old memories flooded her mind as Eliza talked. She thought back to a weekend when, after they returned from the market, she had suggested they try something new. Lee frowned. She suggested going to see an amateur play in town that she had read about on a small flyer someone had given her in the marketplace. Lee dismissed it with a wave of his hand and chuckled, shaking his head as he retreated to the office.

"You OK about it?" said Eliza.

"Oh God, yeah, I wouldn't care if I never went to Switzerland again. I bet he takes all his conquests there." Ashleigh tried a smile. "Doubt he tells them it's Daddy's, though. God, he's such a—" She stopped herself. "Oh, who cares? She's welcome to him. I've got Dave. Anyway, Samantha only wants him for his money—"

"And Lee only wants her to make you jealous," Eliza added.

"D'you think so?"

"I *know* so, and Samantha is so shallow she doesn't even care. All she wants is what you used to get."

"Oh God, she's welcome to it. In fact, I feel sorry for her. All the affection and gifts he'll give her will come at a price—she's going to get hurt just like I did."

"That's for sure. Look, I just didn't want you to find out from her about the trip. I doubt she would have been tactful."

★   ★   ★

Ashleigh thought about Lee and Samantha as she dressed for dinner with Dave. She wished Samantha could see what he was doing, and she wished she could stop Lee from trying to imbed himself back into her life. She thought of Dave—her Dave, a kind man who treated her right, and felt grateful. The food was gently cooking, and she was dressed and waiting for him to arrive. She hadn't been waiting long before a knock came at the door, and she ran to answer.

Mr. Schnitzer stood in front of her. He was holding a bunch of lilies, Ashleigh's favorite flower. He held them out toward her.

"Mr. Schnitzer, er . . . you shouldn't have," she joked.

"Sorry, theez are not from me," he said. "Delivery." He raised an eyebrow and smiled. "You woz out."

Ashleigh didn't take the flowers but instead reached into the middle and removed the card to read it:

> *Have fun in Ibiza. I love you, Ashleigh Lands.*
> *Please use this time to think about us.*
> *I miss you more than you know.*
> *See you when you're home.*
>
> *My entire love now & always – Lee x*

She ripped the card in two and smiled back at Mr. Schnitzer.

"They're not from who I thought they were. I've no need for flowers but wouldn't want to waste them. Would you like to have them?" she asked politely.

"You seem to be a much desired voman. Enjoy it vile you can!" He chuckled. "But I can take de flowers if you vish."

"Oh, I do. Thank you, Mr. Schnitzer, thank you so much."

Ashleigh closed the door.

She couldn't take them and have them on display. She and Dave had discussed past lovers, but not that hers was not quite as past as his in many ways. Disregarding the card, she knew that either she needed to tell Dave about Lee's advances, or she needed to put a stop to Lee once and for all.

"Or both," she spoke aloud.

The doorbell rang, and Ashleigh smoothed down the front of her silk dress before answering. She paused and looked at the room for a last check that everything was set correctly, readjusted her hairclip in the mirror and ruffled her long brown hair around her shoulders.

This time, it was Dave at the door.

"Hey," Ashleigh said.

"Hi," said Dave, holding out a bunch of flowers. "I didn't know which ones you liked, so I got a mixture. If you don't like them, blame the girl at the florist's, not me."

She laughed. "They are just perfect," she said, taking the flowers and kissing him on the lips.

Inside, Ashleigh fixed Dave a drink.

"This is nice. You shouldn't have gone to such trouble for me." Dave looked around the dimly lit room.

"No trouble," she shouted from the kitchen.

"Do you need a hand?" He made for the kitchen but then stopped.

"No, no, stay there. It's all under control," she lied, trying to sound calm, stirring the now too-thick sauce and wondering how anyone but her could mess up a packet sauce. "Take a seat. I'll bring it out."

She ran the goopy white sauce over the chicken and carried two plates out into the living room.

"Sorry I didn't do a starter; it's just that—"

"It's lovely. Don't worry, just sit down and eat. It looks really good."

"Might not be so good when you taste it, though."

"Don't be silly." He cut and chewed a piece of chicken. "Mm, it's good. Try it," he said, cutting a larger slice.

Ashleigh smiled. It was as if Dave had a way of reading her emotions and could say the right thing at the right time.

Now, she urged herself. *Talk to him about Lee now; he'll understand.* Ashleigh thought about her packed suitcases ready for her holiday the day after tomorrow. She wished Dave could have driven her to the airport, but he had taken on a last-minute job in Milton Keynes and would be leaving the day before she flew out.

It will keep.

"You seem on edge. Everything OK?" Dave pressed.

She hesitated. "It's my ex."

Dave nodded. "Is your holiday bringing back bad memories? It's OK, you know. I'm totally fine about it."

"No, no. I know you are, and I'm so thankful you're being so supportive. No, it's not that simple—looks like it's my turn to open up to you about more stuff. Full disclosure."

"OK?"

Ashleigh told him everything. He listened patiently, and she saw his lips twitch at parts, but he kept quiet until she had finished.

"So," she said.

Dave was silent for a moment longer, as if choosing his words carefully.

"Would you like me to do anything?"

"No. Oh God, no."

"Then what? Just let him do what he wants to you even though he's not with you anymore?"

She couldn't tell if Dave was upset or not. His tone was calm, but his eyes darted as he talked.

"You're right. But Dave, please, let me deal with this my way." She reached out for his hand and saw his eyes soften.

"Of course. Thank you for telling me." He leaned forward to kiss her. "I'm here if you need me, OK?"

"Thank you."

After packing up the last of Ashleigh's carry-on belongings, they settled down on the sofa to watch a film. Ashleigh felt so much happier after talking to Dave about Lee. The night seemed to fly by, and Ashleigh clung to Dave, suddenly regretting booking the holiday—in fact, it felt as if they were both secretly dreading their impending separation.

It was past eleven before Dave made to leave. Ashleigh hesitantly walked him to the door, then stood holding him for a long moment.

"I'll miss you," he whispered.

"'I'll miss you too."

"Ashleigh?" Dave looked down at her.

"Yes, Dave?"

He lowered his voice. "Ashleigh, I love—"

A quiet knock on the door startled them. Instantly, she knew who was on the other side and gripped Dave's arm. He, in return, mistook her anguish as fear, moving her behind him to open the door.

The two men looked at each other. Two beautiful specimens, two beautiful, polar opposite specimens. There was Lee with his ocean blue eyes and blond hair, and Dave with dark, dreamy eyes and brown hair—one where chivalry thrived, the other where chivalry went to die.

"Lee," Ashleigh breathed over Dave's shoulder.

"Ashleigh, I didn't know you had company," Lee replied, smiling smugly at her.

Dave did not speak.

"Why would you?" Ashleigh asked. "What are you doing here again? Just leave me the hell alone, will you?"

Dave still said nothing but stepped aside.

"Did you not get my flowers?" Lee looked puzzled.

She knew what Lee was doing, but Lee did not know that Dave knew everything, and Dave had a very good poker face right now.

Go, Dave.

"Lee, get off my doorstep." Ashleigh stepped forward, spitting the words. This was it—this was her chance to make him see she meant it. "If I ever see you here again, or if you send me any more gifts, I'll have a restraining order slapped on you. Now get the hell away from me, and stay away."

Lee stared at her.

"You heard the lady." Dave moved Ashleigh behind him again.

Lee's eyes didn't move from Ashleigh at first, but then he slowly turned and walked silently down the steps. Ashleigh stepped backward, watching Dave stand in the doorway to see Lee off until he had gotten into his expensive car and driven away.

"Are you OK?" Dave asked, closing the door.

"I'm fine. Thank you. I'm glad I did that with you here."

"I know his type. I live with one, remember?"

"He won't stop," she whispered into his chest.

"Do you want him to?"

"Yes." She pulled away, looking him square in the eyes. "Yes, I do." And she meant it.

"Sorry, I—"

"Dave, are you jealous?"

"I s'pose I am." He chuckled.

"Well, don't be, because I love you," Ashleigh said, finishing his earlier sentence.

CHAPTER
12

"THIS IS THE LIFE." Jules splashed some more water onto her stomach as she floated around the hotel pool on a blow-up inflatable lilo. "Have you seen Gemma and Rachel?" Lifting her head, she looked over the top of her Dolce & Gabbana sunglasses to see where they had gone.

"Yeah," said Ashleigh. "They were over at the floating bar, chatting up some hotties last time I saw them."

It had been five days since she had last seen Dave, and she missed him. San Miguel was about thirty minutes out of Ibiza Town, and the locals were friendly. The girls were staying at a harbor where people would stop as they sailed around the island. One of the locals had told Ashleigh that lots of famous stars stopped overnight in the bay, and if you took a pedalo out past the yachts, sometimes you could see them onboard in their natural habitat. Ashleigh had smiled at the local man's enthusiasm for rich people, imagining her family's own yachting holidays. She enjoyed the humble life she had carved out for herself, even if Daddy did still send her expensive gifts and pay her rent. She couldn't change where she came from, but her intentions were in the right.

The girls had arrived in Ibiza three days ago. The sun was a brilliant yellow and growing hotter as the days moved on. The girls had worked hard on their tans from the first day, lazing around the pool drinking cocktails. The holiday was just as Rachel promised: relaxing.

Ashleigh and Jules had no interest in chasing hot, toned Spanish men with perfect tans, and Ashleigh was glad Jules was there. Gemma and Rachel, on the other hand, currently had no interest in anything else.

"So have you spoken to Dave since you landed?"

"Nope. He had just gotten home from Milton Keynes and said he missed me already."

"That's good."

"Hmm," Ashleigh mumbled.

"It's not, then?" Jules moved her glasses down her nose.

"He bumped into Lee just before we left."

"What? Girl, why are you only just telling me?" Jules paddled closer to Ashleigh and grabbed her inflatable. "I'm going to start taking this personally."

Ashleigh giggled, holding her inflatable steady. "I told him I loved him."

"That's quick." Jules let go of Ashleigh's inflatable lilo.

Ashleigh told her everything. "But now I'm worried because he's not called me. Have I scared him off?"

"Listen to yourself. You're being paranoid. He said he missed you—what do you want from the guy? Chillax, girl. Just call him if you're bothered. He's not Lee." Jules floated toward the edge of the pool.

"I know," Ashleigh said. "How are things with Jon?" She followed Jules with small wrist paddles.

"Oh, he is everything I've ever wanted, and to think all this time I've been looking in the wrong places at the wrong type of men. He's down to earth, funny, has a good job, and won't sponge off me—"

"Like you've ever been out with a man that would need to sponge off you, Jules."

"I know, I know. I'm just saying it's a plus. Anyway, last week—"

"Jules, Ash, come on," Rachel interrupted, much to Jules's annoyance. "Come to the bar. Have a drink, girls. We're on holiday."

"We'll come over in a bit, sweetie." Jules waved Rachel away with a flick of her hand.

"Okie dokie." Rachel swam back to the bar, where Gemma was laughing with the bartender.

"Lee canceled the holiday in Switzerland with Samantha," Ashleigh told Jules.

"What did he do that for?" Jules reached for Ashleigh's inflatable again.

"Hey, get off!" Ashleigh splashed her. "Eliza called me the day we left. He told Samantha he wasn't over me and that Switzerland was 'our place,' which is ridiculous, because I hated that bloody place."

"Jesus, poor girl."

Ashleigh shrugged. She didn't have a lot of compassion for her and wasn't about to pretend that she did. "Eliza said that she begged him not to leave her. Told him she didn't need a posh holiday with him and to give her another chance."

"And?"

"And he said yes, of course." Ashleigh laughed. "Lee loves pathetic women; it make us easier to control."

"Us? You mean them!" Jules corrected her.

"Right," Ashleigh said.

And Jules *was* right. She wasn't pathetic; she was strong. She had stood up to Lee, had fallen in love again, and was sunning her new, empowered self in Ibiza. Life was on the up and up. Her only stumbling block was cutting down on her drinking, and being on a girls' holiday wasn't really the time or the place to address that life change. She made a silent deal with herself. She would limit her alcohol consumption and allow herself only one major hangover for the whole holiday. Content, she smiled, ironically sipping on her cocktail.

★   ★   ★

The girls opted to stay in the hotel resort later that night for some good old family entertainment that turned into a drinking fest with other guests after the children hurried off to bed. Ashleigh still missed Dave, but she was satisfied that she had done the right thing booking a girls' holiday away without him. Absence makes the heart grow fonder, and Dave didn't seem the disloyal type. She suddenly had a gut feeling that this holiday was going to be just perfect. Ibiza was just as she had pictured it. It was hot and arid, and the infrequent rain could barely penetrate the hard, cracked soil. A little way up the road from the resorts was a discotheque, as they called it in Europe. It was small, cheesy, and full of underaged teens and randy Spanish boys, as they had found out on the second evening. This holiday was measuring up just the way she had hoped.

★   ★   ★

The sun rose early, and the girls nursed hangovers—all except Ashleigh, who had stayed true to herself and paced her night. At midday, they took a stroll down to the seafront for some lunch. The restaurants on the resort were exquisite, but the girls wanted to try a traditional Spanish restaurant outside of the resort complex, with authentic, local Spanish waiters. They found a small restaurant with wicker tables outside that overlooked the ocean, and they chose a table pushed up against a small wall built from different shaped stones.

Ashleigh adjusted the parasol. The sun was bright as it hit her eyes over the top of her sunglasses, and she looked out at the sunbathers spread out across the beach like a deck of cards. The beach was a small horseshoe shape, tucked away from the rest of the island with huge cliffs and caves towering over the sides of it.

As they sat chatting, Rachel caught the eye of a Spanish waiter called Antonio—they had all met on the walk home from the discotheque a few nights before. He spoke perfect English with a strong Spanish accent.

"Ah, you four beautiful girls could not resist my wonderful restaurant, ha?" He looked at Rachel and smiled.

"So this is your restaurant?" Rachel looked at Antonio. "Very nice."

Antonio's skin was a lighter shade of gold and shimmered beneath his rolled-up shirt sleeves. It is my uncle's restaurant. I 'ave been working inside. But if I'd known you were 'ere, I would 'ave seen to you all myself." He looked at Ashleigh and winked. "Maybe I could show you some places the locals go tonight, ha? Me an' my friend Matias can take you to a *pequeño* bar down the road."

"Sounds good." Rachel looked at the others for approval. No one objected.

Antonio smiled. "Okay, good. We meet 'ere at ten tonight. I will take you. Now what can I get you?" He took down their lunch orders.

As Antonio walked away the girls giggled nervously. Ashleigh leaned forward so no one nearby could hear.

"Do you think it's safe going off with two Spanish men to a bar that no one knows? Anything could happen."

"Like what? They're OK." Jules sat back, taking a sip of sangria.

"Anything could happen. Like rape."

Jules looked at the others. "I'd let him rape me if I hadn't just found a dishy English bloke back home."

Ashleigh quickly turned her head to look at her. "Jules!"

"I wouldn't mind either," Rachel said boldly in support.

"Rachel. . . that's not normal." Ashleigh could not believe what they were both saying.

Gemma leaned over the table to Ashleigh. "Come on, Ash—they are kidding. Winding you up." She patted her hand.

Jules let out a giggle. "It will be fine, Ashleigh. We know where he works. Anyway, there will be no need for Antonio and his friend to take one of us off against our will, because Rachel will go freely."

They burst out laughing, except for Ashleigh, who felt horrified.

But now it was for different reasons. If she was meeting up with strange men, what was Dave doing while she was away? It had been four days since she had last talked to him. She quickly shook the thought out of her head and tried a timid laugh. She should just call him.

They took a walk along the beach. It was almost four o'clock in the afternoon, and most of the locals were at home for a siesta, so everyone on the beach was British or German—other than the locals making a living from the tourists by renting out pedalos and banana boat rides. The girls strolled along the sand and chatted away without a care in the world except for Ashleigh, who kept looking at her phone, hoping for a text from Dave. She had called him when they landed; why had he not reached out to her? He called her every day at home. She tapped a quick message and hit send.

Loving the sun.
You OK?
Not heard from you?
Ash xXx

They walked down to some rocks they had seen in the distance, and there they found a small, narrow sand path.

A reply to Ashleigh's text came within minutes.

Hey. Glad you're loving it.
I'm OK. Didn't want to bother you.
I'll call you later?
Dave x

Excited, she told him what time to call and slipped the phone away.

"Where does it go?" Jules asked, looking down the path.

Rachel edged forward, and the other three girls followed behind. The path became wider; tiny seashells mixed into the sand, and gray rocks along the side of the path led them on. Then they heard voices in the distance. As they walked further, they heard the sound of water splashing. Reaching a small rock pool with cliffs surrounding it, they found people diving off the rocks into the water below like professional Olympic divers. The water was so clear you could see the various colored fish deep below the swimmers' feet.

The girls stopped to watch for a while, taking in the amazing surroundings. Ashleigh caught sight of an opening further along the path and pointed it out. They walked on, leaving Jules watching the divers in the rock pool.

As they got closer to the opening, they smelled barbecue in the air. They turned into the opening on the other side of the rock pool to discover a small beach. Like a secret alcove, it was hidden by tall, overcast cliffs. There were men and a few topless women sunbathing on towels. They could see a group of people splashing around in the sea, shouting something in Spanish to a group of girls standing on the sand.

110

To the rear of the beach stood a small wooden hut that sold food and drinks. The girls took off their flip-flops and walked over to the food hut for a cooling drink. Then, they found a spot on the sand to sunbathe.

Not long after, Jules appeared with Spanish friends she had made by the rock pool. Rachel threw her arm into the air, waving them over.

"This is amazing. Look at this place." Jules took in the surroundings before introducing everyone. "This is Gina and Gabriela," she said, pointing to the young women, "and this is Zane," she added, indicating the man that joined them a few seconds later.

After a quick introduction around the group, they sat drinking and getting to know each other.

Gina explained how they had all left school at sixteen years old; Zane, who had family in Manchester, came up with the idea of living in each country for six months of the year. Five years later, they were still doing the same thing but in different countries. Gina had spent six months in France so she could learn the language, Zane still went back to Manchester, England, and Gabriela had picked a different country to live in for the last two years.

"Do you not want a career or to start a family?" Ashleigh asked Gina, hoping not to offend her.

"I no worry about career much. As long as I'm happy wiv enough money." She paused. "But maybe family one day."

Zane handed everyone a bottle of cold beer. "So where are you lovely girls off to later?" He waited for a reply, looking at Gemma.

"We met a guy that works in the fish restaurant over on the seafront. Him and his friend said they'd take us to some local bar tonight."

"What is this guy's name?" said Zane, a smile teasing the corners of his mouth.

"Antonio. His friend is called Matias, I think."

"Ah . . . Matias. I know Matias, and Antonio is my cousin. Dat is our uncle's restaurant. I work dere sometimes. This is good—we can all meet up tonight and 'ave a big party, ha?"

Ashleigh felt better now that there would be girls going with them; however, all she really wanted was speak to Dave.

★   ★   ★

The afternoon grew late. The girls left their new friends on the beach to take a slow walk back past the rock pool, where only one girl remained lazing on a stone ledge, dangling her foot into the crystal-clear water. A feeling of complete ease suddenly rushed over Ashleigh as she trailed behind the others. Dave was the best thing that had happened to her in a long time. She let all bad feelings of Lee and Samantha vanish, and her longing to be close to her family in New York was forgotten. There was only Dave in her thoughts now. She was in love again. She stopped.

"Come on, Ash," Rachel called out, dropping back to wait for her.

Ashleigh confided in Rachel about her feelings for Dave and her new concern.

"That's amazing. Hell, I wish I could fall in love once." Rachel laughed.

"You don't think Dave is a player, do you?" Ashleigh asked suddenly.

Rachel laughed at the description. "No. Do you?"

"No, but how can I be sure? I mean, look at his brother—they live together, and they're twins."

Rachel threw an arm around Ashleigh's shoulder. "Just because they are twins doesn't mean they are the same."

"Yeah, you're probably right."

"Girl, I am *always* right."

"If you say so." Ashleigh grinned, hoping she was right.

★   ★   ★

Back at the hotel, Jules helped Gemma choose an outfit to wear while Ashleigh and Rachel sat on the balcony with a glass of champagne, smoking Ashleigh's slender cocktail cigarettes as they looked out at the evening views.

Ashleigh looked out beyond the hotel pool to the beach, where only a few people still occupied their temporary patches of sand. She watched a local man walking his dog by the shore, which was now a deep purple color as the sun sank below the horizon; a cool breeze was drifting in from the ocean beyond. In the distance, it looked as if one of the yachts were having a party—she could just about hear the music and see the people on the deck. She looked over at Rachel.

"I wonder what Dave is doing now."

"It's Friday night; he's probably already drunk. Has he not called you yet?"

Ashleigh stared at her with wide eyes. "I hope that Issi behaves herself. He's calling soon."

"Ash, stop worrying. He's not the type to cheat."

"I know. Just used to Lee's antics, I suppose." She put down her glass of wine and walked over to the end of the balcony. Rachel joined her, watching the distant waves in the dark.

"Here." She passed Ashleigh a cigarette. "You know him better than any of us. What's your gut telling you about him?"

Ashleigh laughed, taking the cigarette. "Like I can trust what my gut tells me! Look what happened last time I trusted those feelings."

"No—last time, you knew Lee was a rat; you just didn't listen to yourself." Rachel walked back to the table and topped off their glasses. "Honey, you must always go with what you feel. Instincts, they're never wrong. Just listen to them this time."

They both looked down to the hotel pool, where some men were setting up a karaoke stand and what must have been a stage for the evening entertainment. Ashleigh turned to look at Rachel.

"What about you? When are you going to settle down and find a nice man?"

Rachel rolled her eyes. "I'm not ready just yet; I'm happy," she said simply. "My time will come."

Both girls jumped as Gemma turned on the stereo in the lounge.

"Come on," Gemma called.

They laughed, putting out the cigarette.

"OK, let's go get ready," Rachel instructed Ashleigh. "Time to have some fun."

CHAPTER

13

"DAVE. COME ON, BRUV." Peter banged on the bathroom door. Half dry, Dave opened the door and stepped past his brother with a black bath towel wrapped around his waist, raising his eyebrows and shaking his head.

"Dave, what the hell are you doing? We have to leave." Peter looked panicky as he walked down the hall after him.

Isabella ran into view. "Dave, you're not ready?"

"I told you both I'm not coming."

"No, you said you didn't *think* you were going to come." Peter paused for a reaction, but Dave walked into his room and shut the door. "Dave!" he called after him. "Dave, come on. It will be a good night. You'll love it. Lots of girls, drink, more girls, more drink. Did I say girls already? Look, I'll even buy you a kebab on the way home—a tonna meat and fries with a shit-ton of mayo—come on, that's a bloody good deal." Peter pushed open his brother's bedroom door, walking in.

"Pete, mate, I'm getting dressed, and I'm still not coming." Dave dropped the bath towel from around his waist then bent over to pick up his tracksuit bottoms from the floor. Peter jerked his head away.

"Dude, I don't need to see that," Peter said as he recoiled.

"Then leave. I'm not coming, end of discussion." Dave could feel his brother's frustration.

"What?" Peter asked. "What else is there to do?"

"I'm going to watch a movie and order a takeaway."

"What is up with you? Jeez. OK, fine, well . . . you know where we are if you wanna stop dwelling on the fact that your new girlfriend is in the clubbing capital of the world with three other hot, sexy women, and you aren't."

"Funny, mate, funny . . . Enjoy yourself, and shut the door on your way out of my room." Dave smiled sarcastically.

"Oh, I will," he whispered. "And I won't apologize if Issi screams too loud later as I roger—"

"I heard that," Isabella shouted from other side of the door.

"You're a dick, Pete. You know that, right?" said Dave. "Now out—leave. Go." He picked up the towel to throw it at his brother, but Peter didn't wait, slamming the door shut behind him.

"Bye, Mr. Boring," Isabella called out.

Five minutes later, Dave heard the front door close. He walked out of his room to a calm, quiet household. Picking up his phone, he dialed Ashleigh's number. As he listened to the international ring tone, he heard his brother crash back through the front door. He hoped he had just forgotten something. The last thing he needed was Ashleigh hearing Peter telling him to come out drinking and getting wound up.

★   ★   ★

Dressed and dancing around the hotel room drinking wine, the girls filled the air with the scent of perfume. From the balcony, Ashleigh could see Rachel looking around to see where she had disappeared to. Catching sight of Ashleigh pacing the balcony with her mobile phone against her ear, Rachel ran out to see if she was OK.

"You good?" Rachel mouthed. She looked relieved when Ashleigh smiled, nodded her head, and then pointed to her phone, mouthing back, "It's Dave." Rachel went back inside.

"Are you going out tonight?" Ashleigh asked Dave.

"Not tonight. You?"

"We're all off in a minute."

"Where? Ibiza Town?' Ashleigh wondered if Dave felt jealous.

"No," she said. "We met some locals on the beach today. I got on really well with a girl called Gina. They're taking us to a bar up the road."

"Sounds better than my night. I'll let you get off, and I'll see you when you're back."

"Right, OK. Well… bye, then. See you when I'm back, I suppose?"

"Or I can call you," Dave offered. "Whatever works for you."

Ashleigh hung up, looking down at the phone as the screen faded. *That was odd. Didn't he want to talk to me for longer?* "See you when you're back." Did that mean he wasn't calling her again? Or was he implying Ashleigh wasn't to call him? She tightened her lips. *Doesn't he care? Or maybe he has a girl coming around while I'm away. Maybe he doesn't like me enough . . . Or maybe he is insanely jealous and can't bear to hear me talking about going clubbing, so he can't talk to me, or maybe . . .* She pondered for a moment. *Or maybe he just trusts me. Yes, that's it—he trusts me. He's a decent man that respects and trusts me enough not to suffocate my holiday.*

She moved to join the others.

★   ★   ★

Waiting excitedly outside Antonio's restaurant for their new friends to arrive, Ashleigh lit a cigarette. The sea was calm, and a gentle breeze tickled the girls' bare shoulders.

Sitting down on a cobbled stone wall, they looked over at Antonio's restaurant. It was full to the brim with tourists waiting patiently for food to arrive at their tables. They could see Antonio behind the bar talking to a man who looked very angry; he was waving his hands around, pointing at the customers in the restaurant. Antonio looked as if he were trying to calm the man down. The man turned and pointed out of the open-fronted restaurant to where the girls were sitting.

Ashleigh jumped. "That doesn't look good; maybe we should hide." The others didn't reply.

"Hola," a voice said, drawing the girls' attention away from the angry restaurateur. Zane walked over to Rachel, kissing her on each cheek, and then walked along air kissing all of them in turn.

He swung around to see the end of the argument that the girls had been watching previously.

Antonio stormed out of the restaurant toward everyone. Once he stood in front of them, he changed his frown to a welcoming smile.

"Hola, everyone."

"Antonio, where is Matias?" Zane asked his cousin.

"Uncle Pablo needs him to work in da kitchen—'e he is not listening to me."

Ashleigh looked around, puzzled. "Where are Gina and Gabriella?"

"Ah . . . They will come later. Let's go."

"OK." Ashleigh felt a little uneasy.

They walked out past the resort to where Zane's jeep was parked. Gemma climbed in the front while Rachel, Jules, and Ashleigh climbed into the back seats, and Zane sat casually with his legs hanging over the back of the old, dusty black jeep. They drove down country roads with small villas on either side. There were fields that looked like vineyards running for miles, though Ashleigh couldn't see well in the night with no streetlights.

San José was the next town up. The bar was quietly tucked back from the tourist resorts down a small road with a few villas. The jeep neared the end of the undeveloped road, and Zane pulled up right outside. They jumped down onto the sandy grit road, looking up; there was a large, dimly lit orange sign over the entrance with what looked like the word "Paradox," but none of the vowels were illuminated anymore.

Ashleigh wondered if this was such a good idea after all. Rachel was the first through the doors, and reluctantly, Ashleigh followed. To the left stood a rustic bar where local people sat drinking. She looked down, noticing fine grit scattered on the floor that had obviously been walked in from outside. It was definitely authentic, she realized, pleasantly surprised—just a lot smaller than she had imagined.

The girls lined up along the bar to order tequila. The bartender laughed, gesturing to a row of many different types of tequila; then he reached for a golden bottle, saying something about a worm. The music was loud and his accent was strong, so they all just smiled, nodding their heads as he held up the bottle for approval.

Antonio laughed with the Spanish locals while Zane bought a round of beers for everyone. Drinks in hand, Antonio then led them to the back of the bar. Rachel nudged Ashleigh as they realized there was no more to the bar apart from the toilets to the left and the dimly lit stone stairs they were being led up. Ashleigh glanced back at Rachel. As they got to the top, they came out to an open-roof terrace. In front of them was a large square with stone tables, wicker chairs, and candles lit on each tabletop. To the front of the terrace was a large, raised concrete platform onto which Antonio and Zane had jumped, beckoning the girls to come and sit down.

As they sat facing each other in a semi-circle, Ashleigh noticed something orange in color out of the corner of her eye. She realized they were sitting at the top of the building above the partly illuminated sign.

"Wow, how cool is this?" Rachel had noticed the same and peered over the top. "Hey, there's Gabriela and Gina. Hola, up here!" Rachel waved down to them.

The stars above glittered in the dark; it was late. They listened to music playing from the bar below as they laughed and drank, telling stories and acting like drunken idiots. Tomorrow was shaping up to be Ashleigh's one hangover day. The drinks kept flowing, and the laughter kept growing. The girls danced with each other, taking lessons from Gabriela and Gina on how to do the flamenco and failing. After that, Zane showed Gemma his nimble Spanish hips as he spun her around long into the night as the others clapped.

Ashleigh straightened as she heard the music stop and the downstairs door to the bar being locked for the night. Had the night come to an end already? She started to sulk—she had more dancing to do. She looked over at Antonio for reassurance, and he pointed at some external stone steps on the side of the building.

"The locals use them to leave with no need to worry about closing time," he explained.

She checked her watch. One a.m., she managed to read.

Zane and Gemma sat at another table talking while the others played drinking games without them. Their drunken voices rolled off the top of the building into the night. Ashleigh's thoughts had been occasionally jaded by thoughts of Dave's abrupt phone call.

Fleeting thoughts of another woman curled in his arm watching a movie pinched at her better judgment. She distracted herself by reaching for another liquor shot that Antonio had poured. Her vision blurred as the alcohol rushed her veins.

"You OK, Ash?" Rachel asked. "You look a bit drunk. We can go home if you like."

"Me? No . . . I'm not drunk at all." Ashleigh laughed, believing she was far less drunk than she felt. "No, the night is young. Let's drink more."

Rachel smiled, swaying. "Well you just downed the last shot, so that isn't happening."

"Really? You mean we drank all the booze?" Ashleigh glanced at her watch.

"I have a bottle of vodka," Gina announced.

Ashleigh could feel her eyes light up.

"No, Ash, you really don't need any more." Rachel pushed the bottle away from Ashleigh's grasps.

"I have an idea," Antonio said. "Let's go to the fisherman's beach—go naked swimming."

"Skinny dipping. Yeah, let's go. Where is it?" Rachel was up and rearing to go.

"Just over dere—you can see it from up 'ere if you stand." Antonio pointed into the distance. The moonlight reflected off the sea behind the rocks.

"Let's go." Ashleigh stood up and reached for the vodka bottle.

"No . . ." Rachel giggled precariously, guiding Ashleigh down the stone steps that snaked the side of the building. They followed Antonio across the road, making no effort to lower their voices.

Zane ran ahead, holding Gemma's hand. "Naked swimming!" he shouted.

Ashleigh heard Gemma laugh. "You mean skinny dipping."

As they approached the sand, there was a stampede to take off their clothes. The only light was from the moon. Gemma and Zane ran as fast as they could, stripping as they ran, leaving a trail of clothes scattered down the beach.

Rachel and Antonio watched as they splashed into the sea, Zane in all his glory and Gemma wearing just a small black thong, laughing loudly. Gemma gasped as the lukewarm water soaked her naked torso; she jumped up and down, waist-deep in the sea, holding her double D breasts, as Zane stood next to her, mesmerized. She let go to reveal her naked body and turned to face him; the water splashed over the large mounds of flesh.

Gina tried to convince Ashleigh to strip; the others were all naked and running down the beach, laughing as they splashed into the sea.

"Come on, you keep panties on—it is fun," said Gina as she stepped out of her jeans, quickly pulling off her small vest top.

Ashleigh stood looking at the others, suddenly lacking in enthusiasm.

"Come on, come on," Gina shouted. "Come on, it ees so much fun. You on holiday, live a leetle . . ."

Ashleigh swayed and started to giggle. Perhaps because of the alcohol, she pulled her white dress up over her head.

"Sod it, but I am going to keep my panties and bra on."

They ran to the water's edge; the others had started to swim out to an old wooden fishing boat. Gina grabbed Ashleigh's hand, and they fell into the water.

★   ★   ★

At three a.m., Dave woke up with a stiff neck, realizing he had fallen asleep on the sofa. Yawning, he stretched out his arms and then picked up the half-eaten Indian takeaway boxes. He walked toward the kitchen and paused, thinking he heard a bang from outside. Walking up to the front door, he put his eye to the spyhole to see Peter, Issi, and another girl messing around in the hall. He quickly stepped away from the door and walked back in the direction of the kitchen. The front door opened with a bang. All three piled in.

"Dave—you're still up," Peter said, standing in the doorway looking at his brother with one hand around Issi and the other up a blonde girl's top.

"OK, I'm off to bed. Enjoy!" Dave smiled.

"No. Have a drink with us, bro."

"Yeah, come on, Dave, you can meet my friend Sassy," Issi said, smiling as she walked up to Dave, throwing her arms around his neck and kissing him on the lips.

Dave pulled away, wiping his lips. "You're drunk, Issi."

"Yep, I am, and you must stay up with us," she said. By this point, Peter had Sassy pinned up against the hallway wall and was undressing her.

Dave rolled his eyes. "Thanks, but no."

"Do you want some company in bed, then?" Issi put her hand out, tugging at Dave's belt buckle. Dave grabbed her hand.

"Wow, Dave," she said. "You're strong. That turns me on."

"What are you doing?" Shaking his head, Dave walked to his room.

Closing his door, Dave undressed and slid into bed. He lay there, unable to sleep. His mind was fixated on Ashleigh, as it had been all night; his heart yearned for her to come home.

Four more days. He tried to close his eyes to see if he could slowly drift off to sleep, but all he could think about was her, and all he could feel was his brother's bed banging against the wall. He lay there on his back with his eyes closed, trying to clear his mind. Was Ashleigh still out drinking, or was she in bed sleeping? Was she missing him? He hoped so. Eventually, he drifted into a shallow, steady sleep.

★　★　★

He dreamed of Ashleigh lying with him, and his penis hardened as he felt her hand touch him. In his dream, he saw Ashleigh dip below the covers in front of him, massaging him, her hand rubbing him gently, firmly, and ever more feverishly, her mouth close. He groaned out loud, pushing his pelvis forward so he could slide into her mouth. Dave suddenly felt a warm, moist feeling. He woke and quickly opened his eyes to see Sassy leaning down over him, her mouth sliding down his manhood.

"What the fuck are you doing?" Dave pushed her off. "Get the fuck off me! Get the fuck out—*out*, before I throw you through the fucking door!"

Dave had never sworn at a woman before, but he was in such a rage, he felt violated. His head felt like a pressure cooker ready to blow.

Peter and Issi ran into the bedroom in a blind panic as Sassy ran out, also in a wide-eyed panic. Issi looked at Dave, who glared back at her like she was the devil's best friend as he held the sheets against his pelvis.

She stared back for a split second before running after Sassy.

"Dave, what are you doing?" Peter stood in the doorway, one hand on his head, not quite awake.

"What am I doing? What am I fucking doing? That girl just got into my bed, trying to give me a blow job! I was asleep! Fucking asleep, Pete."

He reached for his tracksuit bottoms and moved for the door, but Peter held his hand out. "Wow, Dave, wait! She's leaving; just stay here and calm down." Peter closed the door.

"What happened? If some girl tried to give me head while I was asleep, there's no way I would be throwing her out."

"Yeah, well, I'm not you, am I Peter?" Dave spat. An urge to wash spread over him. "She has to go," he said.

"She's gone."

"Issi, Peter. Issi has to go."

"What? Why? She didn't try and suck your fucking cock!"

"Don't say that. Shut the fuck up." Rage burned like nothing he had ever felt.

"Dave. Bro." His brother looked taken back by his reaction.

"Don't say that. Don't ever say that again." His hand fidgeted, and he could see Peter watching him with concern. "I said if it didn't work within three months, then she would go—it was her friend." Dave started pacing the room.

"Dave, it weren't Issi's friend. We met that girl in a bar, and she was up for some fun, so she came back with us. It ain't Issi's fault."

"Well, where is Issi, then? Why did she run after her?"

Isabella opened Dave's door. "I went after her to check that she didn't take anything." She stared at Dave in alarm. "You OK? You look pale, Dave. I checked. Nothing is missing, and she has gone."

Dave slumped down onto the bed. "What am I going to tell Ashleigh? How could I have let this happen?"

Issi sat down next to him, putting her arm around his shoulders. Dave flinched.

"Don't." He pulled away.

Issi stood up. "I'm so sorry, Dave." She glanced at Peter.

Dave saw the exchange of pity in their eyes and felt sick.

"Tell her nothing," Isabella said. "It's not your fault; you didn't want it to happen. Anyway, what's the point in saying anything? It would only upset her. If it was me, I would rather not know."

Dave looked at her. "She's not like you."

"Bro." Peter frowned.

"Sorry, Issi," Dave tried. "I can't lie to her."

"You can if you don't want to hurt her, because you will if you tell her. Trust me, I'm a woman. I know how we think."

"How can you say that? You sleep with multiple men, and by the looks of it, women as well. What do you know about being faithful?"

"Bro, stop it," said Peter. "I know you're upset, but it's not Issi's fault."

"It's OK," she said. "I can take a low punch—I'm used to it. Look, just because I like sex doesn't mean that when I finally meet Mr. Right, I won't be faithful."

Dave noticed her look toward Peter and remembered his conversation with Ashleigh. Maybe Ashleigh did see her crying. Maybe she felt as dirty as he did now.

She carried on. "I'm single and can do as I please. I do know, however, that Ashleigh likes you a lot, and it might upset her to find out a girl sucked her man's cock. Some things are best kept to yourself. That's all I'm saying."

"She's right," Peter agreed. "Come on, let's go to bed—it's been a weird night. Get some sleep, bro."

Dave lay in bed on his back yet again for what seemed like ages, mulling over the situation. He wondered if this was how women felt when men touched them without permission. His skin felt odd, itchy.

He quietly took a shower, trying to wash away the violation. He stood facing the showerhead, water running over his head and down his body. Strange feelings stirred inside him. If it were not for Ashleigh, he would have loved a good-looking girl sneaking into his bed. But somehow, he felt angry—guilty, even. It had been completely beyond his control, but he still felt an overwhelming amount of guilt. Was Isabella right? Would Ashleigh even believe him if he did tell her? Would she think there was something cynical in it?

He thought of his brother's reaction. *How are we even twins?* Then, he thought again of what Isabella had said. Should he really take her advice? The girl who apparently seemed to violate herself regretted it but still went back for more. Ordinarily, he would feel compassion for her, but he just didn't have the emotional real estate for anyone else at that moment.

Once dry and lying back in bed, Dave decided the best thing was to forget it ever happened. How would she ever find out, anyway? He would tell her in his own time, when the time was right.

CHAPTER
14

A SHLEIGH BRIEFLY WOKE TO hear the hotel door close. Small, quick footsteps ran over the ceramic floor tiles into the bedroom. She observed Gemma sneak into bed and smiled to herself.

Later that morning, at a more sociable hour, Ashleigh woke again and went to bask in the morning sun on the balcony with croissants, jam, and strawberries. Rachel sat beside her, managing to squeeze out a small "Morning" before reaching for a croissant.

The two girls sat in silence, looking out over the resort as other guests went for their morning swim in the pool. A strong morning wind was blowing across the sea, and they could see the beach filling up with sunbathers. The banana boatman was getting his lifejackets out of his locker, and the pedalos were lying motionless on the sand, waiting for another day's use. Ashleigh sighed; the days were going so fast, rolling into one. She put down her cup of tea.

"Just think; this time last year, I planning a girly holiday with Kelly," she said.

"Why didn't you go?" Rachel asked.

"Lee talked me out of it." She turned at a sound, looking into the living room, where she saw Gemma stumble to the bathroom, hungover.

"Don't worry," said Rachel. "You live and learn."

Ashleigh wasn't missing Lee, just wishing she had left him long before she had. How different her life would have been without him! She didn't dwell on it for too long—there was no point in consuming herself with thoughts of events she could not control.

An hour passed; all the girls except Gemma were dressed and sitting out on the balcony, ready to head off into Ibiza for a day. San Miguel was so far away, they didn't have the luxury of the town on tap and wanted to explore the clubbing capital of Ibiza.

Ashleigh went to check on Gemma, as she could no longer hear noises coming from her room. She found her sleeping, head in arms, hunched over the dressing table with her hairbrush still in her hand. Ashleigh put Gemma back to bed, telling her to phone her cell once she was up. She returned to the balcony and explained that Gemma was in no fit state to be walking around Ibiza.

"You old drunk!" shouted Rachel into the living room from the balcony.

"Oh, don't be mean," Ashleigh protested.

Excited, they went down to wait in the hotel lobby for a cab. Ashleigh grew quiet, however, concerned about leaving Gemma in such a helpless state on her own. She felt a pang of guilt spread over her, knowing that if she were the one feeling that hungover in a strange country, especially after making such a life-changing decision as Gemma had just done by leaving her husband, she would want a friend around to comfort her.

"Guys, I think I'm going to stay here and look after Gemma. Don't tell me not to, because I would do the same for any of you if you were in that state—"

"Ash, that's nice of you, but it's your holiday too," Rachel protested. "You were looking forward to today. She will be OK."

"I don't mind," Ashleigh said. "Really. I can bathe by the pool, check on Gemma, and then come along later with or without her . . . I want to stay—that's final." Her words were stern.

She waved them off and then made her way back up to the room. Gemma was being sick in the bathroom; quickly, Ashleigh ran in and held her hair up while rubbing her back. Gemma sat on the floor, panting, sweat dripping from her forehead as she retched uncontrollably and then threw up again. Ashleigh helped her back to bed and put a bucket on the floor beside her. She sat outside on the balcony reading a book and listening for any whimpers, checking on Gemma every now and then.

★   ★   ★

The sun slowly dried the chlorine-filled water from Ashleigh's skin after a long dip in the pool. Laying out her towel on a wooden sun-lounger, she bathed in the hot midday sun. She closed her eyes behind her sunglasses, feeling the warm rays pour down onto her soft, wet skin, gently drifting off into a light, lingering sleep. She was still aware of noises around her but had no muscle movement or any particular thought bothering her mind. This was pure relaxation.

Suddenly, a beach ball was thrown out of the pool by some children and landed on her legs. She sat bolt upright, startled by the wet plastic ball. The children looked sheepish and waved to say sorry. Brushing the water off her legs, she threw the ball back to them.

Pure relaxation over, then. The children screamed at each other and kept playing.

Leaving her towel on the sun-lounger, she wandered along the side of the pool and went to check on Gemma.

Gemma was sitting on the balcony with a tall glass of ice-cold water.

"Feeling any better?" Ashleigh looked at Gemma, whose hand was shaking slightly as she smoked a cigarette.

"Kinda . . . still feel like shit, but no more puking, thank God."

"Have you tried to eat anything?" Ashleigh sat next to her.

"Yeah, I had a bit of toast. Sorry I messed up your day, Ashleigh."

"Don't be silly. You haven't messed anything up. We can meet Rachel and Jules later if you like."

"Sounds good to me," Gemma said.

"I'm going to go get something to eat," Ashleigh told her. "You just chill out here."

Gemma smiled, grateful. "You're so kind. I wish I was more like you."

"Don't be silly. Stay here and rest." Ashleigh smiled, getting up to walk toward the door.

In truth, Ashleigh was content with the way things had panned out. She was enjoying the day to herself but still hoped Gemma would be well enough to meet the others later, as that would make a perfect end to a lovely day.

Ashleigh sat alone, looking out over the harbor as a waitress took her lunch order. Life had changed over the last six months, and for the better. Lee may have finally gotten the message, and she even had found the courage to handle a confrontation with Samantha. And then there was Dave.

Amazing Dave. She remembered their phone conversation and then thought back to before her holiday and how they texted each other every day in England. Why was it different now? She had just told him she loved him. *This is silly.* She pulled out her phone.

> *Hey honey*
> *What you up to?*
> *I miss you*
> *Ash xXx*

Seconds later, there was a response, just like normal.

> *Hello you*
> *I miss you too.*
> *Just at work but so glad you texted.*
> *Are you enjoying yourself?*
> *I love you x*
> *Dave*

Excitement flooded her face. She was right. This holiday was the perfect way to mark the start of a new beginning—drama-free, filled with happy days ahead.

★　★　★

Later that afternoon, Ashleigh came back to the hotel room, sandals in hand. A gentle scent of perfume drifted past her nose. She saw

Gemma, bright-eyed and fully dressed, wearing white cotton shorts, a vest top, and an oversized red belt sitting nicely around her hips.

"Wow, look at you . . . diva." Ashleigh stood admiring her for a second.

"Right, get a move on. I called Rachel, and they are already pissed. Now come on, we have men to find." Gemma said.

By the time Ashleigh and Gemma arrived in Ibiza Town center, the sky had darkened and was softly lit by the street lights. They found Rachel and Jules perched high on barstools, sitting outside a noisy bar on a busy lane. The lane was packed door to door with other bars, all full to capacity. The road was swamped with English clubbers, and a parade promoting a dance venue flooded the cobbled road. There were people on stilts, muscular men in black dinner suits with naked chests and bow ties around their necks, skinny girls in green leotards jumping around with ribbons in their hands, and even a flamethrower and a tightrope walker. People cheered, and drinkers from the bars joined in, dancing to the music as the parade passed by.

Ashleigh looked up to see a man standing on a balcony dancing and waving his arms around in time with the beat. She realized he was a DJ who had his decks set up above a bar on the balcony opposite them.

"That's awesome," she said, but no one heard her over the music.

Ashleigh joked with a man dressed as a Victorian lady wearing a huge, light pink wig, his face heavily painted in makeup; he held out a flyer for her to take. It was for a nightclub that she had been told was the best club in Ibiza, and from the look of the parade, she could see why. It was a spectacular way to advertise a club.

"This is brilliant," Ashleigh shouted to the others, who were downing strange-colored drinks at the table.

"I know. We've been here ages. What took you so long?" Rachel shouted back, shaking her head. "Never mind . . . here, down this, girls. You've got some serious catching up to do." She thrust a shot glass into Ashleigh's hand and one into Gemma's.

"What's this?" Ashleigh eyed the strange green liquid.

"Just down it!" shouted Jules.

They stayed in the bar until the parade had passed, and then they stumbled in and out of bars packed with drunken clubbers before stumbling off to the venue on the flyer that had been given to Ashleigh by the Victorian transvestite.

"Whoop, whoop!" Rachel cried as they wobbled unsteadily down a cobbled alleyway.

"Oi—hey!" came a voice behind them.

They spun around and saw three boys who looked English. Gemma stared at them suspiciously.

"What's up, boys?" Rachel asked as if she knew them.

"Where you heading?" one of the boys said in an equally familiar way.

"Er . . . and you are?" Gemma placed her hands on her hips.

"It's all good, Gem. We met them earlier today," Rachel explained.

"Yeah, Gem. It's all good," one of the boys mocked, staring directly at Gemma's cleavage. Gemma smiled sarcastically at him.

Rachel introduced them. "Gemma, Ashleigh, this is Dylan, Rees, and Eddy."

"So where you girls taking us?" Dylan, the largest boy, put his arm around Rachel's shoulder.

"Er . . . well, here, if you're up for it." Rachel passed him the flyer.

"What? Don't go there—it's fucking expensive. Let's go to a place I know round the corner."

"No, thanks." Rachel pulled away from his grip.

"Babe, listen . . ." Dylan tried to put his arm back around Rachel, but she walked on quickly. Rachel was not acting quite so friendly toward the boys any more. Ashleigh suddenly felt uneasy with Dylan's demeanor.

"Come on, girls, let's go—this guy is freaking me out now. He's drunk." Rachel pushed Gemma to walk with her; Ashleigh clung to Jules's hand.

"Hey, don't walk off!" Dylan shouted. "Hey, I'm talking to you!"

Gemma looked at Rachel. "Thought you said they were all good."

"They were earlier." Rachel glanced over her shoulder. "Shit, girls, speed up. They're following us—we need to get to the end of this alley." Ashleigh followed with Jules.

They could hear music and shouting coming from the streets around them. All they needed to do was get back onto the main drag.

Ashleigh suddenly felt sober as blood pounded in her ears. The boys started to walk faster and were gaining on them, and Dylan was laughing and calling them to stop. Ashleigh could hear another boy telling Dylan to cut it out; however, that just made him shout louder. They were halfway down the alley now, but the cobbles made it hard to walk in heels.

Dylan slapped his hands together and shouted, "Come to Daddy."

That comment was enough for Ashleigh. They had to get out of the alley—and fast. "Quick, start running!" she said in panic. They started to run.

"Oh, don't run away!" Dylan shouted, then sprinted after them.

They reached the end of the alley at the same time as Dylan reached for Rachel's arm. Tugging at her, he pulled her toward him, laughing, and gripped her upper arms with both hands.

"Aw, don't—get off!" she cried.

Gemma tried to pull at Dylan's arms while Ashleigh and Jules shouted at him to let go, but it was no good. He pushed Rachel against the wall and leaned his heavy weight on her. Rachel screamed, looking at Ashleigh desperately.

Eddy ran toward Dylan and Rachel. "Dylan, what the fuck you doing, mate?" He yanked Dylan away from Rachel. "Rachel, you OK?" Rachel didn't answer. "Fucking hell, Dylan mate, what's got into you?"

Dylan squared up to Eddy, pushing him with his chest.

Ashleigh grabbed Rachel and ran out of the alley. Jules and Gemma followed, leaving the three boys arguing. They ran a few steps and were back into the hustle and bustle of Ibiza Town. Clubbers pushed into the girls as they fell out of food outlets and bars, singing and shouting.

"Shit, what just happened there?" Gemma asked, panting as they slowed down to a walking pace.

"Don't know, but let's get into a bar and off the streets for a bit." Ashleigh pointed to a busy bar opposite them.

Rachel followed close, still holding onto Ashleigh for support, her face drained of color and her hands trembling as adrenaline pulsed through her veins.

"Fuck, Rachel, who were those boys? I thought you said they were OK?" Ashleigh snapped.

"They were," Rachel said. "We met them earlier, and they were fine—I'm sorry."

"It's not her fault, Ashleigh," Jules said.

"Sorry." Ashleigh clung to Rachel. "Just shook me up a bit."

"Me too." Rachel looked pale.

Inside, they managed to find a table to one side, away from the packed bar. Clubbers danced on the small dance floor next to them. The girls didn't care that people were pushing into them as they sat there. The more people around, the better.

"You OK, Rach?" Jules returned from the bar, placing four bottles down on the table. Everyone drank large mouthfuls.

"Yeah, thank God for Eddy," Rachel said. "I thought Dylan was going to get nasty."

"Me too," said Jules. "Jeez . . . Dylan was totally different from when we first met him."

Gemma looked at Rachel with concern. "You sure you're OK? We can go back to the hotel—"

"No, let's just stay here," Rachel insisted. "There are plenty of people around, and anyway, Eddy and Rees wouldn't have let anything happen—I hope, anyway. Plus the cabs are just at the end of the road, so we can get home."

"I'll call Zane," Gemma suggested.

'No, really, it's fine. I'm fine."

"No, no, let me; he can come and meet us after his shift. He wanted to come out anyway, but I told him it was just girls, so he won't mind, really."

Rachel smiled knowingly, glancing at Ashleigh. "Go on, then. Call him, and I'll get us all a shot to get this night back on track."

Ashleigh giggled as Gemma bounced off. She was pleased that Gemma liked Zane and hoped Zane would let her down gently when they left for home.

★ ★ ★

Stepping outside the bar so she could hear, Gemma told Zane to finish work and then come to meet them, but Zane had ripped his apron off before Gemma had even told him the whole story. Zane told his uncle he had to leave work early and made Antonio drive him into Ibiza Town.

Turning to go back inside, she heard someone call out to her.

Stunned, Gemma looked across the road to see Eddy standing on his own, eating a kebab.

"It's OK, he's gone," Eddy said. "Rees took him back to the hotel. Is Rachel all right?" Eddy stood opposite her chewing a piece of meat. "He was drunk. Don't think he would have hurt her; he just gets a bit out of it when he's had too much to drink. He's not even my mate. He works with Rees."

"Well, it's disgusting behavior, whoever's friend he is. But at least you were there. Do you want a drink with us?"

"Nah, said I would get back to meet Rees, but tell Rachel I said sorry for what happened."

"Just one and you can tell her yourself." Gemma smiled warmly.

★ ★ ★

Ashleigh noticed Gemma returning to the table with Eddy at the same time as Rachel was picking up a shot glass.

"Down the hatch, girlies," Rachel shouted over the music.

"Rach, look who I found loitering outside," Gemma said.

Rachel swung round, stumbling slightly. "Eddy," she said, looking past him with wide, anxious eyes.

"It's OK," Eddy assured her. "Dylan ain't here; Rees took him to the hotel, and I was going to—"

"Down this; I'll get another." Rachel thrust a shot glass into his hand and rushed back to the bar.

"I'll get them," he shouted. He downed the drink and rushed after her.

Returning with replacement shots, they both knocked the clear liquid back and laughed at Rachel's reaction to the sour taste.

"So where do you live?" Ashleigh heard Rachel ask Eddy.

"Epsom Downs, by the race track."

"No way, I'm only in central London."

"Oh, really?"

Ashleigh smiled, stepping away as Rachel tried not to giggle like a schoolgirl with a crush.

She turned back to the others just in time to see Zane appear beside them. He gathered Gemma up into his arms.

"You OK? The Englishmen over here are no good. They get drunk and act like pigs."

"It's OK, Zane—they're no different in England. Sit down, have a drink." Rachel pulled a stool out for him. "This is Eddy—he saved me."

"You know this pig who did this thing?" Zane looked sharply at Eddy.

"Unfortunately, I do."

"You have bad taste in friends."

"I wouldn't class him as a friend," Eddy corrected him.

"But you are on holiday together, no?"

Rachel jumped in, wanting to put an end to the conversation. "He is a friend of a friend, Zane. Forget it; I'm fine. Eddy protected me."

"OK, well, your friend has bad taste in friends." Three fine lines slowly deepened across Zane's forehead.

"You're not wrong there, mate," Eddy agreed.

"Anyway," Ashleigh interrupted, "where to next?"

Rachel quickly turned to Eddy and asked him if he could afford to go to the big club, remembering Dylan's comments that it was too expensive. Eddy said he didn't have a lot of money left but told Rachel to go without him.

"Everyone up for this club, then?" Ashleigh asked in a loud, drunk voice.

"Let's find somewhere around here," Rachel replied.

"Thought you wanted to go," Ashleigh said.

"Er, well, I've changed my mind."

Ashleigh looked at Eddy and then laughed. "Jules, Gem, Zane, you lot OK with staying around here?"

There was a movement of heads up and down—everyone was in agreement.

"Well, let the night begin then."

CHAPTER
15

"YOU READY?" PETER BANGED on his brother's locked bedroom door.

Dave was not ready and had no intentions of getting ready, either. He had been staring at his reflection for the past ten minutes. His brother's demand pulled him from his thoughts.

"I'm not coming." Dave opened the door.

"What's wrong with you? Why are you locking your door now?"

Dave pushed passed him in his bathrobe. "Thinks it's best practice given the circumstances."

"Bro—c'mon now. Are you still mad over that? Just come, will you? It's only dinner. You love this restaurant."

"Guys, I'm fine," Dave said. "To be honest, I think I have a cold coming on, and I'd like to be better for when Ashleigh's home."

Isabella waited by the door for Peter. "We can get takeout and stay in." Her offer felt sincere.

"No," Dave told her. "Go have fun. I'll come next time."

"You sure, bro?" Peter asked, frowning.

"I'm sure, Pete," Dave replied. "Bring me back some leftover dessert."

"Leftover? Ha, unlikely."

The door closed, and he was alone again. Ashleigh was back in a few days, and he still didn't know if he should tell her about the other night.

After fetching a cold beer, he ordered pizza and then opened his phone and typed "Male rape." He read the list of Google search options:

Male rape
Male rape statistics
Male rape victims
Male rape hotline

He closed the browser. He felt ridiculous—he hadn't been raped. He had just given off the wrong signals, and she had acted on it. It was his fault, and he needed to get over it—and soon, because Ashleigh would be home in two days. That, or he tell her.

★   ★   ★

"Ashleigh, order me another drink while you're up there, darling." Jules waved her hand toward the open-fronted bar.

"If you want a water, sure, but I'm not even looking at a cocktail tonight. Not after last night's shenanigans." She walked up to the bar on the beachfront and requested a large glass of water, returning to the table where she had met Gemma and Jules.

"This holiday has gone way too fast for my liking, wouldn't you say, Gemma?" Jules said, looking out over the dimly lit sea.

"I know—I wish Zane didn't work every night."

"Gemma, that's what he does," said Jules. "He's not on holiday like us, sweetie."

"I know. I'm just saying."

"Now, now, girls." Ashleigh placed her water on the small wooden table. She noticed the sand move under the table as a small crab scuttled sideways across the sand. Ashleigh moved her foot but didn't mention it, knowing that Gemma would have cried blue murder and made them move seats from their prime location at the front of the stage. They were waiting for the night's entertainment to start. The MC tapped the mic, and Ashleigh caught a glimpse of brightly colored material from a costume hovering behind a screen.

"So, what do we think of Eddy, then?" Gemma asked.

"All right for a bit of rough by all accounts, I'd say." Jules took a sip of her cocktail and carried on. "Seems to have all his morals in good order."

"Rachel looks to be set on him." Ashleigh looked up to the small, dimly lit restaurant on the top of the cliff, where Rachel and Eddy were sharing a canal-lit dinner.

"She's in luurve with him," Gemma chimed in, and the girls all laughed.

Silence fell; the MC cleared his throat and spoke into the mic with a thick, muffled Spanish accent. He introduced the first act, and a group of small girls no older than eight or nine ran onto the sand dressed in beautiful Spanish dresses. They looked exactly like small versions of the grown-up Spanish dancers, with red lips and blushed cheeks, their hair tied tightly back in buns and large fans in one hand. Midway through the dance, the adult dancers joined them, and everyone clapped in time with the music. Gemma nearly stepped on the crab inadvertently, and Ashleigh winced and then exhaled as the creature scurried away unharmed.

Later, Rachel and Eddy finally emerged with a tray of fresh cocktails, sitting down to enjoy the show.

"Missed much?" Rachel whispered to Ashleigh.

"No, not much. How was dinner?"

"Lovely—he is so nice. I've got so much to tell you. Oh, and I said he could stay tonight. Is that OK?"

Ashleigh smiled. "It's fine by me, and I'm sure the others won't mind, honey."

"How's your hangover?"

"Much better." Ashleigh smiled. "I think I'm going to give drinking a rest once back in the UK. Think I've been overdoing it since I left Lee, you know?"

"I agree. You don't need to drink to have fun. So do you like him—Eddie, I mean?" Rachel asked.

"He's perfect from what I've seen so far. Makes me miss Dave, watching you two together."

"Sorry."

"Ha, don't be. It's lovely. You look good together." Ashleigh glanced over to Eddy and smiled.

"Have you spoken to Dave again?"

"A few times." She smiled. "Can't wait to get back now."

Rachel gave Ashleigh a knowing smile. "Not long to go."

★   ★   ★

The last day was finally upon them. Rachel waved goodbye to Eddy, and he promised to call her when he returned home. They had already arranged a place and time to meet. Watching the cab pull away, Ashleigh saw Rachel's eyes glaze over and squeezed her hand.

Gemma also had a long, tearful farewell with Zane outside their hotel before the girls managed to pry her away from him and onto the coach that took them to the airport.

Unable to speak through her tears, Gemma clung to Ashleigh the whole way. They unloaded their suitcases outside the airport; Gemma's makeup streaming down her face, her hair a mess, and her body shaking from the alcohol she had consumed the night before. Ashleigh knew deep down that Gemma was not upset about leaving Zane—she was terrified about going home to face reality and the prospect of a new life in a strange and very large city. Her heart ached for Gemma as she held her close under her arm while pushing their luggage piled high on a trolley to the check-in desk.

"Come on, sweetie, let's get a coffee." Ashleigh passed Gemma her carry on luggage and boarding card and beckoned for the others to follow them.

Once through security, they found a café and ordered some sandwiches and espressos to nurse their hangovers. The airport was filled with red-faced young people, and others showed off their new golden skin, shouting at each other as they bounced around the duty-free shops.

"It's been good, girls," Jules said with a sigh.

"It's been messy." Rachel winced. "Same again next year, yeah?"

"Definitely. I'm so glad you guys came," Ashleigh said. "It's been really nice to spend time with you. You OK, Gemsie?" Ashleigh nudged Gemma. "Come on, honey, you'll see him again."

"No, I won't."

"Course you will. He has family in Manchester that he visits—didn't he say he was going there in a few months? Manchester isn't that far away. You can nip up on the train."

"No." Gemma sniffed.

"Why?"

"Because we agreed to leave it in Ibiza."

"What? Why?"

"He said that what we had in Ibiza was so perfect that if we met up in England, it might spoil it. He said we should never forget the memory—that way, it can be perfect forever." Gemma stared into the distance.

"The smarmy twat," Rachel said in outrage.

"He's right," Gemma said.

"What do you mean, 'he's right'?" asked Rachel. "Gemma, he has just fobbed you off."

"No, he hasn't. He was really gutted, and he had tears in his eyes. He told me he loved me."

"Jesus, girl, you are gullible!" Jules exclaimed.

"No, I'm not."

"Gemma?" Ashleigh interrupted. "Why didn't you tell us all this at the hotel?"

"Zane told me not to. He said you wouldn't understand."

"Ha—the cheek of it." Jules laughed.

"Jules, stop it. Of course we understand." Ashleigh looked at Gemma's red, puffy face. "Look, you're right. It was probably for the best, honey."

"What? Don't mollycoddle the girl." Jules sat up. "Look, Gemma, I know you are hurting, but if you don't want to get messed around with by men, you really need to recognize and accept when someone has pulled the wool over your eyes so you can learn from it. We've all been there at some point in our lives—look at Ash. Shit, she should be an expert by now."

"Thanks, Jules," Ashleigh said.

"Not a problem. Look, all I'm saying is, think about it. You know deep down I'm right in what I'm telling you. So you fell for it. So what? We have all fallen for it too."

Gemma sniffed. "I really liked him."

141

"There'll be others, and anyway, long-distance relationships never work out," Jules told her. "Darling, stick with me. I'll teach you a thing or two about men."

★   ★   ★

Before they knew it, the plane was climbing up into the sky, passing through the clouds and away from the Mediterranean island toward home. Gemma had managed to cry herself to sleep while Ashleigh finished a crossword on the back of her newspaper. She found herself distracted by thoughts of Dave. Excited to see him she made a silent pact with herself. *No more worrying about things—just trust him.*

Looking over the aisle, she saw Jules showing Rachel something in a glossy magazine. She sighed.

"Ashleigh, you OK?" Rachel reached across the narrow aisle, passing her a magazine. "Look at page nineteen. It's a new anti-aging face cream. Jules said she can get it for me; she knows the woman who developed it, right, Jules?"

"Sure do," Jules replied simply.

Ashleigh smiled as she looked at the magazine, thankful for such good friends. She flicked the pages.

Not long till I'm home.

CHAPTER
16

I T WAS PAST MIDNIGHT before Ashleigh walked in through her front door, arms full with bags, struggling to close the door behind her. After making a hot cup of cocoa, she unpacked her bags. Eventually, having overfilled the laundry basket and restocked her bathroom with the borrowed toiletries, she climbed into bed.

★   ★   ★

Waking the next morning, she stretched her arms above her head, glancing over to see the time: 11:27 a.m. Ashleigh reached for her phone to call Dave, noticing one missed call on the screen. Her heart raced with anticipation. Dialing his number, she listened anxiously for an answer as she perched on the edge of her bed.

"Hey. Sorry, can you hang on a minute?"

"Er, yeah, of course." Ashleigh waited patiently on the phone, listening to his deep voice as he spoke to another man. She could hear the sound of glass being moved and van doors being opened and closed, and a few moments later, she heard a van driving away.

Finally, Dave spoke. "Hello, you still there?"

"Yeah, I'm still here. You sound busy—shall I call later?"

"No, no, just needed to help load some windows up for a job. Peter will be back in the yard soon, so how about I come over and take you out for the afternoon?"

"Er . . . OK, sounds good to me. I have so much to tell you."

"Really? So you had a good time, then?"

"It was brilliant," Ashleigh said. "I'll tell all when you get here. Did you do anything exciting while I was away?"

There was a slight hesitation before he answered. "No, not really. Same old, same old."

"OK, see you in a bit, then."

Ashleigh rushed around the flat, getting ready and pondering what to wear. Was it too hot for jeans, or should she opt for a summer dress? Should she wear her hair loose or stylishly tied up? Should she wear flip-flops or strappy, kitten-heeled sandals? She was so happy to see Dave again, an excitement she had never felt with Lee, and she liked it. Deciding to leave the clothes decision for last, she sat down in front of the mirror to apply her makeup.

A few hours later, she looked out of the window to see Dave handing a cab driver some money. Checking herself in the mirror, Ashleigh smiled, thinking how she had made the right choice by wearing jeans with a small white vest and kitten-heeled sandals. She ran to open the door just as Dave raised his hand to the bell.

"Hello, sexy." He pulled her close, running his hand through her long hair, kissing her softly on the lips. She giggled, pulling him inside her door.

"David, whatever would the neighbors think?"

"That a hot, sexy man is ravishing their sweet, beautiful young neighbor."

His touch felt familiar. She kissed him back, content to be back in his arms.

Ashleigh laughed nervously. "Cheeky, so what do you have planned for today?"

"Before or after sex?"

"Oh, you bad man."

"Yep, very, and if you'd stop rushing around, I'd show you just how bad."

Ashleigh picked up her small, pale pink handbag, walking straight past him toward the door with a wink. This man was everything she had ever wanted. Why had she been questioning his motives? She had been such a fool.

★   ★   ★

Ashleigh stood on tiptoe to look into a shop window, pointing to Dave on the other side.

"That one?" he mouthed.

"Yes, yes, that one there, at the top, there . . ." She beamed with excitement, clapping her hands together like a performing seal and then running back into the shop.

"Dave, I was only joking."

"No, you said you'd die if you didn't have this bracelet! And I can't have you dying on me the first day you're back from holiday."

"Oh. My. God."

"How did you know my real name?" he joked.

She stared down at her wrist as the shop assistant fastened a stunning slender, white gold, diamond-encrusted bracelet around her arm.

"Oh my God."

"You don't need to keep calling my name. I am here."

Ashleigh looked up at him, laughing. "So what would my God have me do to make up for such a divine gift?"

"Oh, you know—the norm."

"Like . . . ?"

"Cooking, cleaning"—Dave leaned down to her ear—"endless blowjobs." Dave's smiled faltered as he said the last word.

"You OK?" Ashleigh asked.

"Yes, sorry—just remembered something I had to do for a job. So where were we? That's right, making a deal."

"Ha, the cheek of it."

"Well, I could make an exception to the rule and do away with the first part just for you," he said.

"It's a done deal, O great one."

"I could get used to you calling me that." He looked at the shop assistant, who was smiling at their juvenile conversation, as he passed his credit card across the glass counter.

"And I could get used to you doing that," Ashleigh retorted.

"Oh, really?" Dave tickled her for a second, laughing as she wriggled away.

The shop assistant tapped in the amount, smiling at their affection. Ashleigh stood looking down at her new gift glittering under the shop lights, feeling like Pretty Woman with her very own Richard Gere.

★   ★   ★

"Please check the amount, sir, and enter your PIN."

Ouch, Dave thought as he punched in his four-digit number. *This is going to be an expensive day.* He waited for the receipt before following Ashleigh out into the sunshine, which reflected down onto his face from a glass building above.

They walked hand in hand up Knightsbridge toward the park. Ashleigh was smiling the whole way along the road, glancing down at her wrist from time to time. He enjoyed being with her, and if he wanted it to work, he would have to be honest and tell her. But not today—today was their day, and he wanted it to be perfect.

"Look, there's one boat left. Let's walk faster." She walked ahead, pulling slightly at his arm to hurry him up. His eyes fixed on the rowing boat floating on the lake, and he matched her pace.

A man held out two lifejackets as they walked toward him with excessive haste, stepping into the boat and causing it to sway off balance.

"Sit down, Dave, quick! It will tip over."

Dave sat facing her, slowly rowing them out to the center of the lake.

"Go right, go right," Ashleigh demanded. "Let's get away from the other boats."

Dave rowed in the opposite direction as the swarms of boats approaching them, pushing the murky water aside with the long wooden oars. He watched her sunning herself, one hand dangling over the side, brushing the water with the tips of her fingers as she relaxed with her eyes closed. They floated near some tall grass far away from any noise or people. He felt content with her. He had never met a woman with such natural beauty before, and such genuine kindness. He'd never realized that personality could exist in such a beautiful woman. If only he could let her know that the word love didn't even come close to how he felt. But how could he explain that without frightening her away? A renewed pang of guilt chilled his body as he remembered the other night.

The afternoon drew on, and late beams of weakened sunrays fell over their faces as they left the boat lake and walked through Hyde Park in the direction of Ashleigh's flat.

Once the sun lost its heat, Ashleigh drove them back to Wandsworth. They stopped at a small supermarket, and Dave picked up some food to cook a nice welcome home meal, and a DVD for afterward. Once they got inside, he put the food on while Ashleigh relaxed on the sofa, flicking through the TV stations.

"D'you want a glass of wine with me, Ash?"

"Sure, just a small one, though."

Dave walked into the living room with two glasses of rosé. Then he relaxed back into the sofa, draping his arm around her shoulders.

"So, excited about the DVD?" He nudged her.

She laughed. "I still don't understand why we can't just watch Netflix."

"Because we are trendsetters, my lovely, not followers."

"The DVD trend has already moved on, though."

"You'll see. Give it a few years, and Netflix will be a distant memory."

She shook her head. "We'll see."

★   ★   ★

The evening rolled by. Ashleigh was having such a good time, she didn't want the day to end. The DVD was so poorly directed, they laughed the whole way though.

"Ash, I've got something for you," Dave said, turning off the TV.

"Really? Don't you think you've given me enough already?"

"Wait here." He walked out the living room.

He returned a few moments later with one hand in his pocket.

"What's in your pocket?"

"Why don't you come and find out?"

She got up hastily to pull his hand out of his pocket.

"Show me, then," she said, struggling to open his hand, eager to find out what was encased inside. Suddenly, a thought ran through her head: a ring. She stepped backward sharply. "You didn't buy me a ring, did you?" She laughed nervously, unable to contain her thoughts as the words blurted out uncontrollably, not quite sure what she would say if he said yes.

Laughing, Dave opened his hand to reveal two bronze keys. "Ha-ha, no, I didn't buy you a ring . . . but I can buy you a key ring if you want."

Ashleigh blushed. "Are these door keys here to your flat— for me?"

Dave nodded.

"Are you sure?" She took the keys before he answered, kissing him quickly on the lips. "Dave, you're the best. This has been the perfect day." Stepping forward, she kissed him again. "I love you."

There was an appropriately awkward moment before he replied, "I love you too." He kissed her.

She realized it was only the second time they had actually said the words to each other not in a text. It felt so right.

This is it. She kissed him back. *This is what real love actually feels like, and it's really happening.* She let her whole body fall into his strong arms, all her insecurities drifting away.

17

THE SOUND OF LAUGHTER from the kitchen woke Dave. Ashleigh was no longer in the bed next to him, so he scanned the room and saw his bathrobe gone and the door ajar. He closed his eyes. Yesterday had been perfect, but today he needed to tell Ashleigh the truth about what had happened while she was away. He had to tell her. It was time to get out of his own head and deal with the situation. He kicked off the duvet. If she really loved him, she would understand. That was his hope, anyway. He felt anxious and irritated, and guilt snapped at his emotions as he thought about how he would tell her and what her reaction might be. His thoughts were disturbed by a smash that vibrated through the flat, startling him back to reality.

Jumping out of bed, Dave dashed for the kitchen. Standing in the doorway he gasped as Isabella, Ashleigh, and Peter all stood with hands over their mouths looking down at broken glass all over the floor.

"What the fuck!" Dave glared at them.

Ashleigh stood motionless at the sight of his anger.

Dave felt guilty for losing his temper. What had gotten into him? This Sassy secret was eating him up inside.

"Mate, I have no idea how that happened," said Pete. "The shelf just fell off the wall."

"It's true, Dave," Ashleigh's small voice said.

"Ashleigh, come out in case you get cut." Dave held out his hand.

She walked carefully over to him, taking his hand to avoid stepping on the shards of glass and crossing into the hallway.

"Honey, go and watch TV," said Dave. "I'll clear this up. Issi, you go too."

Issi stared at him. "Who died and made you the boss?"

"Do not even start with me, Issi."

"Why? Can't I clean up just as good as a man or something?"

"Issi, please just go," Dave said through tight lips.

"I'm just joking with you," she said. "Jeez, chill out."

"Oh, you two—do me a favor, and shut up already," Peter said, interrupting their apparently petulant argument. "Issi, just go and keep Ashleigh company for me, please. You know he gets grumpy in the mornings. Don't wind him up."

Isabella glared at Dave as she walked past.

"Dave, what's up?" Peter asked once she had left the room.

"Nothing. Forget it."

"Dave."

"I said forget it."

"OK."

Dave walked into the lounge, holding two cups of coffee.

"Peter's making you one, Iss." Dave tried to sound polite.

Isabella got up and strolled out of the room.

"What's up, honey?" Ashleigh looked at him. "D'you not like her anymore?"

"She's OK—just gets under my skin sometimes, that's all. I'll get used to her."

"She was telling me about a friend of hers," Ashleigh said.

Dave stiffened as she went on, "She said I could go out with them for a drink."

"Who? What? Why?"

"Are you sure everything's OK, Dave?"

"Yes, yes, honey. I just didn't think she was your type, you know what I mean?"

"Oh, maybe I'll leave it, then."

Dave felt a tug of guilt; it wasn't for him to control her social life, and he liked Isabella. On all accounts, she was fun to be around, and before the Sassy situation, they had been getting on well living together. More guilt settled in as he realized he was taking his anger out on poor Issi, when it was as much his brother's fault as hers.

"No, go if you want to," he told Ashleigh. "I'm just being a dick; take no notice." Dave changed the channel, trying to deflect the conversation. He pulled Ashleigh under his arm and kissed the top of her head as she snuggled close.

"What d'you fancy doing on your last day off?" he asked.

"Not much. Maybe I could make you lunch at my place to say thanks for yesterday."

"I could think of a better way to say thank you."

She pinched his side and giggled.

"Me and Pete need to head into work for a bit, but I'll meet you at your place later, give you time to slip into something . . ." He paused and whispered, "Nice and sexy for me."

Ashleigh laughed. "So cliché."

★ ★ ★

Dave left Ashleigh in the flat and headed off to the yard, followed shortly by Peter.

Once Ashleigh was dressed, she said goodbye to Isabella and let herself out, thrilled to use her new keys.

Stepping out of the communal door at the top of the large stone steps, she breathed in deeply through her nose. A wave of contentment filled her chest. She was in love. Life was light and full of adventure again.

After putting down the roof of her car, she jumped inside, scorching her legs on the hot leather seats. As she sat in traffic at the end of the road, her phone rang, and Dave's number flashed on the screen.

"Ashleigh, sweetie, have you left my flat yet?"

"Yeah, why? I'm only at the end of the road, though."

"Good, OK—would you mind popping back in? I forgot to get a DVD for us to watch tonight. I bought one the other day called *Dark Mist*. You'll love it. It's sitting on the windowsill in the living room."

"Oh, Dave." She laughed. "OK, but it sounds scary."

"I know; my plan is to watch it behind a pillow."

"Ha, you big wimp. I'll go back and get it."

"Thanks, sexy lady. See you soon."

She turned around, accelerating back up the road and pulling into the space she had just left. She made her way up the stone steps, smiling to herself as she opened the communal door with her key, heading up the stairs and in through Dave's front door. She called out to Isabella but didn't get an answer; she could hear her talking on the phone in her bedroom. Ashleigh walked into the living room and retrieved the DVD from the windowsill, and then she turned to head out.

"Yass, ha-ha, sexy Dave—Pete's twin brother," Ashleigh heard Isabella say.

She stepped into the hallway, taking a few footsteps up the hall toward Isabella's bedroom. Careful not to get too close as the door was slightly open, she strained to hear the whole conversation.

There was a bang and rustling from inside the room, making it harder for her to hear. She stood still, listening for more of the conversation, growing apprehensive that Isabella might come out at any minute.

"Yes, way. She was in his bed," she heard Isabella say.

Whose bed? Ashleigh tried to hear over the clanging of things being moved around inside the room.

"Ashleigh"—*Bang. Rustle. Bang*—"Ibiza."

Oh my God. Ashleigh's head spun at the thought of hearing any more. This was a conversation about Dave when she was in Ibiza. Her heart thumped. She lost the thread for a moment as Issi clambered around the room.

"Yeah. She was giving him a blowjob." *Scuffle. Bang.*

Ashleigh steadied herself against the wall. *No. Wait. What?* She panicked. He legs wanted to run and then give way. She told herself to stay and listen. She had to find out for sure.

"Some drunken girl in a bar—her name was Sassy, or that's what she told us, anyway."

Ashleigh quickly stepped backward, hearing Isabella approaching the door.

"OK, I'll call ya later. Yeah, yeah, speak soon. Bye."

Walking as fast and as quietly as she could, Ashleigh dove out the front door, down the stairs, through the communal door, and down the stone steps to the pavement. She ran as fast as she could to her car, starting it frantically. Tears stung her eyes. He cheated, he really cheated. She had heard it with her own ears. Dave cheated on her when she was in Ibiza. She looked at the key Dave had given her, dangling on the key ring hanging out of the ignition.

So that's why he gave me a key to his flat—guilt. Now it makes sense. The expensive bracelet, the way he made gentle love to her the night before, the key—it was all out of guilt. She sat in her car, trying to make sense of the conversation she had heard. Sassy, a random girl from a bar, had given Dave—her Dave—a blowjob. The thought of it cramped her stomach with pain. Over and over, she played the conversation out in her head.

I did hear it correctly. Of course I did. I was there; I heard it . . . Sassy—what kind of name is that?

"Oh God, this cannot be happening to me again." She sobbed into her hands, hitting her head onto the steering wheel. "Why?" She let out an ear-piercing scream and hit her fist on the steering wheel hard. How had she missed the signs? It wasn't as if she didn't know them. Dave never bought her expensive gifts—that was one of the things she liked most about him. So why had she not realized that yesterday when he bought her an expensive bracelet? She looked down at the bracelet on her wrist. It was a guilt gift. It was all guilt, the whole day.

Rage surged inside. Thoughts of Lee clawed their way back into her mind—memories of him laughing with girls at parties, and the lavish flower deliveries that he would send to her work if he had stayed out all night. How had she missed it? Her thoughts turned to yesterday—Dave's gentle lovemaking and the key. It was all lies. How had she been so stupid not to see it?

She looked over at the DVD on the passenger seat and snatched it up into her hand, removing the disc and breaking it in two.

"Who watches DVDs anymore?" she spat. Then she felt remorse as she looked at the broken disc.

"Ahhh," she cried, tears now rolling down her cheeks.

She left the parking lot and drove slowly down the road with no destination in mind. She drove aimlessly around the streets of South London, eventually finding her way over to the other side of the Thames and finally ending up at Rachel's flat in Belgravia.

Her makeup running down her face with every teardrop, she stared at the grand red door, waiting for Rachel to answer.

"Hey, babes," said Rachel cheerfully as she opened the door, but then she stopped dead in her tracks at the sight of Ashleigh's face. "Oh my God, what's happened?"

Gemma rushed up behind her, peering over Rachel's shoulder. "Babe, honey, is it Lee? Has he done something?"

"Come inside." Rachel ushered her through the hallway to the kitchen.

She slumped onto one of the kitchen chairs, placing her head in her hands as she leaned on the table, trying to speak.

"Dave," she sobbed, "Dave . . . is a fucking . . . chea—"

"Dave did what?" Rachel stood next to her, rubbing her back.

"Cheated." She raised her head, her bloodshot eyes blinking at Rachel and Gemma's gob-smacked faces.

"What?" howled Rachel. "Are you sure, Ash? What happened?"

"Issi . . . Issi was—was talking on the ph—phone. I heard her . . ."

"OK, in your own time, sweetie, no rush. Let me get you a tissue."

Ashleigh jumped at the sound of her mobile ringing. She looked at her phone, mesmerized, as Dave's name flashed on the screen.

Gemma quickly picked up the phone with Ashleigh watching. She felt as if she were having an out-of-body experience.

"Fuck off, you pig!" Gemma shouted into the phone and slammed it down.

Ashleigh felt her face crumple up again, ready to cry. "Why me? Why me?"

"Oh, babe." Gemma rubbed her back.

"I'm sorry, Gem."

"Whatever for?"

"I kn—know you're upset about Z—Zane . . . this must be hard for you to see."

"Ashleigh, don't be silly. You be as upset as you want. Zane is a twat, and good riddance to him."

A few seconds later, Ashleigh's phone rang again.

"Don't." Ashleigh raised her hand, stopping Gemma from picking up the phone.

"Just leave it to ring," she sobbed.

Rachel placed a box of tissues on the table.

Ashleigh picked up the phone, switching it off, and then took a deep breath.

"I overheard Issi on her mobile, telling someone that when I was in Ibiza, Dave met a girl in a bar." She took a moment before continuing. "The girl came back to his house and gave him"—her stomach clenched tight—"a blowjob."

"No!" Gemma gasped.

"What an asshole," Rachel said, reaching out to hold Ashleigh.

"Sassy," Ashleigh spluttered.

"Sassy, is that her name?" said Gemma.

"Yeah."

"What kind of name is that?" added Rachel.

"The blowjob kind." Ashleigh's voice quivered.

"Oh, sweetheart, I'm so, so sorry," Rachel said with a pained voice. "I can't bear seeing you so broken up again."

"Me too, Ash," Gemma said. "Can I do anything for you?"

"Can I stay here tonight? With you two?" She glanced up at Rachel.

"Yes, stay as long as you like," said Rachel. "Maybe I should call your work. I could tell them you have a tummy bug. They'll never know."

"Oh, I don't know. What if they find out I'm not sick? I'll get fired."

"They won't find out. How will they find out? Gemma can look after you while I'm at work."

"I don't know if I should . . . it's not right."

"Ash, you never take time off work sick. They would never suspect you to be lying. I can say you got a bug last night. One of those forty-eight hour bugs."

Ashleigh's shoulders dropped. "Maybe."

"Good, that's settled, then. And no one will ever know."

★   ★   ★

That evening, the girls all jumped into Rachel's jeep, heading over to Ashleigh's flat to pick up some things—a washbag and a few days' clothes—for her stay. It was dusk, and Ashleigh guessed Dave would head over to her place after work.

She left the girls in the car and hurried through her front door to gather her things. She removed the bracelet Dave had bought her, placing it on her dresser. A fresh wave of sadness engulfed her entire body, and she fell to her knees alone on her bedroom floor. She had been so sure of him; she had been convinced he was one of the good ones. Anger motivated her to continue gathering her things, wiping tears away as she went.

Once finished, she rushed back down the steps into the jeep, ready to head back. A small white van pulled into the mews just as she shut the car door. Ashleigh's heart jerked, blood spontaneously pumping through her body as she realized it was Dave.

"Oh, oh God, it's Dave," Ashleigh said, hitting the floor of the jeep.

"Stay down. I'll talk to him." Rachel got out of the jeep, walking back toward the flat in the hope that Dave would stop his van away from her jeep, where Ashleigh was hiding under the dashboard. Dave did just what she had planned—he jumped out of his van next to where she stood. In a frenzy, he didn't even seem to notice Gemma in the jeep. Ashleigh could hear the whole thing from her hiding place.

"Is Ashleigh in?" he asked.

"No."

"Where is she?"

"Don't know."

"Something has happened."

"No shit, Sherlock."

"What? What is that supposed to mean, Rachel?"

"Why don't you tell me, Dave?"

"Tell you what? What is it?" Dave raised his voice in frustration.

"Try *you*, you cheating pig."

"What? Cheating?"

"Oh, bugger off. I don't have time for this." Rachel stormed off, jumping into her jeep.

"Wait!" he shouted after her.

"Tell it to Sassy, you pig!" She put her foot down, wheel spinning off down the cobbled road, knocking Ashleigh's head against the dashboard.

"Dumbass," Rachel spat. "Probably trying to work out how we know the name of that girl."

Ashleigh jumped up to see Dave watching Rachel's jeep turn onto the main road.

★　★　★

Dave slammed the door of his flat, storming up the hall to the bathroom, where Isabella was standing in front of the mirror, blusher brush in hand. She saw Dave in the reflection over her shoulder and turned to face him.

"Hey, get out, you pervert!"

"So what was your plan then, Iss?"

"Plan—what plan?" She looked genuinely confused.

"Why did you tell Ashleigh about Sassy?"

"What the fuck are you on about?"

Dave could feel his blood boil as his voice rose. "Don't lie."

"Don't shout at me," Isabella said. "I don't know what you're talking about."

"Just be straight with me, Issi. What did you tell her?"

By now, Dave was pacing the doorway, hands on his hips to keep them from hitting anything. This was exactly why he had been frightened of telling Ashleigh. She thought it was his fault. Had he led her on in some way? Was Ashleigh right to think it was his fault?

"Dave, what are you on about?" Isabella repeated. "I don't know what the fucking hell you're talking about!"

"Issi, just fucking tell me!"

Isabella stepped backward quickly, her eyes staring straight into Dave's.

The front door slammed. "What's going on?" Peter walked up to his brother, poking his head around the bathroom door to see who

Dave was shouting at. Concerned, he looked at Isabella fixed against the far wall. "Well? Is anyone going to tell me? Dave, what's up?"

"She has told Ashleigh about Sassy," Dave said, "and I wanna know why."

"Iss? Is that true?"

Looking slightly more confident now that Peter was there, Isabella stepped away from the wall, straightening her blouse. "Right, well, like I said, I didn't tell Ashleigh about Sassy."

"Then how does she know?" Dave barked.

"I don't know," Isabella said again, "for fuck's sake, how she knows."

"Bro, Dave," Peter interjected, "what happened?"

"Fuck knows," Dave said. "Last time I spoke to her, I was at work. She was coming back here to get a DVD. I rang her later, and one of her mates swore at me and put the phone down, so I headed over to her flat after the job. Rachel was outside and shouted Sassy's name at me and then drove off . . . what the fuck is going on? Someone in this flat has told her." Dave looked at the floor, trying to retrace the day in his head before looking up at Isabella, who looked horrified.

"What's up, Issi?" Dave surveyed her face.

"Oh God!" she said.

"What?"

"Oh God!"

"What, for God's sake, *what*?"

"Oh God, I think I know what happened."

"What? Tell me what happened."

"I think what may have happened was when she came back to get the DVD, she overheard me talking to a workmate on my phone. I heard a noise. Thought it was one of you two, but no one was there."

"What are you saying, Iss?" Peter probed.

"She must have misheard my conversation about that night Sassy was here."

Dave walked off down the hallway to the front room, arms stretched up to the back of his head, trying not to explode with anger.

Why had he not just told her? He had been so worried that she would think he'd led the girl on that he had put it off for too long. Now she thought he'd cheated on her, just like her ex used to do.

What a mess. All he needed to do was explain the full story of what had really happened that night and hope that she would believe it was not his fault.

He heard the front door shut and walked over to the window. A few moments later, Isabella walked off up the road.

"Dave, she didn't do it on purpose." Peter's voice was measured.

"Yeah, I know." Dave watched her walk away until she was out of sight.

"What you gonna do?"

Dave shrugged his shoulders, still looking out the window.

Peter handed Dave his phone and nodded.

"I've tried," said Dave. "It's switched off."

"Leave a message."

"I was going to, but she has switched that off, too."

"And she ain't at home?"

"Na, probably at Rachel's, but I don't know where she lives."

"So what are you gonna do?"

"Don't know. Go to her work tomorrow, I suppose. What harm could it do?"

CHAPTER
18

ASHLEIGH WOKE EARLY, STARING up at the ceiling, eyes fixed on a small blob of BluTack above the bed. She could hear Rachel whispering to Gemma outside the door before leaving for work. She closed her eyes, feeling a tear roll down her cheek and onto the pillow. She clutched her stomach, curling up into the fetal position. The door slowly opened; it was Gemma. She didn't say anything, just sat on the bed next to Ashleigh, stroking her hair. Nothing could take the pain away; only time would heal that.

★   ★   ★

It was past midday when Gemma suggested a stroll up the road to get some food, shopping for Rachel. Ashleigh reluctantly washed and dressed.

Outside, it was overcast and not as hot as it had been over the last few days; schoolchildren were still on summer holidays and had taken over the local park with footballs, skateboards, rollerblades, and general noisy, happy, irritating mayhem. Ashleigh didn't say a word as they walked through the park. All she could do was concentrate on not crying, studying the grass as it passed under her feet.

Just as they reached the other side, away from the noise, she heard her phone ringing in her pocket. Pulling it out to answer and hoping it was not Dave, she looked down at the screen.

"It's my work."

"Don't answer it," Gemma said firmly.

"Did Rachel call them this morning?" Ashleigh asked.

"Yeah, they're probably seeing how you are. You can call them later."

"Yeah, you're right." Ashleigh put the phone back in her pocket.

They reached the local convenience store, and after filling their baskets and paying, the girls walked back through the park, struggling to hold all the shopping bags. They stopped to rest on a bench, away from the noise of the children. Ashleigh's phone rang again. Jumping, she wondered if it had been such a good idea to switch it back on today.

Hoping again that it wasn't Dave, she saw Eliza's number flashing up on the screen. She looked at Gemma, concerned as to why Eliza was calling.

"Who's that?" Gemma asked.

"The dentist I work with."

"Don't answer."

"But it's her private number, and she's a friend."

Gemma shrugged. "It's up to you."

Ashleigh stood, walking away slightly. "Hello."

"Ash, it's me," said Eliza. "Are you OK?"

"Er . . ." Ash hesitated, trying to think of something to say, not wanting to lie.

"Look, Ashleigh, I know you are not ill."

"How?"

"Mr. Matson was here today."

Ash gasped. Mr. Matson was the principal of the practice. "Oh, no, the one time I call in sick, the principal comes in."

"That's not the problem."

"What's the problem?" She glanced over at where Gemma sat on the bench with an equally worried look on her face.

"Dave is."

Ashleigh's stomach clenched at the sound of his name, and she doubled over as if in pain. Gemma quickly walked over and guided her back to the bench.

"Why? What has he got to do with it?" she managed.

"He came to see you. Mr. Matson was at reception and overheard."

"So . . . what does that matter?"

"Well . . . now, don't get stressed, but Samantha—"

"What?" Ashleigh cut her off. "I don't understand. What has she got to do with anything?"

"Dave must have bumped into Samantha on her break or something, who knows, but she told Mr. Matson that Dave was looking for you because you two had an argument. She said you are not sick."

"Oh, great, so he thinks I have faked a sickie because of a row with my boyfriend."

"You have." Eliza laughed slightly.

"But no one knew that." Ashleigh felt sick.

"Are you OK, Ash? What has happened between you two?"

After explaining the whole thing, she said goodbye to Eliza and burst into sobs again. She felt as though throughout her entire adult life, she had tried to look out for others, and yet she had nothing to show for her efforts except heartache.

"Ashleigh, honey, it will be OK. They can't just sack you."

"Can't they?"

"You had a good reason."

Ashleigh wiped her eyes and sat up, looking at Gemma.

"I think I'm going to leave," she said. "I've had just about all I can take."

Gemma stared at her, puzzled. "What do you mean, 'leave'? Leave your job?"

Ashleigh didn't answer. She stood up and walked slowly toward the children playing in a nearby playground. She stopped at the edge of the grass, kicking at the loose stones on the concrete path.

Behind her, Gemma struggled with all the bags. "Ash—Ashleigh," she said, panting as she put them down.

Ashleigh turned to her, feeling slightly distant.

"What do you mean?" Gemma asked again. "Leave where?"

"England. Leave England. My family never wanted me to stay here. Now me and Lee are done, and Dave . . ." She dropped her head. "What's the point?"

Gemma's face drained of its color. "Look, let's walk back to the flat and have some lunch. See how you feel after that, eh?"

"I need to ring Kelly." Ashleigh's head sprung up at this epiphany.
"Your sister?"

"Yeah, I need to call her. I've been such a fool, thinking I can live here without her. I could have made a whole new life in New York with my family, but instead, I chose a life full of bloody betrayal with asshole men. I should be in New York with my family. I'm such a fool. God, I'm such an idiot."

"No, honey. No, you're not. OK, look, sweetie, let's not be rash. Why don't we just go home and make some tea and wait for Rachel to come home before you go calling Kelly and waking her up over there?"

★ ★ ★

Dave walked into the yard, hot, bothered, and clean out of ideas as to how he could contact Ashleigh. Pulling his phone from his pocket, he dialed Ashleigh's number, expecting it to be switched off.

To his amazement, the phone rang. He listened, hoping for an answer that did not come, nor did her voicemail message; instead, it just rang and rang. Deflated, Dave pressed the reject button on the phone. The whole situation was one big mess. Finally, he had found a girl that he truly cared about, a girl that he had fallen in love with. He had even confined in her about Caroline.

He deeply regretted not talking to her about the Sassy situation. Why had he not? She would have believed him; he knew her well enough to know that. She was compassionate and trusting; that's why he loved her. So what had stopped him? Why did the situation feel like a dirty secret? He opened his phone and re-typed the words "Male rape."

Dave noticed a shadow and looked up to see his brother standing over him. Quickly, he slipped the phone away.

"Did you see her?" Peter asked.

"She called in sick. What do I do now?" Dave hung his head.

"Look, she obviously wants to be on her own right now, and a job has just come up. It's in Cumbria, so that means we will be away for three days." Peter waited for a reaction.

"Fucking great." Dave stood up, walking off in the direction of the porta cabin.

His brother followed him inside.

"Dave, there's nothing you can do if she doesn't wanna see you. Why don't you drop a note through her door before we go?"

"Yeah, you're probably right, mate. So when are we leaving?"

"Tonight."

"What?"

"The bloke needs it done by Thursday. It's OK—the job's been priced accordingly. And to be honest, Dave, we could do with the extra money. If we do this job, it will put us back in the black."

Dave sighed. Money was the least of his worries. He leaned back in the office chair. Maybe when he got back, Ashleigh would be ready to talk to him.

★ ★ ★

Rachel didn't get home until late that night to find Ashleigh, Gemma, Jules, and Leon sitting in the garden with one empty bottle of wine plus another half-drunk bottle being poured. Ashleigh saw her looking around the patio where they all sat. Her patio floor lights had been fixed and were shining dimly under the early evening light. Gemma also noticed her looking and proceeded to explain proudly how she had fixed them. Rachel beamed at the sight of her lights working again and joined the others, sitting down next to Ashleigh.

"How are you bearing up, Ashleigh? Sorry I'm so late home."

Ashleigh gave half a smile, taking a sip of wine. She wasn't bearing up at all. She didn't think it possible to be hurt worse than she had been with Lee, but this it was.

"I spoke to my sister in New York today," she said.

Gemma had not been able to convince Ashleigh to wait until Rachel got home before calling her big sister, and now the wheels were in motion.

"Oh, really? How is she?"

"Yeah, good," Ashleigh said, finding it difficult to hold Rachel's stare.

She knew Kelly's intentions would be to come to England in order to take Ashleigh back to America, but how could she tell Rachel that? And how could she tell Rachel that she *wanted* her to?

"So what have I missed?" Rachel looked around at everyone for some kind of explanation as to the sudden change in atmosphere.

"She's flying out first thing."

"OK! So why are you looking funny at me?"

"Rach . . . I might be going back with her—to live."

"What?" Rachel jumped out of her seat, screaming at the top of her voice every reason why Ashleigh should not leave. After a good minute or two, she sat down again, looking around the table at everyone staring back at her.

"Well, we didn't think you'd go that cuckoo," Leon joked, though Ashleigh knew he was equally upset at her decision.

She felt awful. She was letting down all her friends, but what else could she do? A fresh start in a new country was the right thing to do.

"Ash, please don't do this," Rachel pleaded.

Ashleigh swallowed, placing a hand on Rachel's leg. "Rachel, honey, I said 'might be.' That could mean for a holiday." Ashleigh tried to avoid the confrontation.

"Don't patronize me, Ash. I'm not a child."

"OK, OK," Ashleigh said. "Seriously, nothing is set in stone. But let's be honest—things don't seem to be working for me here." Ashleigh wondered whom she was trying to convince, Rachel or herself. The magnitude of the situation had suddenly hit home. Kelly was on her way to England, and Ashleigh knew her family would be expecting her to bring Ashleigh home this time. She wondered if calling Kelly had been the right thing to do.

"We work!" Rachel's voice had risen again.

Ashleigh gave a small laugh. "Yeah, we work. All of us work."

"So then don't go," said Rachel.

Silence fell around the table. Ashleigh didn't have a reply—not a truthful one, anyway.

Ashleigh noticed Leon looking at Jules with an odd, apprehensive look. Then Jules nodded as if in agreement, and he stood. Scanning the table for everyone's attention, he cleared his throat to speak.

"So maybe now is the perfect time to tell you all something." He gave an awkward laugh.

Rachel threw her hands up in the air. "Don't tell me you're bloody moving countries, too."

Ashleigh swung her head around to look at Rachel. "I *might* be."

"OK, OK," Rachel apologized sarcastically. "Leon, sorry, tell us your news."

Leon took a quick sip of wine and placed it back on the table with everybody watching him intensely. "I am moving to France."

"You are fucking joking me!" Rachel stood, her hands on her head, and paced the length of the patio.

He burst out laughing so hard he practically doubled over in his chair.

Jules shot him an ice-cold look. "Leon, that's not fair. Tell them the truth."

"What?" Rachel stopped dead in her tracks. "That is not funny, you idiot."

"All right, sorry—bad joke. Sit down, Rachel. I think you will need to for this."

They all sat still, waiting for him to speak again.

"I'm gay," he told them. "Well . . . bisexual, I think, more than gay, because I do like women still."

Silence fell over the table. Ashleigh looked at Gemma, smiling.

Gemma didn't know Leon as well as the others, and she was looking slightly confused at the announcement. Ashleigh was glad of the distraction.

Leon looked around the table and sat down slowly.

Rachel leaned over toward Leon, shaking her head. "Honey, we could have told you that years ago."

"What? What's that supposed to mean?"

"Oh, come on, Leon." Rachel's face had lit up with the new conversation. "You have three girl best friends, you love fashion, and you've never had a proper girlfriend."

"So? What does that prove? I sleep with loads of woman."

"Babe, you are one of our best friends. And it appears that we know you better than you know yourself."

"Well, that went down better than I thought." Leon gulped down the rest of his wine. Ashleigh sensed Leon's disappointment that his announcement had not been met with more astonishment, and giggled to herself.

"Which is why Ashleigh should stay in England." Rachel reignited the conversation. "Look how well we know each other, Ash. Look at the acceptance we have for each other. You'll never find that in New York."

"You don't know that," Ashleigh said defensively.

"I do," Leon said. "Rachel's right. Before I met you guys, I lost so many friends after telling them I liked men. They knew I was gay the same way you did, but as soon as I admitted it, the invites stopped coming, and people seemed to always be busy when I invited them out. Jules was the only one who stood by me."

"So Jules, you've known all this time and not said anything?" Rachel shook her head.

"I would do the same for you, Rachel," Jules said. "It wasn't mine to tell, like when you guys didn't tell me about Ashleigh and Lee splitting up."

Rachel nodded.

"Why now? Why are you telling us now?" Ashleigh looked at Leon. "I feel so bad, Leon." She pulled up a chair next to him and gave him a hug. "I should have just said something to you, and this would have been all out in the open ages ago. Did you think we would disown you? Really, did you?"

Leon shrugged. "Yes, no. Jules has been on me to tell you for ages. I just—I don't know. But I couldn't have you leave without telling you, and even if you don't go, I just—"

Ashleigh pulled him close. "It's OK. We know now, and we still love you the same."

"Hey, Leon," Rachel said, changing the subject. "Your dad was getting you a painting, right? What painting did he get for you?"

"Ah. Now here's a story . . ." Leon sat forward with a sparkle in his eyes again. "So I went to meet the dealer. He was some French art guy called Trent."

"Trent? That's a name?" Ashleigh frowned.

"Apparently so . . . Anyway, he showed me a few paintings, none of which took my fancy, and then offered to take me out for lunch. I thought it was some kind of soft sale tactic, but I went, course."

"Was it?" Rachel rolled her eyes. "A soft sales tactic?"

"Probably. I ended up buying the damn painting, but not before getting absolutely wasted on red wine. Second date tomorrow night."

Ashleigh stood. "Well, on that happy note, I'm off to bed, guys. Don't stay up too long. Leon, I look forward to hearing more about *Trent*." She emphasized his name.

"Don't go," Leon whispered up at her.

Ashleigh squeezed his hand and disappeared inside, with Gemma following. After saying good night and reassuring Gemma again that her sister Kelly was just coming over for support, she got undressed, lay down on top of the bed, and stared back up at the blob of BluTack on the ceiling. She didn't like misleading her friends, but it was easier this way. She was sure Leon knew her true intentions, and telling her about his sexuality was his way of telling her how much he wanted her to stay.

Was she really leaving England? Maybe Rachel was right. Friends like hers weren't easy to find, and they needed her as much as she needed them. Ashleigh wiggled under the sheets. The last thing Leon needed was to lose a friend now, but the last thing she needed was to be in England now. She wondered what Dave was doing. Then, the endless loop in her mind began again, replaying the conversation she had overheard, and Ashleigh's anguish intensified.

"Dave, Peter's brother . . . She was in his room . . . Ash? Ibiza . . . . Giving him a blowjob . . . some drunken girl . . . Sassy."

She turned on her side and started to cry. *How can this be happening to me again? I must trust my feelings. Whatever happens, I am to trust my gut feeling.*

Slowly, after a river of tears, she eventually managed to drift off into a shallow, troubled sleep.

CHAPTER
19

WANDERING INTO THE KITCHEN the next morning, Ashleigh found Rachel, who looked like death and sat slumped over the kitchen table trying to drink a cup of coffee before work. Ashleigh put down two pieces of toast, asking her if she wanted some too. All Rachel could do was shake her head, pulling a face, repulsed by the thought of her offer.

"I heard you lot go out last night. What time did you get to bed?"

"Four."

"Oh, dear," Ashleigh said, looking down at her watch. It was 7:33 a.m.

Rachel stood up. Picking up her bag, she slowly walked out of the kitchen.

Ashleigh listened as the front door opened and closed. "Poor thing."

Moments later, Gemma came tottering into the kitchen in a pair of oversized dog slippers and a undersized pink nightie.

"I'll have a slice. How are you feeling today, honey?" Gemma chirped brightly.

"The same." Ashleigh pulled out more fresh bread. In her bedroom, she heard her phone ring. Her heart skipped at the prospect of speaking to Kelly. She ran off to answer it, leaving Gemma to finish off the toast.

★ ★ ★

Twenty minutes later, Ashleigh found Gemma sitting out in the garden.

"Everything OK, Ash?" Gemma asked.

"Kelly is at JFK Airport, waiting to board. She said she'll be landing in England at three thirty this afternoon."

"Blimey, that was quick. Does she need a lift from the airport?"

"No, Dad booked her a car."

"It'll be nice to see her again," Gemma commented. "Feels like a lifetime ago now. Just wish it was under different circumstances, you know?"

Ashleigh grimaced.

★ ★ ★

The day passed by, and Gemma and Ashleigh messed around with clothes and makeup. Before they knew it, both girls were jumping into Ashleigh's car and heading over to her flat to get it ready for Kelly to stay. Gemma hurried out of the car at the end of Ashleigh's road to have a look in Harrod's, agreeing to meet Ashleigh at her flat shortly. She seemed completely overwhelmed by the dazzling variety of goods on offer. Ashleigh smiled, watching her in her review mirror as she drove on. Turning into her cobbled road, she stopped the car at the bottom of her steps just in time to see Mr. Schnitzer leaving.

He walked over to update her of the goings-on over the last few days, telling her about the shouting outside. He hadn't seen who it was but had heard them. Ashleigh was, of course, well aware of this, as she had been there, hidden away at the time, so she just listened, trying to look appreciative at the information. He then informed her that two identical men had come around last night and put something through her door. Ashleigh's smile faded. She thanked him and walked up to her front door, anxious to find out what was on the other side. On the doormat was a piece of paper. She picked it up, turning it over to see a note from Dave.

★ ★ ★

Ashleigh,

*Please call me, I'm begging you. You misheard Issi's
conversation. Please! I can explain everything if you
just call me.*

*I love you. I would NEVER do that to you. You're the
best thing in my life right now. Please don't shut me out.*

*Let me explain. If you don't believe me after that,
then fine.*

Dave x

★　　★　　★

She couldn't get Dave's request to explain himself out of her head.
She tried to Hoover and dust; she even remade her unslept-in bed.
Finally, giving in, she dialed his number.

He answered right away. "Ashleigh, thank God you called. Listen,
you have it all wrong."

"Oh, really?" her tone was blunt. She walked out onto her
balcony.

"It was Pete. Listen, him and Issi brought back a girl from a bar
one night. I didn't even go out; I stayed in. Some girl snuck into my
room, and I woke up to find her in my bed. Ashleigh, I went mad,
kicked her out. Honestly, nothing happened. It's the truth—you
have to believe me."

"You have to be joking me! You know how made up that sounds,
right? Why would a strange girl sneak into your room? A strange
girl whom you say you never met just jumps into your bed?"

"Well, I met her, but only as I was going to bed."

"Oh, so you *did* meet her, then?"

"Ashleigh, I saw her for a second on my way to bed as they were
coming home. Honestly, that's the truth."

She didn't say anything. They remained quiet on different ends
of the line.

"It just doesn't make any sense," Ashleigh finally said. "You pass up on going out, knowing your girlfriend is in Ibiza. Issi and Pete bring some random girl home, and she aimlessly wanders into your bed after seeing you for a split second."

"God, Ashleigh, please believe me. I honestly haven't done anything wrong, I swear to you. Look, I'm away on a job. I'll be back the day after tomorrow. Then can I see you?"

"No," she said, flustered.

"Please, Ash."

"I need to think. Just stay away for now."

"Ashleigh! Please don't do this."

Ashleigh put the phone down. It rang again. This time she did not answer as she watched Dave's name flash up on the screen. The landline rang, but again, she didn't answer. She stood on the balcony, looking over the streets of London. Did he honestly think she would believe that story, even if everything in her body wanted to?

She remembered the advice Rachel had given her. *Trust your gut.* But her gut felt like believing him. No. Not this time. Not again—last time, her gut feeling had been wrong, and this time was no different. Or was it? Ashleigh slumped back inside in time to hear a knock at the door.

Gemma had returned from her shopping trip, and Ashleigh was thankful for the distraction of cooing over her new Fendi bag and Jimmy Choo shoes. Gemma looked very pleased with herself, and Ashleigh wondered aloud how she could afford them.

"Some things you just have to have," Gemma said, "even if your credit card limit shouts at you."

Ashleigh nodded.

She held out the note for Gemma to read. "It was on the mat when I came in."

Gemma read the note twice, as if seeking some kind of hidden clue that would uncover the truth. Ashleigh told her about the phone call over a cup of coffee. They sat together on the balcony, mulling over Isabella's conversation, the note, and Dave's explanation; by the end of their talk, Gemma was sure Dave was lying through his teeth. Dave and Isabella had clearly made sure their stories corroborated each other's once they realized Ashleigh had heard

Isabella's conversation. Both Ashleigh and Gemma had decided not to fall for a man's lie this time.

Ashleigh glanced down at her watch—six forty-five. She pulled her phone out to call Kelly and check if she was all right when a knock on the door interrupted her. Knowing it must be her, she rushed to the door. Arms open, she threw them around Kelly's neck as her sister stood on the doorstep, bags in hand.

"Oh, Kelly, I'm so glad you're here. Come in, come in. I'll make a coffee." Ashleigh hugged her sister tightly and whispered, "No one knows you're here to take me back, OK?" She placed her finger against her lip.

Kelly looked over Ashleigh's shoulder. "What?" she hissed.

"Come in, come." Ashleigh took Kelly's bags and ushered her out to the balcony before she could ask any more questions.

"Oh my God, Gemma, what are you doing here?" Kelly asked when she saw their old friend sitting there. She now had an American twang to her English accent.

"Hey, Kelly, long time," Gemma replied. "How was the flight?"

"Good. A bit of turbulence, but I'm here, you know?"

"Sit down, sit down," Ashleigh said, rushing around her like a mother hen.

Kelly pulled up a chair, happy to relax after her travels. She looked like an older version of Ashleigh with long legs, slender neck, dark, wavy hair, and a lovely golden tan. As the evening drew on, Ashleigh caught up on what her family had been up to. Kelly had brought over photos of everyone, telling stories of how brilliant their lives were in the states.

Inevitably, the conversation led to Dave. Kelly listened quietly to both Ashleigh and Gemma. It was clear that Gemma did not believe Dave, making many connections to her own divorce on the grounds of infidelity.

"So have you sat down with Dave and asked him all these questions, Ash?"

"No need," Ashleigh said. "I know when someone is lying, and I've hashed it out with Gemma all day."

"Is that right?"

"Look, Kell—"

"OK, OK . . . look, it's your life." Kelly held up her hands. "I'm just here to pick up the pieces."

Ashleigh winced. "What did Dad say?"

"He's delighted—delighted you're coming home with me, not that you're heartbroken again, but, you know."

Gemma looked concerned.

"*Might* be coming home," Ashleigh corrected her, hoping her sister would play along. "And Mum? Why haven't they called me?"

"She is fine about it; everything is fine. I told them not to call. Mum's itching to talk to you, but I wasn't sure how you were dealing with it. Call them now. Mum has her cellphone on her, waiting. I said I would get you to check in once I got here."

Ashleigh rushed to the phone in the hallway and dialed the international code.

★   ★   ★

At nine thirty p.m., Dave stood at the bar in Cumbria's small country pub, which was situated in the middle of nowhere, watching the barmaid pull him a pint of Guinness. He stared at the glass, concentrating on the liquid settling inside as it sat on the other side of the bar, still under the tap.

"It won't be long, sir—£3.80, please." She held her hand out, breaking Dave's trance.

"Er . . . yeah." He quickly rummaged around in his tracksuit pocket for some loose change, spreading it across the bar and counting the correct money out.

"I'll bring it out to you."

Dave smiled, turning to walk out into the evening air to where Pete was sitting at a table, waiting for him to return. Dusk had started to fall.

There was the smell of a bonfire drifting over from a small farmhouse in the distance. He sat down at the table opposite his brother. There was a thud of dead weight as the bench took the heavy load of his tired body.

Not long later, the barmaid followed him out with a perfectly poured pint of Guinness, placing it down in front of him. He smiled and thanked her, watching her walk away.

"This place is nice," Pete said.

"Yeah." Dave looked over at the field next to them.

"We can start early in the morning tomorrow and get finished."

"Yeah." Dave sulked.

"Got quite a lot done today, didn't we?" pressed Peter.

"Mhmm."

"It's quite a small town here."

"Yep."

"For God's sake, man," Peter said, "snap out of it, will ya?"

Dave looked back at his brother. "What the hell am I going to do if she won't believe me?"

"She will. Mate, she's a woman. They like to stew over things and blow them out of proportion before they listen to reason."

"She didn't seem to believe it when I spoke to her *or* blow it out of proportion. She didn't even wanna talk about it."

"Look, don't worry. I'll go around and talk to her if you need me to; it will be fine. I'll make sure of it."

"Pete," Dave said, "can I ask you something?"

"Fire away."

"What that girl did. Sassy. Would you call it rape?"

"What? No." Peter laughed. "Girls can't rape men." He thought about it for a few seconds. "Can they?"

Dave shrugged, and silence fell between them.

A horse walked over to the fence next to them, stretching its head over as if trying to reach for their drinks.

"Wow!" Peter pulled his pint away, looking at Dave in surprise.

"Easy, boy!" Dave smiled.

"'Easy, boy'? How about 'go away, boy'?" Peter didn't look impressed.

"Ha, what's up, bro? Scared the horse can down it faster than you?"

"That's exactly what I'm scared of," Peter said.

"Sorry, lads," said a female voice. "Sebastian, leave it alone."

Peter looked up at the long-faced gray horse, still clutching his beer close to his chest.

"Sebastian, move on, boy," said a young girl whom Dave could now see standing next to the horse.

"It's OK. He's not doing any harm," Dave objected.

"What?" Peter looked at his brother in disbelief but then glanced at the source of the female voice beside him.

When he saw the beautiful red-headed girl peering over at them, he corrected himself. "I mean, what a lovely horse you have."

The girl laughed, turning to stroke her Sebastian. "He likes beer."

"We can see that. How about you? I don't mind sharing my pint with you." Peter held his pint up.

"Maybe I will. Depends how long it takes me to finish up over at the stables."

"Well, how about if we both help you?"

Dave nearly choked on his beer. "What? We? Oh, no, not me. I'm off back to the house after this pint."

"Dave, the lady needs a hand."

"I do not." She took hold of Sebastian's bridle, walking him away.

"Hey, no, please don't go!" Peter called after her. "Sorry, I didn't mean it like that."

"Well done, Pete."

"Shut up, you moron." Peter stood up on the table, placed his hand over the top of the pint to stop it from spilling, and then jumped over the fence.

"What the hell are you doing?"

"Going to help the lady and have me some fun."

"What, with the horse?"

"Funny, funny. Don't wait up."

★   ★   ★

Dave finished his cup of coffee under the morning sun; then he headed over to the barn conversion to start work with no sign of Peter. Half an hour later, after he had unpacked his tools, he saw his brother walking up the driveway, smiling as he approached. Dave squinted in the sunshine, trying to look stern.

"What time do you call this?"

Peter glanced down at his watch. "Eight o'clock—or should I say, she ate my cock."

"Get to work, mate. And we need to be finished by the end of the day. The bloke needs it ready for his son's wedding reception, remember?"

★ ★ ★

They worked hard into the day, not stopping for lunch and keeping the tea breaks to a bare minimum. The sun had started to lose its heat by the time they had packed their tools away into the van. Satisfied with their hard work, they stood side by side, arms crossed, looking up at the newly fitted windows.

"A barn fit for a king, hey, Dave?"

"Yep," Dave said, not caring about anything other than getting home and talking to Ashleigh.

In the distance, Dave saw the owner storming up the driveway toward them, arms moving like pistons.

"Hey, Robert. What's up?" Peter put his hand out for the man to shake. Robert—a small, stocky man with a red face and thin, orange hair—returned the gesture.

"Hi, lads. It looks good." He took a quick look up at the building behind them. "May not even be a wedding now, though." He pulled out a bundle of money, passing it to Dave for him to check.

"Why is that?" asked Dave, counting the money.

"One of the local farmers saw my son's wife-to-be in the stables last night, having it off with some scumbag. I've spent all day looking for him." The man's face had gone a deeper shade of red. "I thinks it's one of Maggie's boys. Just wait till they get home from work. I'll find out which one it was, and—well, anyway, you boys don't need to hear about that. So you're leaving tonight, then?"

Peter's eyes widened in disbelief. Dave looked over at him, but his brother refused to make eye contact.

Dave quickly took the envelope of money. "That is terrible, Robert . . . yes, we need to head off home now, actually."

Dave discreetly nudged his brother toward the van.

"Stay for dinner," Robert said. "I can have my wife fix you something hot for the road."

"That's a really kind offer," said Dave, "but we have another job back home. It just came in—you know how it is."

By this point, the two brothers were inside the van, talking to Robert through the window and trying very hard to end the conversation.

"OK, well, you'd better get off, then. Thanks for your work, even if there is no wedding."

"Well, we hope it won't come to that. Thanks for letting us stay; see ya around."

Dave watched him out of the rearview mirror the whole stretch of the driveway until they had successfully turned onto the main road toward safety.

"Fuck, that was close." Peter breathed a sigh of relief.

"What the hell were you thinking?"

"What—how was I meant to know she was marrying his son? She never said anything. That has to be the funniest thing that has ever happened to us on a job."

Dave rolled his eyes. "Pete, you always walk into trouble. It's like you're some kind of fuck-up magnet."

"Thanks, bro. Just keep the compliments coming. It's a long drive home."

"And Issi?"

Peter glanced over at Dave. "And Issi what?"

"Well, you're fucking that one up."

"There's nothing to fuck up. I'm not even bothered about her."

"I'm not sure she sees it that way."

Peter reached for the envelope of money from the dashboard and tucked it into his bag. "I'll put that somewhere safe. Do me a favor—stay quiet the rest of the way home if you're in one of these moods! Anyway, how can I mess something up when it isn't even something? And how do you know the way she sees things? What's she said?"

"You seem very bothered for someone who isn't bothered."

"Why do you care? You were hating on her only the other day," Peter retorted.

"Should have been hating on you, too, and for good reason, don't you think?"

They drove on in silence.

"So, do you think it was rape?" Peter asked.

The question startled Dave for a second. Had his brother actually listened to him for once?

Dave glanced over at him and then back to the road. "I didn't at first."

"But you do now?"

After a moment of silence, Dave said, "I do."

"Me too," said Peter quietly.

Dave didn't reply; he wasn't sure how to reply. It had been a long time since they had talked about anything deep.

"What are you going to do?" Peter continued. "Go to the police? I can go with you."

Dave smiled. "Cheers, Pete. I'm not going to report it. I just needed to tell someone, you know? I kept thinking I led her on in some way."

"What? Why would you think that?"

"I don't know. And I know it sounds odd, but you don't think of men being . . ." He didn't finish the sentence. "Anyway, I just needed to tell someone, that's all." In his peripheral vision, Dave could see Peter staring at him. "What?"

"Do you need to talk to a doctor or shrink or someone?"

"What? No, no." Dave laughed. He knew his brother was trying to say the right thing, and he appreciated the concern. However, he didn't need therapy—or he didn't think he did. "Look, it happened, and if it wasn't for Ashleigh, maybe I'd have handled it differently. More like you would have."

Peter gave an awkward laugh. "Well, I'm here if you need me, bro. Sorry I took so long about it."

"Thanks," Dave said, glad that he had told his twin what was on his mind. He continued his prior conversation. "And Issi?"

"And Issi what?"

Dave laughed. "She likes you. You must see that?"

"Most girls do."

"But Issi isn't most girls."

He wanted to see his brother happy, and what Ashleigh had told him about Isabella the other day had put things into perspective. He loved the way Ashleigh could see the best in people, and she had shown him that Isabella wasn't as tough as she made out.

Peter glanced at his brother. "Where is this all coming from?"

"Just something Ashleigh mentioned."

Peter didn't say anything.

"So?" Dave pressed. "Let's face it, she spends more nights in your room than her room."

Peter smiled.

"Maybe you two should go exclusive?" Dave suggested. "I mean, if you had done that in the first place, I wouldn't be chasing Ashleigh right now."

"I'm sorry, bro. Really, I am."

"Just give it some thought, and don't mess her around, Pete. She might not be as tough as she appears."

"Yeah, I know that. And don't worry about Ashleigh. She's a smart girl—she'll come around."

Dave smiled, hoping he was right.

CHAPTER
20

EARLY THE FOLLOWING MORNING, Ashleigh drew the blinds in the kitchen. She jumped as a blackbird flew off the windowsill outside. She had a lot to think about after her talk with Kelly the night before, and such a short time to do it in. Kelly had told Ashleigh that she was due to leave for home for a work commitment in just two days' time. Could Ashleigh really be leaving all her friends in two days? This was such a life-changing decision; would two days be enough?

She stared out the window, watching the bird as it flew away over the streets of London, wondering if she should do the same thing but on a big metal bird destined for the United States of America. It all sounded so easy. Her father had a position open in his company with something called an L1 visa. Kelly told her that she would need to fly back to London in a few weeks to sort out the visa but could stay in a hotel. It all felt surreal—visas, coming back to London to stay in a hotel.

I could stay with Rachel, she thought. However, her excitement faded when she thought of a second goodbye.

"Morning, Ash." Kelly stood in the doorway, wearing Ashleigh's bathrobe.

Ashleigh jumped for the second time that morning. "Kelly, you scared me." She offered Kelly a cup of coffee.

"Sorry. Here, let me make it."

Ashleigh refused.

"So, you could have warned me that no one knew I was here to take you home," Kelly said. "You need to tell them."

"Sorry. And I will."

"Still avoiding confrontations."

Ashleigh didn't answer.

"So what d'you want to do today?" Kelly retreated back to the doorway.

"I need to think. I need to figure out what I want."

"Are you going to call him?"

"No."

"No?" Kelly repeated.

"No. I'm going to make my own mind up."

"Are you sure you want to do that?"

"And what do you mean by that?" Ashleigh put the teaspoon in the sink and faced her sister.

"Nothing . . . just thought you would want to speak to him properly. To be honest, when you called me, I presumed you had done it."

"We went through this last night. I'm not talking to him. If I do, it will just cloud my mind."

Kelly hesitated for a second. "So do you love him, then?"

"What? No. No, I just *think* I love him. Anyway, that's not the point. He cheated."

"Did he?"

"God, Kelly, whose side are you on here?" Ashleigh handed Kelly the hot cup.

"No one's—I'm playing devil's advocate. I just want you to be sure."

"Well, don't," Ashleigh said firmly. "I *am* sure. I'm leaving."

"Ashleigh, come on—you're upset, and like you said, you need more time to think it through."

"No, Kelly, I do not. I need you to book me a one-way ticket, and that's final. Now, if you will excuse me, I've got packing to do and a job to quit."

She pushed past Kelly with a fake smile, closing the door behind her.

Ashleigh looked up at her bedroom ceiling for inspiration, wondering if she truly knew what she was doing. She couldn't help but think maybe it was her past clouding her judgment and not Dave clouding her mind, but it was no good—something had to change in her life. Her phone vibrated in her pocket. Ashleigh swung open the bedroom door, rushing out to find Kelly.

"It's Dave." Ashleigh stared down at her phone, yearning to answer but staying strong to her word.

Eventually, the screen stopped flashing. She exhaled loudly, looking at her sister, and then her phone suddenly started to ring again. Frustration that he was calling for a second time masked the desire to answer. She glanced at the phone; however, she did not see Dave's name flashing across the screen but Lee's.

"Oh, for God's sake, it's Lee ... Kelly, get me out of this emotional hellhole."

Ashleigh threw the phone onto the sofa, watching Kelly pick it up just as it stopped ringing. Kelly told her sister to go and get dressed and watched as Ashleigh stormed into the bathroom.

★　★　★

Ashleigh sat on the side of the bath sobbing. She heard a gentle tap on the door before the handle turned.

"Hey, sweetie, do you need a hug?" Kelly's voice was soft.

All Ashleigh could do was nod as tears rolled down her cheeks. "That's what Dave said to me when I was at Rachel's grandparents' house."

Kelly held her sister close, listening to her trying to catch her breath in between sobs.

"OK, I'm going to book your ticket if that's what you want," Kelly said. "I just didn't want you thinking you had to leave, but the last thing I want to do is upset you. Just get dressed. I'll help you pack, and then we will go to your work together."

"I'm really doing this, aren't I, Kelly?"

"Only if you want to, Ash."

"I do."

"You're sure?"

"Never been more sure of anything in my life," she lied.

★   ★   ★

Ashleigh sat next to her sister on the bus as it edged slowly up Oxford Street on their way to Ashleigh's work. Butterflies jumped around inside her stomach at the thought of quitting and then having to tell them she would not be working out her notice period either. This would not be received well by the practice owner, Mr. Matson. Even though Ashleigh worked for Eliza, the head dentist, Eliza was not the practice owner and not Ashleigh's employer.

Ashleigh wished she was. Eliza would be so much more understanding than Mr. Matson—he was just scary. He also spent eighty percent of his time teaching at the Eastman Dental Hospital, so there was a good chance he wouldn't even be at the practice. She could resign to Penny, the practice manger, grab her things from the locker, say goodbye to Eliza, and leave. She was also well aware that once Samantha got wind of the drama, she would tell Lee, who quite possibly would create a scene before she left. Her heart pounded inside her chest as if she had just run a marathon. The bus slowed down outside John Lewis. Jumping off, they took a shortcut through the store, which led them out to Cavendish Square.

"My God, this has to be the scariest thing I've ever done."

"Well, don't worry. I'll be there with you."

"Do you think he will shout at me?"

"Not if he knows what's good for him, he won't."

Nearing the practice, Ashleigh tried to breathe deep, controlled breaths. She looked at her watch—one forty p.m. They should all be at lunch. She opened the door, stepping inside and nervously looking around to see if anyone was about. They wandered down the hallway quietly.

A whisper made her jump. "Ashleigh." She looked around and saw Eliza coming out of reception.

"Ashleigh, what are you doing here?" Eliza asked

Ashleigh kept her voice low. "I know you will be mad at me, and I'm really sorry, but I'm here to resign."

"What?"

"Eliza, I'm so sorry to leave you in the lurch, but I have to do this. I am going to America."

"What?" Eliza glanced at Kelly.

"This is my sister Kelly," Ashleigh explained. "She has come over from New York to take me back with her."

"When?"

"Day after tomorrow."

"What?" Eliza shook her head.

"I know, I know, it's short notice."

"Ashleigh, Mr. Matson is here."

"No way." Ashleigh winced.

Moments later, they heard footsteps along the corridor. Ashleigh held her breath, praying to see Samantha or Penny, the practice manager, walking toward them—anyone but Matson. Suddenly, Ashleigh's day hit rock bottom as Matson stopped dead in his tracks, looking straight at her.

"Ah, young Ashleigh. I thought you were heartbroken—sorry, I mean ill."

"I am—I mean . . . anyway, Mr. Matson, can I have a word with you in private, please?"

"I think that would be a wonderful idea," he said. "Follow me."

Both Ashleigh and Kelly followed him along the corridor to the back surgery where Ashleigh had first met Dave, which she thought ironically fitting for the occasion at hand. Matson held the door open, looking inquisitively at Kelly as they walked past.

"So what seems to be the problem, Miss Lands?"

"Mr. Matson, I am here to hand in my resignation."

"Well, due to your behavior since you came back from holiday, I am not surprised. But I am confused as to why, after being such a good member of staff over the last few years."

Ashleigh felt terrible at hearing his response. She had always prided herself on being a reliable, hard-working, no-nonsense, straight-talking kind of employee; suddenly, she was being unreliable, making no sense, far from a straight-talking employee.

"Er . . . well . . . unfortunately, something has come up. I have to go back to America with my sister." She gestured toward Kelly.

He turned, looking at Kelly with a look of annoyance on his face. "Well, if this is what you need to do, then you can work out your notice starting tomorrow."

"Er . . . well . . . er . . ."

Kelly came to her rescue. "What my sister is trying to say, Mr. Matson, is that due to a change in her circumstances, she will be unable to work out her notice period."

"What?"

"I'm really sorry, Mr. Matson." Ashleigh panicked, looking at her sister for guidance.

"You're sorry?" he asked. "What good is that to me? I do not care if you are sorry; it is in your contract. You must work your notice out. And you will if you know what is good for you, young lady."

Kelly's posture became rigid. "Mr. Matson, is that a threat to my sister?"

"Yes, it damn well is."

"Well, you will be hearing from our family lawyer, then."

Ashleigh stood riveted to the spot, staring at Matson's face as he turned bright red, watching his upper body starting to shake slightly with rage.

"And just who do you think you are?" he roared.

"My name is Kelly Ann Lands, and we do not wish to continue this conversation with you any further due to your intimidating, threatening behavior. If you feel you need to take this matter any further, feel free to call our family lawyer. Good day to you, sir."

Kelly handed Matson a business card, opened the door, and pushed Ashleigh out, leaving Matson full of rage, peering down at a posh-looking business card.

"Run," Kelly told Ashleigh. "Go grab your things from downstairs, and let's get out of here."

"Oh, Kelly, why did you have to get all aggressive with him?"

"Will you just go get your things?"

Ashleigh reluctantly ran downstairs to get her things. No one was in the staff room. She hadn't envisioned things ending like this. Ashleigh grabbed a pen and wrote a sorry, thank you, and goodbye note to everyone, including Mr. Matson's name at the top. She had never liked him, but she still respected him and felt terrible that she couldn't work her notice out. Things were going from bad to worse. She met Kelly at the top of the stairs.

"Ready?" Kelly asked.

Looking around at the empty practice and Mr. Matson's closed office door, Ashleigh nodded.

They walked up the road back toward Oxford Street, and Ashleigh burst out laughing.

"What's up with you?" Kelly said

"You, Kelly—you. That was everything I never wanted to happen, but at the same time, it was bloody brilliant. However, I have no idea what to feel any more, so all I can do is laugh. And I don't care."

"Good, because it was all complete bullshit."

"What?" Ashleigh stopped for a second and then ran a few steps to catch up with her sister. "Which bit was bullshit?"

"All of it. You are fully in the wrong. You signed a contract agreeing that you would work four weeks' notice, and that is legally binding in a court of law."

"So Dad's lawyer can't help me, then?"

"Nope. Just said that to frighten him and buy us some time to get out. It's OK; the worst he can do is not pay you your last month's pay. Anyway, it won't matter in America. You have two weeks' notice and something called an 'at will' agreement, so you can just leave."

"At will agreement? What's that?"

"Don't worry—your boss will be Dad."

Ashleigh was confused. "So what if Mr. Matson doesn't fall for you immature bullshit and calls Dad's lawyer?" Ashleigh felt sick with panic.

"Immature? Whatever, anyway, you will be halfway around the world, honey. It won't matter. Like I said, all they can do is not pay you."

"Well, if that's the worst they can do, why did you make a fight out of it?"

"He pissed me off. Look at how he was talking to you; he's a jerk, Ash."

"But he's been good to me, Kelly."

"Well he wasn't just then. Now, come on."

Ashleigh dragged her feet, thankful that she had left a note apologizing. Everything was getting so messy. She had forgotten how obnoxious her big sister could be. Kelly was still a hot-headed, egotistical bitch, and America had not changed that.

This was not the way she had pictured it playing out. Everything suddenly felt messy—Kelly was doing her normal big sister act, and Ashleigh was back to being poor, helpless, little Ashleigh. Was she really doing the right thing? She walked alongside Kelly toward Oxford Street, wondering if her fantasies of living in America with her family had been just that—fantasies. She had been to visit and loved it there, but it wasn't her home. And *could* it be her home?

CHAPTER
21

ASHLEIGH PUT ASIDE HER doubts and threw a goodbye meal for her friends. Her plan was to keep herself busy right up to the point of no return in order to keep all second thoughts at bay, not that she had told anyone that she was having second thoughts.

Finally, the last supper was upon her. Gemma spent most of the night crying into Rachel's arms, which in turn made Rachel cry. All the while, Jules kept telling Jon old, embarrassing stories, making Ashleigh cry. Leon insisted on taking bets on how long it would be before Ashleigh would come back to England, at which Kelly laughed but insisted on keeping her little sister this time.

After dinner, everyone helped clear the table, leaving Kelly and Rachel to do the washing up, reminiscing over old times. Leon, Jon, and Jules opened a bottle of champagne on the balcony, and not long after, they all sat around drinking toasts to anything and everything.

"Toast! Toast! Toast! Toast!" Leon knocked on the table with a coaster to get everyone's attention. Ashleigh saw ten eyes attached to five smiling, caring faces that she was about to abandon looking straight at her. She knew that if she tried to give them a long, heartfelt speech like they wanted, it would start her crying—or worse, change her mind about leaving—but she couldn't turn down the invitation to say a proper goodbye.

"Er, OK . . . um . . . I'm not good at speaking to an audience, but um . . . I just want to say thank you for being part of my life, and . . . I will miss you all. But I will come and visit whenever I can. And you must come to see me. Er . . . that's it, thanks and goodbye."

She quickly sat down, relieved that it was over. Then Leon stood up, rhapsodizing about all her mistakes and blunders, followed by Jules, Rachel, and Gemma.

Gemma spoke up last. "Ash, do you remember the time in the woods—"

Ashleigh quickly tried to stop her. "Gem, shhh—"

"No, no, tell all, Gemmzie." Leon beamed.

"Er . . ." Gemma pressed her lips tight.

"Gemma, no," Ashleigh pleaded. "My sister is here."

"What does that matter?" said Kelly. "Carry on, Gemma."

"Er . . ."

"Gemma!" Kelly prompted.

"Er . . . Ash?" Gemma looked to Ashleigh for guidance.

"Oh, tell the damned story, then." Ashleigh rolled her eyes.

"OK." Gemma smiled. The table's full attention was on her. "Me and Ashleigh were in the woods after school—"

"How old?" Leon interrupted.

"Twelve, I think. We found a dirty mag—"

"Oh God." Ashleigh winced.

"So we started flicking through the pages, looking at all the naked girls and stuff." Gemma stopped for a moment, looking at Ashleigh, who was wishing she had never brought it up. "Anyway, Ashleigh suggested we act out some of the pictures."

"I did not—you did!"

"Oh, come on, Ash—you know you did!"

"You said you wanted to be a Page Three girl!"

"And you said you would be my agent, and we should practice."

"So. Not. True."

Gemma grinned. "So true."

"Bitches, please. Who undressed, and who touched who?" Leon looked back and forth from one to the other.

"Ash did," said Gemma.

"Shut up, you told me to," Ashleigh said. "I didn't want to; I was the agent, but you said an agent has to strip too."

"Ah, so you do remember!" Gemma laughed.

"Yeah, I remember. I remember trying to do one of the positions—with clothes on, may I add—and Barnaby Jones catching us."

"Yeah, we bribed him not to tell because they were his dirty mags that he had hidden. It was one of the best summers I ever had." Gemma smiled at Ashleigh. "Me, Ash, and Barnaby met up every day by this big oak tree in the woods behind the school. We climbed that tree so many times but never mentioned the porn mags again."

Ashleigh smiled. "I remember. I wonder where Barnaby Jones is now."

"I don't remember. Where was I?" Kelly asked.

"That was the year you met Ben Keller," Ashleigh reminded her.

"Oh yeah," said Kelly. "Sounds like you guys had more fun than me that summer." She laughed.

"Another reason you shouldn't go," Leon said. "Let's find this Barnaby Jones fella—he may be your Mr. Right."

"Oh, Leon, stop." Ashleigh scowled.

The night came to a finish far too soon for everyone as they all kissed Ashleigh goodbye, their eyes filled with tears at the thought of losing their friend to the Big Apple. One by one, they hugged her and then departed down the steps, leaving Ashleigh alone with her big sister. In silence, Ashleigh and Kelly cleared the glasses from the table. Ashleigh couldn't bring herself to speak and tried to focus on the task at hand.

★   ★   ★

By late afternoon the next day, Ashleigh had packed all she needed back into her suitcase. She sighed. Just a short while ago, she had used the same suitcase for a fun trip with her friends; now, as she looked at the dark pink suitcase, happy was the last thing she felt. She had said goodbye to all those she felt needed an explanation regarding her decision. She was sad that things had come to an end in this way, and she cast her mind back to the last time she was due to go to NYC and how love had kept her from going. It was ironic that she found herself in the same place, but now it was love that was sending her away.

Love. She hung on the word as it danced in her mind. Love. Did she love Dave? She believed in giving love a second chance, and last week, she thought she was in love.

So what's changed? She wondered if maybe she should have gone to meet him. *No. He cheated. People don't cheat on people they love.* She stood alone in her room, looking around at the mostly empty wardrobes and dresser top. She wished things could be different and longed to stay here in the safe retreat and comfort of her familiar home. But she couldn't stay—something had to change in her life. Something had to give, and she no longer believed she could be happy in England.

A loud bang from outside her room brought her back to reality. She opened the door to see Kelly looking dazed and upset, rubbing her head.

"Kelly, what did you do?"

Ashleigh quickly guided her sister over to the sofa, sitting her down.

"I walked into the kitchen cupboard," Kelly said. "It was open, and I didn't see it."

"Oh, silly, lie down. I'll get you a bag of frozen vegetables to put on the bump."

Ashleigh could see a large red mark appearing on her sister 's forehead. She hurried off to the kitchen, returning with a tea towel wrapped around half a bag of frozen peas.

"Here you are. Hold this on there and lie still."

Kelly caught her breath, holding the cold bag to her head.

"You're my favorite little sis. You know that, right?"

"I'm your *only* sister," Ashleigh pointed out. "And good job, too, because I think I give you enough to worry about."

Kelly removed the ice pack and raised herself onto her elbow. "You don't, and you never have. You've done so well on your own."

"Have I? I've made a mess of everything."

"No." Kelly laughed softly. "No, Ash, you haven't." She swung her legs around. "You've done everything perfectly. You stayed true to your beliefs, and you were so brave staying here without us. You haven't messed anything up."

"I stayed for the wrong man . . ."

"Oh, Ashleigh." Kelly took her sister's hand in her own. "No, don't you see? That doesn't matter. What matters is you were willing to take a risk, trust yourself, and see where it took you."

"I was wrong. I'm always wrong."

"Were you?"

"Yes," Ashleigh said, confused.

"Depends on how you look at it," Kelly told her. "Lee was wrong, but look at all your friends. You have four friends who will love you forever. If you had left with us, maybe you would have drifted apart from them. And you wouldn't have been here when Rachel needed you the most, nor would you have met Gemma again. Look what you did—you helped her move on in life, and that's amazing . . . Ashleigh, I've never said this to you, and maybe I should have, but I have always wished I could be more like you."

"Me?" Ashleigh laughed. "I'm always trying to be more like *you*."

"Oh God, don't do that."

"Why? You're strong."

"Ashleigh, I'm far from strong. I just act like I am. I mess up all the time. The difference is I keep it all inside, away from people. You, though, you wear your emotions on show to the whole world, and I love that about you."

"Oh, Kelly, I've missed you so much, and Mum and Dad." Ashleigh hugged her sister tightly.

"Ashleigh?" Kelly pulled away. "You can change your mind and stay."

"Why would you say that?"

"Because I know you well enough to know you always need options to make the right decision." Ashleigh tilted her head, and Kelly explained. "If you feel backed into a corner with a decision, you will always push against it, even if it is the right thing, because you don't like to feel controlled. But, if you are given a choice, then you always make the right decision. That's why Dad said he would help you stay in England if you wanted to. He knew you needed to make your own way, your own decision. That's who you are." Ashleigh didn't say anything. "No one—not me, Mum, or Dad—will mind if you stay. All we want is for you to be happy."

"See?" said Ashleigh. "This is what I love about you, Kelly. You are my inner voice."

"And I always will be, even if we are thousands of miles apart. You'll always be my little sis."

A knock at the front door disturbed them. Ashleigh left her injured sibling, telling her to put her feet back up and rest. She rushed to answer, not even thinking about who might be on the other side. She reached out and opened the door, turning the latch to reveal Lee Preston, who looked stern and serious.

"Still here, then?" he asked.

Samantha.

"Lee, what do you want?" Ashleigh put the door on the latch, closing it behind her so Kelly wouldn't hear. She led him down the steps, and they stood at the bottom, glaring at each other.

"So after all we have been through, you were just going to run off without a word."

"That's right. I was."

"You're a brazen woman, but I know you better than that," Lee said. "You don't mean it. Deep down, you wanted me to come and beg you not to go, just like last time."

"Oh my God. You self-centered, arrogant, jumped-up little prick. I couldn't give a toss if I never laid eyes on you again," Ashleigh said, and for the first time, she really meant it.

Lee's facial expression didn't falter, but a hint of realization flickered in his eyes as he stood rooted to the spot. Ashleigh had finally gotten over him—and with a vengeance.

"Well, what can I say to that?" he said.

"Nothing. Now, please leave. I have things to be getting on with."

"Ashleigh, before I go, there's one thing I must say." He paused. "You know I always loved—"

At that moment, Ash's front door opened and Kelly stepped out, glaring at Lee.

"And what the hell do you want?" Kelly spat the words.

"Kelly, hi. How the devil are you?" Lee beamed.

"Please, Kelly, don't," Ashleigh protested. "He is just leaving."

"Am I?"

"Yes, Lee, you are." She lowered her tone to match his patronizing tone. "I do not care for your presents, nor do I care for your final farewell words, so if you don't mind, I have things to do."

"Ashleigh, please—"

"Lee, just go."

"Ash?" Hesitating, he said, "I'm sorry for everything. I really am."

"Please, just go, Lee." Ashleigh started walking up the steps toward her sister, feeling the weight of Lee's stare as he watched her disappear into her flat.

Closing her door felt like closing a chapter. It was time to leave England and all its drama behind.

CHAPTER
22

ASHLEIGH STEPPED OUT OF the black taxi outside of the airport. The morning sun was high, blinding her as she glanced around for a luggage trolley. The heavyset Indian driver helped unload their suitcases onto a trolley she found, and Kelly tipped him well. Slowly, they wheeled their luggage toward the main entrance, where they scanned the airport for the check-in desk. The airport was hectic, crowded with holidaymakers and businessmen in dark suits. Ashleigh flinched as families hurried past, disoriented kids bumping into her legs as they tried to keep up with their families.

"There's our check-in desk. Let's get in line." Ashleigh pointed it out eagerly, happy to be out of harm's way from the three-foot-nothing, kamikaze kids.

They stood in the long queue, patiently waiting. Kelly had been uncharacteristically quiet since they had arrived, and this bothered Ashleigh. She cared what her sister thought, and if she was holding something back, she wanted to hear it—even if she knew she may not like it. She guessed Kelly was still worried about her decision to leave, but it was the right one.

"You OK, sis?" she asked.

"Yeah."

"You seem distracted."

"I am a bit," Kelly said.

"Why?" Ashleigh probed.

"Concerned about you."

"I know what I'm doing."

Kelly nodded. They edged forward as the queue moved down a space. Kelly's phone vibrated in her hand—it was a text.

"Who's that?" Ashley asked.

"Er . . ." Kelly looked taken back. "Dad."

Kelly finished replying to the text and then smiled at her sister.

"Look, Ash. I just want you to be sure that what you're doing is what you really want."

"Why wouldn't it be? It's what I want, Kelly."

"Well, that's OK, then." Kelly hugged her sister, stroking the back of her hair like their mum would do.

From behind her, Ashleigh thought she heard her name being called. She looked around, not seeing anyone and wondering if she was going crazy—it sounded like Dave. *There must be another Ashleigh somewhere nearby.*

The queue moved forward again, pushing them closer to the check-in desk; a lady called out, asking for everyone to have their passports in hand. Ashleigh rummaged around in her handbag.

"Ash. Ash . . . Ashleigh, wait."

Her heart skipped, adrenaline raised her blood pressure, and her stomach clenched at the sight of Dave standing next to her, only a rope dividing them. The queue moved forward, leaving only four more people in front of her.

"Dave, what are you doing here?"

"Please, I love you. Please don't do this." Fear and anxiety were emblazoned across his face.

"I have to."

"Why? Look, just come out of the queue. Let's just talk."

"No. Sorry, Dave. I have made up my mind. You cheated, and that is unforgivable."

"Ashleigh, I did not cheat on you."

"Well, you *would* say that, wouldn't you?" she snapped.

Seeing him again felt nerve-racking. Was this the same Dave she loved? She stared at him for a long moment.

Dave stared back at her as the queue move forward, leaving only three people left in front of Ashleigh. Maybe he was telling the truth. She started to question why she hadn't met with him. Was she making a big mistake after all?

"If you really believed that I had cheated, then you wouldn't have avoided me."

Ashleigh screwed up her face. "That makes no sense."

"Yes, it does . . . After speaking to me on the phone, you knew I was telling the truth. Deep down, you know I am not like that. You know you heard the conversation wrong, but you just want an excuse to leave. Well, fine, but why break my heart in the process? Why use me to run away from your past?"

"My past? How dare you!" Any second-guessing thoughts vanished, and Ashleigh's bottom lip trembled, matching the hurt she now felt inside.

"Ashleigh, I damn well love you."

"You have a funny way of showing it."

Dave looked panicked. "Will you just come out the queue and talk to me? I have so much I want to tell you, so much I *need* to tell you."

"No, Dave," she whispered. "It's over. You hurt me. I can't risk it again."

Dave glanced at Kelly.

"Hi. I'm Ashleigh's sister." Kelly gave him an awkward wave.

Dave grimaced and then looked back at Ashleigh desperately.

"Marry me." Dave held out his hand. "I love you. I never thought I'd meet someone like you. Ashleigh, I'm committed to you. Marry me. Stay."

Ashleigh didn't move. She felt a pang of desire, the sudden urge to jump the rope and throw her arms around his neck, but something held her back. Something was stopping her—pride, maybe, or was she just confused? After all, a moment ago, she was doubting her choice.

The queue moved forward, and it was her turn.

"Ashleigh, please," Dave begged, tears welling up in his eyes.

She looked at him, holding his gaze, watching his eyes turn red—her eyes also filling with tears. It was the point of no return. If she gave him a second chance, she would lose her sister again, but if she went through security, she would never see him again.

She remembered the conversation with Kelly the day before—were these her only two options? How could these options make it easier for her to make the right decision? Was it really possible to want both? Love or family—it was an impossible decision.

"I'm sorry." She turned, walking quickly to the desk.

"Passport please, madam," said the young, camp-looking boy sitting behind the check-in desk.

Ashleigh handed over her passport. "I don't want a window seat. I'm a nervous flyer."

The boy looked up and smiled at her, seeming to notice her eyes were glazed over with tears.

"Not a problem, madam. Place your luggage on the scales, please."

As she put her suitcase on the scale, she watched the weight roll up on the small screen in front of her. Was she really doing this? Had Dave really just proposed? She couldn't hold back the tears from falling down her cheeks any longer.

"It will be fine, madam. You will be there before you know it," the young boy said, assuming that fear of flying was the cause of her anguish.

"Thank you; I'm sure you are right."

Ashleigh wiped her cheeks, eager to keep her sadness hidden from her sister. All checked in, Ashleigh looked back to see an empty space where Dave had been standing. She sighed, feeling a wrench of pain and a lump in her throat as she swallowed. He hadn't waited. Why should he? She had made her decision. Kelly joined her, putting a comforting arm around her waist and walking her up to security before going through to the departure lounge.

★　★　★

From a distance on the other side of the queue, Dave watched Ashleigh as she looked over at the empty space where he had been standing seconds before. He saw her eyes frantically glance around looking for him and the disappointment in her face when she could not find him, and he knew she loved him. But it was all too late—they had gone their separate ways. Life had parted them; she had made her decision.

He took one long last look as she disappeared behind scores of people, and then he walked away, dragging with him a feeling of guilt, regret, sadness, and loss, all for something that had not been his own doing. He made his way through the smiling, happy people rushing toward him, all excited about their holiday destinations, knocking into his shoulders as they passed. Slowly, head down, he wandered in the general direction of the car park, trying to comprehend what had just happened. Was this really the end?

★   ★   ★

Ashleigh walked into the departure lounge, her heart literally in her mouth. She made her excuses to Kelly and hurried off into the ladies' toilets, where ten minutes later, Kelly found her in floods of tears as she leaned against a broken hand drier. She was being comforted by a well-dressed older woman who was handing her tissues from her handbag.

"Ashleigh, honey." Kelly put her arms out, holding her as tightly as she could. The woman gave her a kind smile and left them alone.

"How did he know I would be here? How did he know, Kell?"

"Er . . . I told him," her sister whispered sheepishly.

Ashleigh pulled away. "What?"

"I'm sorry, I really am."

"Why? When did you speak to him? Why—why do that?"

"Last night," Kelly admitted. "I had already taken his number out of your phone the day before, when you threw it onto the sofa."

"Why? You knew I had been avoiding him for this one reason."

"I just needed to hear his side."

"I told you his side."

"Don't take this the wrong way . . . but you told me *your* version of his side."

Ashleigh looked down at the floor as a tear fell from her face. Kelly was right; she hadn't given him a chance to explain properly. What had she done? She sniffed, standing up tall.

"Well, I can't go back now."

"Yes. Yes, you can. I'm so, so sorry. I really am. But Ashleigh, I honestly believe him. I didn't mean to make things worse."

"Well, you have."

"I know." Kelly's shoulders hung low.

"Mum and Dad are expecting me. They bought me my ticket. I've quit my job. I have ended my life in England as I know it. It's just not that simple," Ashleigh rationalized.

"Sod the money! Mum and Dad just want you to be happy. And as for the job, stuff it. Do something different. Choose a new career if you want to. Your life in England isn't over—it could be just beginning."

Kelly looked into her sister's eyes. Ashleigh felt a glimmer of excitement but quickly felt a mist of fear drain through her whole body.

"No." She wiped a fresh tear and composed herself. "I have made up my mind," she lied. "Do not meddle in my affairs anymore today." She picked up her bag, walking briskly out of the public toilets back into the swarms of people milling around from shop to shop.

Kelly followed. They wandered silently in and out of the perfumeries, confectioners, and boutiques, and all the time, Ashleigh wondered if she should have just jumped into Dave's arms. She thought about the Sassy situation again. It was possible he was telling the truth, but it was equally as possible that he was not. This was hopeless, she concluded.

"Ashleigh, shall we stop for a coffee and bite to eat?" Kelly asked. "We still have thirty minutes before we can go through to the gates."

They found a quiet table in a small bar with a clear view of the monitor showing gate times. A waitress took their order, leaving them to discuss future plans. Ashleigh tried to distract herself from her own thoughts and told Kelly the first thing she was going to do once she was settled was to find her own apartment.

"Just stay with Mum and Dad. It's not like you will ever see them; the house is huge."

"Er ... no. I want my own place; I haven't lived at home for years. I'm dreading it—Mum fussing over me, Dad wanting to show me his fishing photos. It's going to be painful for a while, I'm telling you. You try being the youngest, Kelly—you'd soon be glad you were the firstborn."

"They don't . . . and anyway, they fuss over me too, and if I have to suffer Dad's fishing tales, so should you. It's only fair."

"Well, anyway, I want my own place sooner rather than later."

"Maybe I could see if there is one available in my apartment block."

"Yeah, that would be brilliant, Kelly. Ask tomorrow."

Kelly smiled lightly. "I'll ask as soon as I get the chance."

"What?" Ashleigh snapped, irritated at her sister's sympathetic smile.

"OK, I know what you're doing, Ashleigh. You're avoiding the elephant in the room. Look, you may not want to hear this, but I'm going to say it anyway."

Kelly was right; Ashleigh didn't want to hear it. She stood up to leave, but Kelly reached for her wrist and dragged her back down.

"Sit—I'm still your big sister. And I'll tell you now or on the plane."

"Tell me on the plane, then."

"Goddamn you. No. It's not a choice; I was just—oh, forget it. Look, Ashleigh, when I spoke to Dave, he said—"

Ashleigh rose to leave.

"*Sit down*," Kelly hissed. "When I spoke to Dave, he said that he was asleep when this girl came into his room. He is really cut up about this, and I don't think he is making this up."

"But—"

"Let me finish," Kelly demanded. "I'm telling you that I believe him, and that's the best conclusion you have right now. Right. So now that that's cleared up, you have about fifteen minutes to decide if you want to leave because you're scared of being in love or if you really want a new life. If you decide it's because you're scared of being in love, then you must stay and face that fear. If not, then we go, and you never look back. Deal?"

Ashleigh understood. This was her last choice—it was time to make the right decision. But what was the right decision? Was she really scared to fall in love again? Was she sabotaging things and using Dave to run away like he had said?

Oh God, that's so mean of me. Did she want a new life? She did—she knew she did—but where? In New York? Or with Dave?

★ ★ ★

The last few minutes had ticked by quickly, and she still hadn't made her decision. They ran along to Gate 57 at the farthest end of the airport, arriving after most of the other passengers. Ashleigh felt a tug of emotion rise up into her throat, causing a shudder of panic in the back of her mind. This was it, the real point of no return, and she hadn't made up her mind—not for real. Not since her final two options. Things had changed; it was all happening too fast. What was she going to do? She could see Kelly watching her out of the corner of her eye, probably thinking the same.

They stood six people away from boarding the plane with only two people behind them. Ashleigh's eyes were fixed on her boarding pass as she tried not to think of anything that might encourage her doubt. She wanted a new life with her family.

"You can back out if you want to, Ash."

"Kell—"

"I'm just saying. No one would blame you if you didn't want to get on the plane."

"Kelly, leave it!"

"OK, OK."

"I just need to get on that plane, and it will all be fine," Ashleigh said, trying to convince herself one last time.

She thought of her new life and seeing her mum and dad again. They must be so excited she was coming home with Kelly. She then thought about Dave—his panicked face as he watched her move down the queue, his perfect smile fading as she moved away from him. Why hadn't she met with him to explain properly? Why hadn't she asked Isabella if he was telling the truth? She might be his flatmate, but she didn't seem the type to lie for any man.

Oh God, I've made a mistake. I've made a big, bloody mistake.

Suddenly, a young, out-of-breath, slightly chubby girl in an airport uniform ran up to the man at the boarding desk in front of them. She whispered something into his ear. Ashleigh couldn't hear what the girl had said, but the gentleman looked frustrated with her. He told her that the plane was nearly full, but the girl seemed to insist on something. Ashleigh tried to use this extra time to think about what she should do. Should she stay? Had she honestly just figured out that she had it all terribly wrong?

Ashleigh was standing directly in front of the man. He looked irritated at the airport girl. Was something wrong with the plane? Still unsure, Ashleigh slowly handed over her boarding pass to the angry man, studying his face as he took a long look at her pass. This was it.

What are you doing? Dave was telling the truth. Stay. I want to stay. I choose love—I choose Dave. She screamed these words in her head, but paralyzed by her realization, she still didn't move. Instead, she just watched as the man showed her pass to the chubby young girl next to him, now rolling his eyes.

"Er . . . is there a problem?" Ashleigh's small voice managed.

Kelly joined her sister, standing next to her, waiting for the man to reply. The young girl stepped forward, holding out a small parcel.

"A man asked me to give you this," the girl said. "He was determined." The girl looked very proud as she thrust the small parcel toward Ashleigh.

Ashleigh took the parcel, stepping out of line.

"Oh, my God." Ashleigh nearly fell over as she opened the little black box, revealing a diamond ring. A note was folded inside, tucked up in the top of the ring case.

Ashleigh Lands

I've never loved anyone the way I love you, and if you can't trust anyone, then trust your gut feeling.

Don't get on that plane.

Marry me?

Dave x

She looked up at both of them, now smiling like a Cheshire cat, tears streaming down her face.

Filled with excitement, the girl explained, "He begged me for at least forty minutes to take his money and buy a ring and then get it to you before you left. It was my lunch break, and he explained the whole thing to me. I may not know you both, but he didn't cheat on you—he loves you, and by the look on your face, you love him too, if you don't mind me saying."

Ashleigh jolted her head around, staring into Kelly's eyes, feeling scared. What were her parents going to say?

As if she were reading her mind, Kelly said, "Don't worry, stay, Ashleigh!"

"But—"

"Ashleigh, what is your gut feeling saying?" She jabbed her finger at Dave's note. "Don't think about it! Just act on that feeling!"

Ashleigh threw her arms around her sister, bursting into tears.

"He is waiting outside W.H. Smith." The girl jumped up and down, excited.

"Now go!" cried Kelly. "Run! Be happy, little sis!"

"I love you, Kelly. Thank you so much for everything."

She thanked the girl and ran as fast as she could.

"Wait," the check-in man shouted. "You can't leave. Goddammit, your bags are on the plane."

Ashleigh ignored his pleas, running down the long, now-empty corridor, following the exit signs back toward the departure lounge. Her heart pounded in her chest. She pushed past anyone who got in her way, taking long, fast strides and stumbling slightly as she negotiated the escalators back toward departures.

★   ★   ★

The man at the boarding desk looked at Kelly, displeased at the turn of events.

"Well, I am afraid we cannot take her bags off this flight. We are delayed as it is."

"Oh, stop being so bloody grumpy and check me on," she snapped. "I can send the damn bags back to her myself."

"Fine. Boarding passes, please." He held out his hand, snatching the card out of Kelly's grasp. If Kelly had not have been so utterly happy for her sister, she would have torn strips off him. True love had beaten every obstacle in its way.

As she walked onto the plane and sat down, she looked at the empty seat next to her, feeling overjoyed but slightly depressed at the thought of another seven-hour flight on her own. Thoughts of telling her parents that their youngest daughter had once again chosen a man over them sat heavy. She knew all they wanted was for their children to be happy, but they would still be disappointed. It made her stop and think about her own love life. When would she meet her Dave?

A male American voice spoke from the aisle. "Sorry, is this seat taken?"

Kelly looked up at a tall, light-haired, well-spoken man. He wore jeans, a T-shirt, and a sand-colored suit jacket and held a newspaper and laptop under his arm. Catching her breath at the sight of this fine specimen of a man, she swallowed, trying to find words.

"Er . . . no."

"Would you mind? I got assigned a window seat, but I'm not such a good flyer."

"Absolutely not—please, take a seat," Kelly told him. "So you don't fly a lot, then?"

"Oh, no, all the time. I just haven't ever gotten used to it." He laughed, sliding down into the seat.

"Whereabouts in America are you from?" she asked.

"New York City."

"Oh, so am I." Kelly smiled to herself, now very happy that the seat had been empty. Kelly eyed the stranger as he talked. *Perhaps this flight may not be so boring after all.*

★   ★   ★

Dave looked down at his watch, then back out in the direction he assumed Ashleigh would come from. It had been over an hour since the girl had taken his money to buy the ring. Maybe she had run—after all, it was £2,000 in cash that he had just given to a young, probably underpaid airport worker in the hope that she would prove that human nature was a sucker for romance. This young girl had the mammoth task of picking a ring from a duty free shop and then finding the love of his life before she got on a plane and left him forever.

Another ten minutes passed; his hope started to fade. What if the girl had found Ashleigh and she had turned him down? Would the airport girl kept the ring? He would lose the love of his life *and* £2,000. Dave winced at the thought. What if Ashleigh thought the ring was cheap? He knew in her world, £2,000 for a ring was pocket money, but for him, it was a month's mortgage payment.

Reluctant to give up the ghost, Dave paced outside W.H. Smith. She wasn't coming, and the W.H Smith workers were starting to look concerned at his pacing up and down. With one more hopeless look across the airport, he walked away, feeling sick to the stomach at the thought of never seeing Ashleigh's beautiful face again.

Dave neared the doors, turning back to have one last look before facing the fact that Ashleigh had gone for good. Swarms of people cluttered his view, but to his amazement, he saw her. There she was, standing outside W.H. Smith, looking around frantically for him. His heart felt as if it had stopped, and then it started to thump-thump-thump as if to burst from his ribcage. His hands were damp with sweat. There she was—a vision of pure happiness.

Quickly, he made his way back toward her, walking faster and faster, pushing people aside without looking at them. Not once did he take his eyes off Ashleigh. He was only a few feet away now, and her back faced him. She turned around, her stare interlocking with his, bringing him to a halt. They looked at each other as if they were the only people there. She ran the last few feet, slamming her body hard against his, grasping the sides of his face and kissing him with all the love she could muster. He lifted her up slowly, swinging her around in circles, inches from the floor.

Passersby smiled at the embrace. Eventually, Dave put her down so he could look into her eyes, making sure this was really happening—she was really there. She had stayed for him. She really did love him.

"I thought I'd lost you," he said, kissing her again. "I love you so much. I'd never—"

"I know." She stopped him. "I've been such a fool."

"Well, you're *my* fool. Ashleigh, will you—"

"Yes. Yes, I will."

www.ingramcontent.com/pod-product-compliance
Lightning Source LLC
Chambersburg PA
CBHW061149170626
46809CB00003B/1034